THE TIME *Rift*

BY

DAVID H. HO

LIWEN Y. HO

The Time Rift

Cover Design: Tugboat Design (www.tugboatdesign.net)
Interior Design: Tugboat Design (www.tugboatdesign.net)
Publisher: 2 Square 2 Be Hip (www.2square2behip.com)

First Edition

DEDICATION

For our children, the pride and joy of our lives.

CONTENTS

Prologue

Ethan Stratford hurried down the staircase, his brown boots clanging against the metal steps. The adrenaline coursing through his body propelled his every move as he exited the military plane. He exhaled when he reached the bottom. Fresh air filled his nostrils and signaled a welcome change from the desert winds he had endured the past week.

"Right this way, Commander."

Ethan greeted his driver with a nod as he entered the black Buick. He sat up tall and drummed his fingers against the leather seat. He noticed his right foot tapping out a staccato rhythm of its own, a habit he had developed after twenty-three years on the job.

The scenery outside his window blurred into a palette of colors as the car sped onto the highway. His heart pumped at a similar speed as he considered the message he would soon be delivering.

This is for the American people, for the innocent men and women who lost their lives. A smile spread slowly across his face. *We're going to get him this time.* He clasped his hands together and brought them to his lips. The smile faded as he narrowed his eyes. *We're going to get that son of a gun.*

The car pulled up to the White House where Ethan received clearance to enter. He paused for a moment outside the doors of the Oval Office to gather his thoughts. Squaring his shoulders, he turned the brass knob and entered.

"Mr. President. General Webb." Ethan took long strides toward the two men standing in the middle of the room.

"Commander Stratford, welcome back." President Obama furrowed his brows as he shook Ethan's hand. "Are you absolutely certain we have Geronimo?"

"Yes, Mr. President. We have a positive ID. Geronimo is hiding in the southern part of Waziristan, a mountainous region of northwest Pakistan. We have long suspected he was in this area, but due to the difficult terrain and tribal leaders' unwillingness to cooperate, we couldn't confirm our suspicions. However, we were successful in tracking down his personal doctor, and the blood sample he provided us with confirms his identity. It's his DNA." Ethan paused and looked directly into the President's eyes. "Sir, we have to move quickly before he realizes we're onto him. We have Seal Team Six standing by for your orders."

President Obama nodded. "Well done. You and your team are doing a great service for the American people. Trust me when I say we appreciate all your hard work." He clasped Ethan's hand and gave him a firm pat on the shoulder. "Operation Neptune Spear is a go. I'll meet you in the Situation Room in five minutes."

THE TIME *Rift*

Chapter One

Lance Everett jolted at the first sound of his alarm. He turned over and strained to make out the time. *Seven thirty already?* He reached over to the bedside table to silence the buzzing, all the while grimacing at the sunlight streaming in through the curtains. The knots in his shoulders and neck caused him to groan as he sat up in bed. Three consecutive nights of working past two a.m. had taken their toll. He rubbed his neck and vowed to sleep in tomorrow. *It's going to be a long day. Good thing it's Friday.*

Lance entered the living room and picked up the remote, aiming it at the 52-inch flat screen hanging on one wall. Floor-to-ceiling bookshelves covered the remaining three walls, each one crammed tight with scientific titles. A heavily dog-eared copy of Einstein's *Relativity* lay open on the glass coffee table in the center of the room.

"Good morning. Welcome to CSS News. Today is May 6, 2011." The anchorwoman relayed the nation's top stories of the day before the broadcast turned its attention to the biggest news of the year, the capture and killing of the FBI's most wanted terrorist five days earlier.

Lance trained his eyes on the TV as real-time video clips from Pakistan played on the air. "It's about time they caught him," he murmured under his breath.

The phone sounded as Lance made his way to the kitchen. He shuffled some paperwork around on the tile counter until he found his smartphone under an empty take-out container. The name *Juliet Bradley* flashed across the screen. "Good morning."

"Good morning, Sir Lancelot. How's my handsome prince doing today?"

The muscles in his neck suddenly loosened their hold, and his shoulders dropped. He closed his eyes and enveloped himself in his fiancée's cheerful voice. He played along with their little charade. "Well, Princess Juliet, it is a glorious day and your servant is doing quite well."

"You're so silly." She giggled. "I'm sure this is a side your students have never seen before."

"I'm just happy. I love hearing your voice first thing in the morning."

"You're such a romantic, Lance. Maybe even more so than me."

"It's only because of you, Juliet. You bring out a side of me I never knew existed."

"I'm sure it was in there somewhere, just buried under all those physics theories. But if this means you'll agree to watch more chick flicks, then I think it's a good thing you have me around."

"I'll even watch *Titanic* again if it means I get to spend time with you." Although he meant his comment as a joke, he knew he would do anything to make Juliet smile. She had brought so much joy to his life. He paused and his voice grew raw with emotion. "I don't even want to think about not having you in my life."

"Don't worry, I'm not going anywhere. Not this time. You are stuck with me."

"Good. You're the only person I'd happily be tied to for the rest of my life. That would give new meaning to the phrase 'tying the knot,' wouldn't it?"

Juliet laughed. "Speaking of tying the knot, did you get a chance to look at the proofs last night?"

Lance glanced over at a pile of engagement pictures on the wooden table. "Yeah, I did. I can't decide which ones to pick. You look beautiful in all of them. Me, I'm just happy to be your prop."

"My boy toy, huh?" Juliet teased. "Don't be silly, you looked amazing in that suit. But your good looks aren't the only reason I'm marrying you."

"It must not be for the money, either."

"It's for your heart, of course. And to be able to one day say that I'm married to a Nobel Prize winner."

"Nobel Prize?" Lance rolled his eyes. Those two words seemed like an unlikely dream. "You have too much faith in me, hon."

"You should have more faith in yourself. You underestimate what that big brain of yours can do."

Lance smiled, pleased that Juliet believed in him so much. "It got you to agree to marry me, didn't it?"

"You didn't have to try too hard to convince me." Juliet sighed. "Just one smile from you across the Stanford Stadium did the trick. And a view of your behind in those tight jeans."

"Ah, so the truth comes out. You *are* marrying me for my good looks."

Juliet chuckled. "Oh yeah, the photographer confirmed our appointment for tomorrow. Can you bring the proofs to lunch? We should finalize which pictures we want."

"Got it, I'll bring them. Same time and place?"

"As always. See you in a bit. I love you, Lance."

Lance's breath caught in his throat when he heard those three words. Each time Juliet spoke them felt like the very first time. He longed to return a part of himself to her as well. "Love you more." He cradled the phone for a few seconds after Juliet hung up. He shook his head and a wide smile appeared on his face. *I'm the luckiest guy in the world. I can't believe I found her again.*

Lance sat down at the dining table and picked up the stack of engagement pictures, flipping through them one by one. They had spent almost an entire day going to all their favorite places in the Bay Area. Half Moon Bay. Golden Gate Park. Stanford University. He stopped at the picture of them taken at the Stanford Stadium. The photo brought him back to the first time they had met on those stands. He had never attended a school football game before, but his roommate had convinced him to go.

"Come on, man, you cannot miss this game," Drew had pled, as if his life depended on Lance's attendance. "It's our senior year. We are so gonna beat Cal this time."

Since it was the 100th anniversary of the Big Game between Stanford and UC Berkeley, Lance had bought a red sweatshirt and worn it with as much school pride as he could muster up.

Alumni and students from both schools packed the stadium that day. Lance could still picture the intense looks on the spectators' faces. Some of them stood and cheered wildly, while others yelled and booed with as much enthusiasm. Lance and his friends had found seats near the aisle where fans from the opposing sides merged, forming a sea of red on one side and blue and gold on the other.

He had just returned from the concession stand with a tray of garlic fries; the memory of the spicy aroma still caused his mouth to water all these years later. As he walked to his seat, Stanford happened to score a touchdown in that moment. The guy behind him jumped up and threw his fist into the air, jostling Lance's arm in the process. The tray slipped out of his hands and the fries flew straight at a guy wearing a *Cal* jacket.

The student whipped around when the fries landed on his head. He stood up with his mouth open wide and fists clenched. When he spotted Lance, his face turned a crimson shade like Lance's sweatshirt. "Hey, watch it, man. Are you stupid or something!"

Lance immediately apologized, "I'm sorry, it was an acc—", but he stopped mid-sentence. He lost his words at the sight of a redheaded girl standing beside the guy.

The girl had turned around and spotted the fries strewn around her. "Greg, it's no big deal. It's just some fries." She placed a hand on Greg's arm.

Wow, who is she? Lance's heart suddenly skipped a beat. He wasn't one to believe in love at first sight, but his body told him otherwise. Just a minute before, he had been under pressure to work the situation in his favor, but now a relaxed grin appeared on his face. His focus shifted completely to the girl.

She locked eyes with him and pushed some strands of hair back from her face. A smile appeared and lingered on her lips.

For a moment, Lance felt like he existed outside the bounds of space and time, unaware of anyone else around him. Too soon, however, Lance's senses snapped him back to reality. He felt two hands on his chest, pushing him back ever so lightly. His vision focused to see Greg lurching toward him again, fury clouding his green eyes. He stood roughly the same height as Lance but sported a lankier frame. *Who is this guy kidding? Both Berkeley and Stanford have more nerds for students than seats in the stadium.*

The petite redhead appeared by Greg's side and quickly pulled him back. "What are you doing! It's just fries; it's not worth it." A look of disapproval crossed her face.

Lance continued his apology. "I'm sorry, it was an accident."

Greg raised his hand, positioning his fist an inch from Lance's nose. "Dude, you try doing that again..."

Greg's friends waved to him, gesturing at some empty seats a few rows down. "Let it go, man. Come on, let's go."

Red-faced, Greg blurted out one final threat. "Don't you ever show your face at Cal. Idiot!"

As soon as the altercation ended, Lance's gaze fell back on the girl. He watched her walk away, hoping all the while that she'd look back. His shoulders fell when she didn't turn around.

Drew waved his hand in front of Lance's face. "Hey, snap out of it. It's over." He motioned to the seat beside him. "Now that those guys are gone, we can enjoy the game."

Lance stared out at the football field as the minutes ticked by, lost in his own thoughts. From time to time, he glanced over in the direction where the redheaded girl had gone. He sat unfazed when the rest of the crowd roared as Stanford won the game by one point.

Following the game, Lance exited the stadium and patted his friend's back as they parted ways. "Hey, it was fun tonight. Thanks for convincing me to come."

Drew chuckled and waved. "Hey, anytime, man. I'm sure you enjoyed that little showdown with that Berkeley moron the most."

"It was probably the most exciting part of the game for me." The word *exciting* only touched the surface of his emotional high. He kept the real reason for his grin a secret. "Anyway, good night."

As Lance walked to his apartment, he kept his head down, still thinking about the girl with the red hair. In his mind, he replayed the moment when their eyes had met, trying to commit her face into his long-term memory. *Will I ever see her again?*

A minute passed before he noticed someone standing in front of him. He raised his head and instantly stopped, his feet frozen. *It's her!* The redheaded girl stood three feet from him. His mouth fell open. She was almost a head shorter than him, and the red locks that had caught his attention fell in soft waves around her shoulders. The smattering of freckles across her nose and high cheekbones complemented her creamy skin. Her eyes held the same vivid blue color as the sweater hugging her curves. After a few moments, Lance realized he had been staring and broke off his gaze. "Hey, it's you."

A smile played on her lips. "Hey, it's you, too."

Lance stood motionless for a moment before reaching out his hand. "I'm sorry, I'm Lance."

"Hi, I'm Juliet." Her cheeks flushed as their palms touched.

"What are you doing here?" Lance wondered. "Where are all your friends?"

"Oh, they left to go back to Berkeley."

"What? They left you here and went back without you?"

"Oh, no, it's not like that. I have an aunt who lives in Palo

Alto. I haven't seen her in a while, so I thought I'd call her and crash at her place tonight."

"I see, that makes more sense. For a second there I thought your friends had abandoned you," he joked. Regardless of the reason she was here, he was glad. So glad.

Juliet gave a good-natured laugh. "No, no, they wouldn't do that. Even though we're from Berkeley, we are decent people, too, you know. Most of us don't mind having a free side order of fries tossed at us."

He smiled warmly. She was beautiful and had a sense of humor, too? "Sorry, that was totally an accident. I would never intentionally toss fries at anyone."

"I know. No harm done."

They stared at one another for a few moments. Lance couldn't believe his luck running into Juliet like this. What he wouldn't do to spend some time with her. He cleared his throat, wondering if he had enough guts to speak his thoughts out loud. Deciding to take a chance, he asked, "Hey, you know, my car's parked right over there. I could give you a ride if you like?"

Juliet pursed her lips as she considered his offer. Apprehension flickered on her face before she nodded. "Sure, if that's not too much trouble."

He pointed at an apartment building a block from where they stood. "Great. My car's right over there."

As they strolled down the road, Juliet kept a gap between them, but she did return every one of his smiles.

"So," he spoke up to fill the silence, "where does your aunt live?"

"Actually, I'm not sure what the name of the street is, but I think I remember how to get there." She grinned sheepishly.

"If we head down El Camino, three or four blocks down, we make a left, and her house should be just around the corner."

Lance squared his jaw and nodded. "Okay, that sounds easy enough. I'm pretty familiar with the area."

He directed Juliet toward a silver sedan and opened the passenger side door. "Sorry about the mess." He tossed a stack of books from the front seat into the back and joked, "Books are my usual passengers. They love sitting in my car with the windows rolled down. I hope you don't mind my little Honda."

"Not at all, thanks." She laughed as she took a seat.

Lance closed the door and jogged over to the driver's side. He flashed Juliet a bright smile as he sat down. He started the car and headed down El Camino, tapping the steering wheel with his thumb and brushing his hand through his hair. He was trying his best to play it cool.

Juliet faced her window, tilting her head to look at the street signs they passed.

After a few minutes, Lance cleared his throat. "Do you see the street?"

"No, not really." She glanced over at him, her nose wrinkling in chagrin. "Are we still in Palo Alto?"

Lance laughed. "We are, but not for long. A couple more blocks and we'll be in Sunnyvale."

Juliet frowned. "Maybe we should turn around. I'm sure the street's around here somewhere. I probably missed it the first time."

"No problem, I'm not in a rush." He made a U-turn at the next intersection and headed back in the direction they had come. Not long after, they reached the Stanford campus. "Here we are again."

Laughing, Juliet threw her hands into the air. "I'm horrible with directions. I have no idea where we are. I'm lost."

Lance gave her a sympathetic look as he laughed along with her. "We are certainly not lost; we are right where we started."

Juliet caught her breath and asked, "Is there a pay phone close by? I'll give Aunt Liz a call. I do know her number."

"Sure, sure." He pointed out the window at the darkening sky. "Uh, it's getting close to dinnertime. Are you by chance hungry?"

"I could use something to eat," she answered without missing a beat.

He didn't miss the enthusiasm in her voice. "Great. There's this place you've got to try out; it's one of my favorite shops. You can also use the phone there. It's just up ahead."

Lance sped up and turned into the parking lot of a small strip mall. They parked and headed out of the car toward a shop with the name Happy Donut written in white block letters. Next to the name read the words *Open 24 Hours.*

Juliet cocked her head to one side as she looked at the sign. "Donuts for dinner?"

Lance chuckled. "It's not as strange as it sounds. They do have other things too, like sandwiches, if you want. But I highly recommend their blueberry cake donut. It is the best."

Juliet eyed his frame, giving him a quick onceover. "I didn't peg you as a donut eater."

"I have good genes, I guess. Come on, you'll like this place."

The excitement in the air was palpable when they walked through the door. Chatter and laughter resounded throughout the small shop. Dozens of customers dressed in red, likely fans from Stanford's Big Game, occupied the tables. He noticed the curious faces that turned toward them made Juliet cower. This was not a good place to be wearing blue. Immediately, he placed a hand on the small of her back and guided her through the crowd.

A petite woman behind the counter greeted them. "Hey, Lance, back for your usual?"

"Hey, Sam, give me two, please. I brought a friend."

"Sure thing, I'll bring them over."

Lance looked over at Juliet. "I hope you don't mind eating before you call your aunt?"

She shook her head as they sat down at a table near the back of the shop. "That's fine with me."

Sam delivered their order shortly after.

Juliet took a generous bite of her blueberry cake donut and exclaimed, "You weren't exaggerating, this is delicious!"

Lance leaned forward in his chair. "I love this place. Even though it may look like any other donut shop, everything they bake here is absolute perfection."

"I can tell. The nutmeg in this really balances out the flavor of the blueberries. And the lemon glaze is the perfect finishing touch." She took another bite and smiled in satisfaction.

"Sounds like you know a thing or two about baking."

"I love messing around in the kitchen. I can't cook worth anything, but I love to bake. Muffins, cookies, pies—you name it, I can make it."

"Well, I love eating. If you ever need a guinea pig..."

"Thanks for the offer, but I wouldn't want to contribute to your freshman fifteen." She blushed as soon as the words left her mouth. "Not that you are in any danger of being overweight."

"No worries. It's about three years too late for that."

"Oh, you're a senior? I didn't realize..."

"It's okay, no big deal." Lance grinned. "I've aged well."

"Well, I hope to look as youthful as you when I'm a senior."

"The secret to my fountain of youth is eating dessert before dinner." Lance winked, causing her to laugh again.

A feeling of ease surrounded them as they continued eating and talking. They rehashed the day's football game and segued to their favorite types of food, Lance's being garlic fries. Hardly a pause interrupted their conversation as one person jumped in where the other left off.

After several hours had flown by, Juliet glanced outside the window and exclaimed, "Oh my gosh, what time is it? I completely forgot about calling my aunt."

Lance checked his watch. "Wow, it's midnight already. You better call her."

Juliet frowned. "Aunt Liz is an early sleeper. She's usually in bed by ten. I wouldn't want to wake her up."

He held her gaze for a moment before remarking, "Well, I don't mind giving you a ride back to Berkeley."

"What? No, it's too far. That's too much trouble."

"I don't mind, really."

She seemed to contemplate his offer then eyed him playfully through her long lashes. "The night's still young. How about another cup of coffee? Or maybe two…"

Lance gestured to Sam from across the room. "Two more coffees, please." He returned his attention to Juliet.

Her cheeks reddened under his gaze. "Uh, what are you majoring in at Stanford?"

"I bet you'll never guess."

Juliet studied him with a raised brow. "Physics?"

"Wow, how did you know?"

She squared her shoulders with a proud look on her face. "You could say I'm good at reading people. I also saw the physics books in your car," she added with a wink. "What do you plan on doing with physics?"

"Well, I plan on going to grad school next year," Lance began then paused as if he were about to reveal a big secret. "And then maybe...I'll build a time machine."

Juliet's jaw dropped. "A time machine, huh? Like Marty McFly in *Back to the Future*?"

"Exactly. I got hooked on the idea of time travel ever since I saw that movie. I've been studying it ever since. I'm also developing a few theories of my own." He paused. "Sounds a little crazy, doesn't it?"

"Crazy," Juliet quipped, "is eating donuts for dinner. It's not crazy to have a dream and pursue it. I'm sure Einstein started out with a dream—look where it got him."

Lance held his hands up in protest at the comparison. "I'm no Einstein, but thanks for taking me seriously. That means a lot."

"I think it'd be cool to go back in time and meet your great-great-grandparents or witness some big events in history." Juliet looked at him with a glint in her eyes. "Or better yet, you could use it to stop yourself from doing something you'd regret."

"Sounds like you have something specific in mind?"

"Just silly, stupid stuff, like telling myself not to dye my hair black in junior high." She held up a lock of hair and grimaced. "It didn't turn out nearly as glamorous as I thought it would. I ended up wearing a ski cap every day that summer. And Southern California is not known for its cool summers."

"I'm glad you didn't change it again. It was the first thing I noticed about you."

Juliet self-consciously brushed some strands back from her

face. She offered a coy smile and asked, "Where do you want to go when you finish building your time machine?"

Lance quirked an eyebrow. "I've thought long and hard about that. I've considered going back to meet Einstein. It'd be so cool to pick his brain, run some of my ideas past him. But then I decided the time I'd really want to travel back to would be when the first donut was invented."

Juliet threw her head back, her chest rising and falling with bursts of laughter.

Lance gazed longingly at her. He never took note of people's hair, but Juliet's had caught his attention. *Red is the most beautiful color.* He also loved the way she laughed so freely. *I've never enjoyed talking to anyone this much before. I could stay here forever.*

To his delight, they continued to share in each other's company over several more cups of coffee. Close to three o'clock in the morning, they ordered sandwiches to satisfy the intense hunger that came with pulling an all-nighter. They continued chatting like old friends trying to catch up after a long separation. The more they learned about each other, the more fulfilled Lance felt. He drank in all the details of Juliet's life, longing to replace curiosity with familiarity. Their conversation finally came to a halt when the bell hanging on the front door rang. They looked up to see a customer coming in to buy breakfast.

Juliet checked the clock on the wall. "It's seven thirty already? I guess I could call my aunt now. She should be up. She usually walks her dog early in the morning."

"Sure." He watched as she walked over to the corner of the store to make her call. He couldn't help staring. Even though he hadn't slept a wink all night, he felt energized in Juliet's presence. *I can't believe we got to spend so much time together. She is absolutely amazing. Where did she come from?*

When Juliet finished her call, she returned to their table. "Okay, I know exactly where my aunt lives now. No more getting lost."

"No problem." Lance took her statement as a cue to wrap up their time together. "Well, should we go now?"

"Sure. Do we pay over there?" Juliet gestured toward the front of the shop.

"No worries, I got it."

"Are you sure?" When he insisted on paying, Juliet smiled. "Thank you."

They left Happy Donut and returned to Lance's car. A heavy fog of silence hung over them as they traveled down El Camino. Lance felt a pit form in his stomach as he pondered their inevitable separation. *Our time together was too short.* He rubbed his chin with one hand and sneaked a look at Juliet. *How do we say goodbye?*

In a matter of minutes, they arrived at Aunt Liz's house and parked. They stood on the driveway facing each other, both silent. Juliet played with a lock of her hair while Lance shifted his weight from one foot to the other. He debated whether to ask for her number. *Should I? Should I not? I think we had a great time together.* He jammed his hands in his jean pockets and started to second-guess himself. *But what if she's with that guy Greg from the game?* He rubbed the back of his neck and made up his mind. *I don't want to look stupid.* He finally reached out to shake Juliet's hand. "I had a really great time, Juliet."

"Me too, Lance." Without warning, Juliet reached out and wrapped her arms around him. She leaned against his chest and gave him a gentle squeeze.

Lance froze. Juliet's sudden show of affection overwhelmed him so much, his body warmed from his head to his toes. *She smells so sweet, like flowers.* He longed to hold her as well, but his limbs felt like stone. He only managed to utter an indistinct sound in his throat.

A few seconds passed before Juliet let go and stepped back. Blushing, she stammered, "I-I better go. Thank you for the ride." She turned in the direction of the brick house and ran up the front steps.

The absence of Juliet's touch woke Lance from his daze. He opened his mouth, but once again, no words emerged. Lance remained still, telling himself that if she turned around, he'd ask for her number.

Juliet reached the front door and paused before knocking. An older woman appeared, pulled her inside with a hug, and closed the door.

Lance found himself standing alone on the driveway. *I'm an idiot! I can't believe I let her get away!*

Juliet had exited his life as quickly as she had entered it.

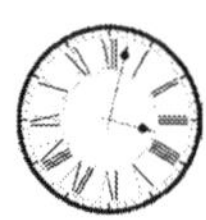

Lance looked up from the engagement picture he had been holding and shook his head free from those memories. He knew too much about living with regret. If he could have had that moment back, he would have done things so differently. *I won't screw it up this time. Thank God for second chances.*

He glanced at his phone. Five past eight. Time to get going. Gulping down the last of his milk, he placed the glass in the sink. He showered and got dressed in his usual jeans and sneakers, pairing them with an azure blue polo shirt Juliet had picked out for him. The color reminded him of her bright eyes and her laugh that had been etched into his memory for the past decade. A smile crossed his lips as he anticipated seeing her in a few hours. Lance gathered up his belongings and stepped outside the apartment. Right after he locked the door, he opened it again. He ran back inside and grabbed the stack of engagement photos from the kitchen table. *That was a close one.*

Chapter Two

Lance entered his office on campus and set up his silver laptop to review his notes. His shoulders tensed from a combination of excitement and focus as he thought about that evening's speaking engagement. He usually gave talks to raise funds for Stanford and to keep his own research going. Tonight, however, he would be speaking at Caltech to undergraduates interested in physics. He had been lucky enough to have done so much in the field in such a short amount of time, so he took every opportunity he had to give back to the community. Inspiring young students ranked at the top of his priorities.

His eyes adjusted to the brightness of the laptop screen as he scrolled to the page where he had left off the previous evening. Sitting up straight with his shoulders back, he projected his voice to an imaginary audience. "Ladies and gentlemen, how would you like to travel back in time to just a week ago and win the biggest lottery in history?"

He couldn't help himself and started chuckling at his own silliness. No other subject energized him as much as time travel did. It was the one topic he could spend hours and hours talking about.

The swivel chair squeaked as he spun around and stopped to admire the complex machine sitting behind him, a product of a decade's worth of research. The model held the potential for creating the first working time travel vehicle in human history. He marveled at how brightly its metals of silver, gold, and copper reflected the sunlight coming through the window. The machine boasted four gigantic posts that had been placed in equal distances from each other to form a perfect square. On each post, two horn-shaped objects—long and thick—protruded out and stretched to the two other horns adjacent to them. At the top, each of these end points merged to form a perfect octagon. Smooth metal tubes surrounded an object in the center of these posts, which resembled a bird's nest. The tubes, evenly and precisely placed, meshed together to form millions of tiny octagons over the entire surface.

Lance's footsteps echoed in the room as he walked closer to the machine. He peered inside the mesh of tubes, among which sat the shiniest silver ball. He saw his own reflection, albeit somewhat distorted, in it. The ball appeared to be made of solid metal, yet with an aqueous quality to it much like liquid mercury. Lance gently blew at the ball, his breath creating a ripple effect that caused it to spread out for a few seconds before returning to its original shape.

He pondered the incredible journey that had led him to this point in his career. Although he had once considered following in his father's footsteps to go into the military, he decided a career in the sciences would serve mankind in a similarly great way. It had all started with a family movie night at the age of ten. Even in his youth, he had determined what he wanted to achieve in life, what he had to make a reality. He spent every waking minute since then reading everything he could get his hands on related to time travel. Things finally fell into place during his post-grad years as his research began to show considerable promise.

In recent years, he published multiple papers regarding relativity in an effort to continue Einstein's work. However, his article in Nature last spring proved to be the most instrumental in elevating his status in the field of physics. His submission on time travel had been a shot in the dark. His own colleagues had questioned his ideas and looked down on him for his young age. Thankfully, he hadn't listened to their criticisms. His article had both shocked and impressed the editor. When it passed the peer review of renowned scientists, Lance knew for certain he had found something groundbreaking. Publication in such a prestigious journal immediately propelled him into the spotlight of the scientific community, as well as mainstream media. Being named one of *Time Magazine*'s "100 most influential people of 2010" also added to his credibility.

Lance shook his head in disbelief to be on the brink of one of the most monumental discoveries in history. *I'm so close, I can feel it.* In the next moment, however, doubt and frustration crept into the corners of his mind as he thought of other, more brilliant people also making strides in the field. *I'm only thirty-seven, what makes me think it will be me?*

His fingers itched to tinker with the machine again and review the data collected from the last trial, but he glanced at his watch and hesitated. *Not today. There's still too much to go over before lunch.* His eyes lingered one more moment on the key to his dreams. *One of these days. One of these days I will discover the secret of time travel.*

He returned to his desk and switched his focus back to his speech. He wanted to find more ways to connect to and inspire the college students at Caltech that evening. Just as he finished editing the final version of his speech, his cell phone alarm went off. *Juliet.*

A wide smile replaced the serious expression that had occupied him for the past few hours. Although the topic of time travel excited him, it paled in comparison to spending time with his fiancée. Nothing else produced in him the same heightened sense of joy as seeing her did.

Often, he thought about how he would give up everything, his lifetime's worth of research, if he could do nothing else but just be with her. Of course, logically, he knew they both had bills to pay, and he also desired to make his life amount to something. But in his heart, he had no greater longing than to retire, live in some third world country, and eat bland potatoes and rice all day if he could do so with Juliet. He finally understood what all those romantic songs talked about, how you could survive on love alone. He grinned as he realized how completely illogical he sounded, so unlike a scientist. He leaped from his chair, packed up his belongings, and left his office with a lightness in his steps.

Happy Donut. To Lance, this little shop not only served up the best food but also the best memories of his adult life. With a childlike grin on his face, he swung open the door and strode in.

Sam, his favorite waitress—honestly, the only waitress there all those years—looked up. "Hey Lance, are you late?"

"No, I'm right on time, but she's always early." Lance replied playfully as he headed toward the back of the restaurant.

Juliet sat at the table where they had spent their first unofficial date together. The light streaming in through the window behind her illuminated her hair, making it appear more radiant and fiery than usual. Lance took in the view and swallowed hard. *My fiancée.* He couldn't help feeling like a tongue-tied teenager in her presence.

She held a glass of iced tea between her hands and looked up mid-sip as Lance approached. A big smile spread over her lips and she tilted her head to the left. She stood up quickly, causing her chair to rock, and ran over to greet him. "Hey, baby, I missed you."

"Me, too." Lance returned her embrace. Holding her like this brought a rush of memories to mind of their unexpected reunion following their separation at Aunt Liz's house.

Since their first meeting at the college football game, over thirteen years had passed. Lance had lost all hope of seeing Juliet again. He had dated a couple of other girls, but he had never experienced with them the chemistry he had with Juliet, that comfortable feeling of being with an old friend. He admitted she had captured his heart already, making it unavailable to anyone else. He had turned to work to fill the void she left.

Ironically, it was his research that had led him back to her. Two years ago, he had been working on a calculation problem in his office that had him stumped for hours. Unable to make a breakthrough, he decided to take a long walk around campus.

Normally, he took a break to give his brain a rest, but that day he couldn't let go of the problem. He wandered around, looking up at the sky as if the equations existed in the clouds. Suddenly, all the numbers and symbols seemed to tumble down from the heavens as he rounded the corner of the walkway and bumped into someone. Startled, Lance held up both hands and apologized. "I'm so…" He couldn't even finish his sentence. Shock held his tongue and left him speechless. He saw her red hair first then her blue eyes. She looked the same as the last time he had seen her, so many years ago.

Juliet's jaw dropped, and her phone slipped from her hands. A clatter resounded as metal made contact with cement. She looked straight into his eyes and squinted for a second.

Lance broke the silence first. "Juliet!"

"Lance! What are you doing here?"

"What do you mean? I work here. What are you doing here?"

"What? You work here? Since when?"

"Since forever? I worked in the lab when I was a student here. I took a break to go to grad school on the east coast, but came back for my postdoc. Now I teach physics here. Anyway, what are you doing here?"

"You're a professor? That's impressive, Lance." Juliet pointed at the name badge on her white coat, which read *Stanford University Medical Center.* "I work at the hospital. I'm a third-year resident."

"A doctor, huh? Now that's impressive." Lance's body warmed with excitement. *She's doing a pretty good job of healing my heart right now.* "If I had known you were working here, I would've broken some bones to come see you." He bent down and picked up the phone lying on the ground, then handed it to her. "Looks like your phone's going to need a doctor."

Her eyes widened when their fingers touched. "You've been here all along. I can't believe we never ran into each other." She shook her head in disbelief. "I didn't think I would ever see you again." A tear slid down her cheek, and she drew in a shaky breath. She placed one hand on his chest then pulled him close.

Lance sensed her body trembling and held her tightly. He was not going to let her go this time. A peace settled over his heart, and he finally felt like he had found his way home.

There they remained in the middle of the sidewalk, holding onto each other as several people passed. Despite the silence, a veil of intimacy hung over them. They stood there for minutes, trying to make up for the years they had lost. They finally pulled away, and their hands found each other. They went from embracing to holding hands as if it was the most natural thing to do.

"Hungry?" Lance spoke softly as he brushed some loose strands of hair from her cheek.

Juliet smiled from ear to ear. "I have the oddest craving for a donut right now."

He raised an eyebrow and grinned. "I think I know just the place."

They restarted their lives together that day and became inseparable. Things were so easy between the two of them. Lance continued to work as a professor at Stanford, and Juliet finished her residency at Stanford and was lucky enough to get a permanent position at the hospital. Now here they were at their favorite hangout where they met for lunch every Friday.

Lance lifted a hand to brush back Juliet's hair from her forehead and paused to look in her eyes. "You look absolutely amazing." He leaned down to place a soft kiss on her lips.

"You look pretty good yourself. I ordered our usual." She motioned to the sandwiches and blueberry cake donuts on the table.

"Thanks, I'm starving." Lance took her hand as they walked to their table and sat down.

As they did every week, they ate dessert first before eating their sandwiches. It was a small reminder of their first time together. When they had finished their meal, they stacked their empty plates to the side of the table and Lance pulled out their engagement pictures from his laptop bag.

"You remembered!" Juliet clapped her hands in delight.

"Of course, my darling." Lance handed the photos to Juliet. "Did you doubt me?"

"Well, there is a reason why someone coined the term 'absentminded professor.'" She grinned and moved aside her glass to make room for the photos. "I've been checking them out on the photographer's website. Let me show you the ones I like, and we can compare them with the ones you like."

Lance continued to smile at Juliet. He was just so happy and at peace with everything that was happening. They had known that one day they would get married; it was simply a matter of when. They had thought about moving in together, but they were both old-fashioned and preferred to have a church wedding before settling down and having kids. Finally, after a year of dating, Lance had popped the question.

"Hey, pay attention." Juliet cupped his chin and turned his head toward the pictures.

Lance chuckled at how easily her presence could distract him. "Yes, yes, absolutely, honey."

She held up a photo and handed it to Lance. "I love this one of us at the beach. What do you think?"

Lance nodded. "Sure."

"Oh, and this one of you by yourself. You look so handsome, don't you think so, Lance?"

"I think that's the one where the photographer told me to look more mysterious and not so constipated." Lance shook his head and laughed good-naturedly at himself. "I like this one of you much better." He pointed at a picture of Juliet sitting on the grass in Golden Gate Park. "You look so happy."

Juliet smiled. "How about we choose both? Oh, and we have to pick the one of us at the Stanford Stadium. After all, that's where we met."

"And where we got engaged. That row of bleacher seats has a very special place in our hearts. Maybe we should have the wedding there, too. What do you think?"

Juliet's eyes grew wide. "You're not serious?"

Lance laughed out loud and reached over to take Juliet's hand. "I'm kidding, sweetheart." He placed a soft kiss on her palm.

Juliet's expression softened as she looked at the engagement ring on her left hand. "You designed such a beautiful ring, Lance."

"A beautiful ring for the most beautiful girl." Lance held her hand up to examine the ring. "I kept wanting to tell you about it the whole month before the proposal. Do you know how hard it is to keep a secret from your best friend?"

"Well, you kinda gave it away when you asked to borrow one of my rings for your sister to try on."

Lance laughed. "Thanks for going along with that."

"I knew something was up. Rebecca and I have totally different tastes in jewelry." Juliet shook her head in amusement. "I almost asked you a dozen times when you were going to pop the question. If you didn't propose soon, *I* would have!"

"It took me some time to make sure everything was perfect with the ring, especially the size."

"I couldn't have asked for anything more perfect." Juliet admired the ring as it sparkled in the sunlight.

"Not bad for a geeky physicist, huh?" Lance cradled her hand in his. He looked at the unique setting, a one-carat diamond set off with a red garnet on one side and a dark blue sapphire on the other. "Our school colors come together quite nicely, don't you think? Just like us."

Juliet raised an eyebrow. "I never thought I'd find love at a football game and, least of all, with a guy in red. My friends still joke that I fell for the enemy."

"But they all came out to support us the day of the proposal. Even Greg."

"Would you believe he's been telling people that he's the one who brought us together?" Juliet laughed. "It was a great idea to ask both our Stanford and Cal friends to join us that day. It was like déjà vu having the same people there just like the first time we met."

"What better place to seal the deal than at another Big Game? But that football game had to have been the longest one I have ever sat through."

Juliet giggled. "You were fidgeting in your seat for the whole first half. You didn't even want to eat your garlic fries! *That* about gave it away."

"It's not every day that I get to ask the woman of my dreams to marry me, in front of all our friends, no less. It was like having our own halftime show."

"I couldn't believe it was actually happening when you got down on one knee. And the speech you made—I get emotional every time I watch it. I'm so glad Drew got it on video." She picked up the smartphone sitting on the table next to her glass. "Do you mind if we watch it again?"

"You've got the video on your phone?"

Juliet smiled sheepishly. "Guess I might be more romantic than you after all."

"Sure, let's see it. I can't pass up watching myself give the best speech of my life."

Juliet started the video, and the two of them appeared on the small screen, with Lance on bended knee. Friends wearing red, as well as blue and gold, gathered around them. A hush descended upon the group as Lance began to speak.

"I have never met anyone in my life who taught me the meaning of *love* and the meaning of *lost* all in one night. When I first met you, my life was suddenly brighter. When I lost you, I spent the next thirteen years thinking about you every day. During those thirteen years, I thought I would likely grow old all by myself and never find you again. But I would always imagine that I'd one day figure out how to time travel. Though I might be old in age, I would travel back in time and go back to that fateful day when we met just to get another glimpse of you. I thought if that were to happen, you may not recognize me in my old age, but for me it would be enough. I love you. I just want to see you happy, to see that smile of yours. If I could, I would freeze time and just live in that one moment."

Juliet held one hand to her heart as she looked deep into Lance's eyes. Fresh tears spilled down her cheeks despite the big smile on her face.

"Well, I'm so glad the big guy upstairs decided to spare me that trouble." Lance paused as their friends' laughter interrupted him. "Life without you is simply a meaningless distraction. I lost you once; I'm not going to lose you again. Before you came into my life, I only knew numbers and equations. Now I know there is so much more. I never knew being in love could bring so much joy and warmth to my life. Sometimes just seeing your smile causes me to forget to breathe. Hearing your voice can stop my brain and whatever it was thinking about and put a smile on my face as if I were on drugs—although I swear I have never taken any illegal drugs in my life. Whenever I'm with you, I feel indescribable joy. Juliet, you are the love of my life. We are made to be partners in crime. We are made to take on this world together." Lance held up a black velvet box and opened it. "Juliet, will you marry me?"

Juliet nodded eagerly as she pulled Lance up. When he stood up, she wrapped her arms around him. She finally answered in a hushed voice. "Yes. Yes!"

Lance held her even tighter to himself at that point. He closed his eyes and sighed deeply. He tilted Juliet's face up with one hand and leaned down toward her, their noses touching. He took the ring and placed it on her finger. "I love you, Juliet."

"I love you, too, Lance." Juliet stood on tiptoes and kissed him fully on the lips.

Cameras went off all around them as their friends cheered and took pictures of the newly engaged couple. When Lance and Juliet broke free of their embrace, their families and friends rushed over to congratulate them.

Juliet sniffed and wiped a tear from the corner of her eye as she stopped the video. "I can't believe you managed to get my parents to keep it a secret from me." She leaned against Lance's shoulder, amazed at how far they had come. All her years of wishful thinking had become reality when they reunited on campus that fateful day. It was such a sweet reunion, sweeter than the sugary scent hanging in the air of the donut shop. Here was the college kid she had fallen for with the same dimples and sense of humor. The only difference was a hint of gray coming in near his temples, which gave her a glimpse of the man she would grow old with. Juliet's cheeks warmed as more tears gathered in her eyes. She loved Lance so much. "I'm crying again. See what you do to me?"

Lance reached his arm around Juliet and brought her close. He gently kissed the top of her head. "I do bring out the best in you, don't I?"

Juliet laughed, looking up at him with tender eyes. "I'm going to be a mess on our wedding day. I don't know how I'm going to keep it together."

"What if I promise to not make any speeches? Or better yet, I won't say a single word. Then you won't have to worry about crying."

"As long as you say 'I do'!" They both laughed. Just then the alarm on Lance's cell phone sounded.

Lance looked at the time. "Oh, man, I better get going. I'm catching the two forty-five flight out of San Jose."

"Is it time already?" Juliet sighed. "Please call me when you're done speaking."

"Of course." Lance returned the photos to his laptop bag. "I should be done around eight and be home just before midnight."

He paid for their meals and walked her out to her car. "I'll give you a call as soon as I'm done speaking to the students, but don't wait up."

"Please make sure you call, otherwise I'll worry." Juliet didn't want to say goodbye just yet. She tugged at the hem of

Lance's shirt as her eyes welled up again. "You've got a brilliant mind, Lance, and an amazing heart. You're going to change the world someday. I just know it." She wrapped her arms around him in a warm embrace and kissed him one last time before letting go.

"Thanks for always believing in me," he replied with an affectionate smile.

Juliet sat down in her car, and Lance closed the door behind her. She started the engine and rolled down her window. "Have a safe trip. Call me."

"You got it. I love you."

"I love you more!" Juliet drove off, waving through the window until she could no longer see Lance in the rearview mirror.

Chapter Three

Lance's flight south had been delayed an hour due to mechanical problems, so he barely had time for dinner. Fortunately, there was a coffee shop at the airport where he landed and he was able to grab a bagel and coffee. Carrying his food in one hand and his laptop bag in the other, he departed the terminal.

As soon as he exited, the commotion of the busy street enveloped him. The rush of cars honking and airport security officers whistling at drivers propelled him to pick up his pace as he walked to the curb. There he noticed a long line of idling cabs waiting for customers. Although the administration at Caltech had offered to pick him up at the airport, he was not the type who wanted people to wait on him like he was a celebrity. He hailed the first taxi in line, opened the door, and stepped inside.

The taxi driver turned around with an eager smile. "Where to, my friend?"

"Caltech. And please try to hurry. I have a seminar starting in about an hour."

"I'll step on it."

Lance devoured his dinner then thought to call Dr. McKenzie, the dean of physics. "Dr. McKenzie, this is Lance Everett. I'm on my way over. My flight was delayed, but I should be able to make it just in time. Yes, thank you, sir. See you soon." Lance sighed as he looked out at the congested roads. *Driving in Bay Area traffic is a cakewalk compared to this.*

As soon as he got off the phone, the taxi driver spoke up. "Sir, I'm not sure if you've been to LA before, but traffic here is pretty terrible. I'll do my best though."

Lance looked at his watch and saw that five minutes had passed, yet they had barely made it out of the airport. *This is going to be a close one.* "Yes, I understand. Please do what you can. I appreciate it."

He took out his phone to send Juliet a text.

Hi hon, flight was delayed, on my way to Caltech now. It'd be great if had a time dilation machine. I could sure use a couple of extra minutes now. Call you when I'm done. xoxo

Lance wished there was something he could do to get to the school quicker. He noticed though that the driver was doing his best to beat the traffic. His body swayed to the left and right as the taxi weaved in and out of the lanes. *I might as well rest a little.* He took the opportunity to close his eyes.

It felt like he had just drifted off to sleep when the driver called out, "Sir, we are here. This school is pretty big. Is there a particular building you want me to drop you off at?"

Lance woke with a start and glanced down at his watch. *I slept for forty-five minutes? Guess I'm more tired than I thought.* "Yes, please go straight and take a right two blocks down. I'm going to Beckman Auditorium." He had become quite familiar with the campus after speaking there several times in the past year.

The taxi arrived at the auditorium with no time to spare. Lance reached for his wallet. "How much do I owe you?" He looked out the window and saw Dr. McKenzie standing outside. Upon seeing Lance arrive, the gray-haired man waved and began to walk over to the taxi.

The taxi driver stopped the meter and turned to Lance. "Seventy-two dollars, sir."

Lance quickly handed the driver his credit card. "I need a receipt, please."

"No problem."

"Can you come back in about two hours? I should be done by then and I'll need to head back to the airport."

"I'll be back." The driver smiled at the offer of more business and handed the receipt to Lance.

Lance signed the slip, adding a generous tip to thank the driver for getting him to the school on time. He grabbed his laptop bag and stepped out. "Thanks. I'll see you soon."

"You got it."

Dr. McKenzie greeted Lance with a handshake. "Lance, it's good to see you. Glad you made it."

"Sorry, sir, for the delay."

"No problem, but we should get going."

They hurried up the stairs to the white circular building. As they entered, some of the students noticed Lance and began cheering. The entire room resounded with applause. When they reached the first row, Dr. McKenzie gestured for Lance to take a seat. "Let me do a quick introduction for you."

Dr. McKenzie stood at the podium and held his hands up to call for silence. "Thank you all for your warm welcome. I wish all this cheering was for me." He paused as the audience chuckled. "We are pleased to have Dr. Lance Everett here with us tonight. I can see you are all very excited to hear about his latest research in the field of physics. Allow me first to take a moment and share with you some of his recent accomplishments."

Lance took a deep breath as he waited for his turn at the podium. He looked up at the golden mesh-like material that hung from the ceiling. The lights flickering behind the mesh appeared like stars in the nighttime sky. *Next time I come I'll have to bring Juliet. She would love this place.* He took off his sports jacket and laid it on the seat next to him. He had thought to change into more formal clothing, but since he was tight on time, his light blue polo shirt and jeans would have to do. Besides, with a younger crowd tonight, casual attire would help him connect with them better.

He took his phone out to silence it and noticed a new text message from Juliet.

Hope you made it on time. Break a leg, babe! Can't wait to hear about the turnout. I bet all those college girls are mesmerized by your good looks. xoxo

Lance smiled as he put his phone back in his pocket. He glanced around the auditorium and was pleased to see so many young faces. *This is a great turnout.* He felt a rush of adrenaline energize his body as he heard his name called out. He made his way up to the stage.

"Thank you, Dr. McKenzie for such a wonderful, gracious introduction." He paused to smile. "For a second there, I thought he was talking about a different speaker for tonight's event. I'm not sure if I should be credited for all those things Dr. McKenzie described. It certainly makes me sound like I've been around forever, but I'm just thirty-seven years old. I'll show you my ID if you like." Laughter filled the auditorium as Lance pulled out his wallet and held it up for the audience to see.

"All kidding aside, I'm very grateful for the introduction and for this opportunity to speak to you all. I'm especially excited because I was told that today's audience would be mostly undergraduate students. Most of my speaking engagements are with an audience who have multiple Ph.D.'s in their titles. They often examine every word I say with a great thought process. And any mistakes I make usually show up in the next issue of *Scientific Journal.*" Lance paused to roll his eyes. "I'm very excited however to speak to this crowd. Younger folks have such a curiosity about science and a vivid imagination, which makes the entire speaking event fun for me and hopefully fun for you as well. I hope tonight we can all learn something and have some fun at the same time."

Lance saw looks of interest on the students' faces. They were listening intently to his words. He smiled and began gesturing with his hands as his enthusiasm grew. "You probably know my specialty is in quantum physics, but to be more specific, time travel. To be even more specific, time travel into the past. I know for many people time travel is a fascinating topic. Why is it so fascinating? Well, who wouldn't want to be able to travel to a distant time and witness the beginning of the universe, or into the future and find out what the world will be like a thousand years from now? Will the human race evolve into creatures with huge heads and small limbs, or perhaps will the entire world become one country with all nations living in peace with each other? The idea of time travel itself holds endless possibilities, and if it is at all possible, it would be an adventure with literally no end.

"As I said before, I'm much more interested in time travel

back in time and not so much into the future. Let me tell you why. Time travel into the future—in a sense, we are already doing it. In fact, we are all forced and bound to travel forward. None of us can say, 'I refuse to travel forward'. As the hands of a clock move, we have no choice but to grow a second older than the last." He stood with one hand on his hip and the other directed toward the audience. "Now, of course, in the traditional sense of time travel into the future, it would involve traveling decades or years or even thousands of years into the future; it would not just simply be a process of aging. However, even that is more or less possible today. I'm sure many of you have already heard of time dilation. This is basically a term describing the phenomenon that as an object travels physically faster and faster, time for this object becomes slower and slower, while everything else still moves at the original speed of time.

"There are many well-known experiments that have been done in the past where this has already been proven. For example, take two people who are each carrying one of the most accurate atomic clocks ever made. One travels into space while another stays on Earth. The atomic clock with the person who travels into space at a high velocity will tick slower than the clock which stays on Earth. This effect is not because the clock malfunctions when traveling at a high velocity. In fact, the person who takes this clock and travels into space would see time passing exactly just like when he was on Earth, but because he is traveling at such a high speed, it literally bends time, and time becomes slower compared to the person who is on Earth." Lance bent his arm from a horizontal position to a slightly curved one to give a visual example to the audience.

"Imagine if this rocket can travel at a speed very, very near the speed of light; time would almost stand still. Yet for the person on Earth, time will continue to move forward with no change. The result would be that when this rocket, after traveling near the speed of light, returns back to Earth in one week's time, thousands of years would have already passed on Earth." Lance paused to let his words sink in. Whenever he spoke, he tended to rush his speech out of excitement. Juliet always reminded him that he needed to talk slower so the audience would have time to digest his words.

"Here comes the reason why I'm not interested in traveling forward. In this type of time travel into space, it is a one-way ticket; you speed into the future, but you can never return. You will in fact land hundreds or even thousands of years into the future. You will surely have missed out on everything that happened while you were out in space. While you were sitting in a rocket for just about a week's time, all your family and friends—the whole world—would have aged and lived their lives without you. Now for me, the idea of traveling thousands of years into the future while all my family and friends live on without me is great science, but a sacrifice I'm not willing to make." He shook his head firmly to emphasize his point.

"Now, my special focus of study is time travel into the past. This idea really, really fascinates me. First of all, traveling back in time is completely anti-nature. Again, everyone naturally travels forward in time. With technology, I believe, in the not-too-distant future, you will be able to choose to travel faster or slower into the future. However, traveling back in time is completely unnatural, completely against the laws of nature. This intrigues me.

"Second, the applications of traveling back in time are completely different than traveling into the future. I'm sure you have seen movies or read books where the main characters travel back in time and rewrite the entire future. Or someone travels back in time to save the life of their loved one from certain death. Or someone travels back in time to witness the beginning of the universe and is able to see the dinosaurs roam the earth and discover what really killed them. The applications are endless. And the biggest difference for me is that traveling back in time, if it is possible, is not a one-way ticket, because as mentioned before, traveling forward in time is in a sense already possible. If one can harness the power to travel back in time, he or she is truly a time traveler, having the ability to travel backward and forward in time."

Lance raised his hand before making his next point. "How many of you have heard of a guy named Albert Einstein?" Murmurs from the audience traveled from one end of the room to the other. "I know, of course, everyone has heard of Einstein. The question should be who hasn't heard of him? Einstein was absolutely a brilliant person. Even though he was born 133 years ago, he discovered many laws of physics that govern our world. He came up with our modern quantum theory, wave-particle duality, and many, many more theories. There is his famous theory of relativity, $E = mc^2$, from which came the discovery of the relationship between time and space, time dilation, and, of course, time travel. According to many theories and laws discovered by Einstein, as an object travels faster and faster near the speed of light, time becomes slower and slower for that object. As the object travels at the speed of light, time basically stands still for that object. Now, if this object can travel faster than the speed of light, the unthinkable happens; time would travel backward."

Lance took the microphone off the stand and began

walking around the stage. He felt more at ease now at this point in his lecture. "Let me use the following example to explain this phenomenon. Let's say, one day you are very upset with me. You disagree with my ideas about traveling back in time, so much so that you want to kill me." He paused with a playful glint in his eyes. "Let's hope none of you are at that point tonight." Laughter rippled once again throughout the auditorium.

"So, you get a gun and point it at me, and you pull the trigger." He used his index finger and thumb to form an imaginary gun. "But you don't know that I already harnessed the power to travel at a speed faster than the speed of light. As I see you point your gun at me, and as you pull the trigger, I travel, at a speed faster than the speed of light, toward you. At that instant, everything changes. Not only does the bullet never have a chance of leaving the barrel of your gun, I reach you so quickly that I get there before you even have a chance to pull out your gun.

"Well, you might think, how is that possible?" Lance held up both hands and shrugged his shoulders. "According to what I just said, I moved after you already pulled out your gun. How can something that happened *after* an event end up happening *before* the event that preceded it? Because by definition, when I see you point your gun at me, that very moment occurs exactly at the speed of light. The light reflecting off your gun, or in other words the photon light particle traveling from your gun to my eye, is traveling exactly at the speed of light. If I can move faster than the speed of light, I am able to get there just before the event of you pointing your gun at me. Thus, I would get there just before you pull out your gun."

Lance noticed several students furrowing their brows in

confusion. "Yes, I know, the concept is difficult to understand. That is exactly why traveling back in time is unnatural. Let me give another example. Again, let's say that I can travel faster than the speed of light. Let's say I plan on running around the earth and start right at this very spot that I'm standing in right now. I start and burst into a speed faster than the speed of light. I would be able to go around the earth and come back just before I started to run. Again, the concept is very difficult to understand. If I can indeed do this, what if I went around the earth, came back, and met myself just before I started my run, and convinced myself not to run? Then would the whole thing have happened? Right, exactly, this does not make sense. The logic doesn't quite work out.

"I've been spending a lot of time working on the equation of time travel, again, specifically time travel into the past, based on some of Einstein's theories. As an object travels faster and faster, and if somehow this object can travel faster than the speed of light, time will begin to roll back. But it will not just simply roll back. Because the energy required for any object to travel faster than the speed of light is so great, the energy involved would literally bend time and space. Not only would that object begin to travel back in time, but its surrounding environment would be pulled into this time warp, and all other objects would also roll back in time. So basically, as an object travels faster than the speed of light, time would begin to roll back for this one object, but as it rolls back in time, it would generate a ripple effect and pull everything in its surroundings to roll back in time with it. This temporal ripple effect theory is the cornerstone of my latest research.

"Let me explain it in these terms. If you can, imagine that time and space are simply a flat piece of cloth floating in space and anchored at its four corners. As an object travels near the speed of light, it gains mass. It is like a marble sitting in the middle of the cloth; it gets heavier and heavier. As the object travels faster than the speed of light, it finally becomes so massive that it drastically pulls down the piece of cloth right in the middle. Depending on how heavy the marble is, the piece of cloth will sink further and further down the middle. At the same time, the surrounding area will also be dragged down because of it. Now, only when the object traveling back in time eventually loses its speed or, in our example, the marble slowly loses its mass would everything return to normal, and the piece of cloth return to a flat piece of cloth floating in space.

"If we can somehow make an object travel faster than the speed of light, everything around it will also travel backward. In fact, the equation that I have developed recently proves exactly this. If an object can be propelled faster than the speed of light, the energy that it requires or the power that it generates would cause everything to roll back in time. We all would have no choice but to begin rolling back in time with this object. It is very much like how we currently have no choice but to roll forward in time. If this event were to happen, we would be in the same situation as now, but rolling backward. Is this beginning to make sense? I hope it does." His eyes scanned the auditorium, and he saw some heads nodding in understanding.

"With this theory, not only can you travel back in time, you can accurately pinpoint an exact time in the past to travel to. How? I'm glad you asked. Using the example earlier, as an object travels faster and faster, time slows down. As it travels at the same speed as light, time stops, and as this object exceeds the speed of light, time reverses. Now, at this speed, it requires a tremendous amount of energy. At some point, this object would eventually use up its energy to keep up the speed in excess of light. As this object slows down, time reversal would slow down as well. And when this object slows down enough to be below the speed of light, time would once again begin to roll forward from whatever point this object has traveled back to—ten years before, twenty years before, or even thousands of years before. It all depends on the energy that initially propelled the object back. With my equation, you insert X, X being the unit of energy that kick-starts this time travel process. Then out comes Y, the number in years you would travel back in time.

"Now comes the million-dollar question. This theory sounds great and all, and the equation looks complicated and impressive, but can this be accomplished? Can there be a machine that actually propels an object to a speed faster than the speed of light? Well, the answer is, undoubtedly, yes."

A collective gasp resounded in the room.

"Such a machine can indeed be built. In fact, I'm already working on a model that in theory would be able to propel a subatomic particle into a speed which surpasses the speed of light. However, I caution in saying that this will only be a model and not an actual machine that can travel back in time. If you can imagine, any one person possessing such a machine would be highly dangerous to all of mankind. If the machine were to be activated, you, me, and everyone on this earth would have no choice but to be pulled back in time to the year when the subatomic particle loses enough energy and slows back down enough to below the speed of light."

Lance paused to give the students time to process his words. "Now, just for fun, who can guess what else my machine is good for, assuming it works?"

Silence ensued until a male voice in the audience shouted out, "Teleportation."

This answer both surprised and pleased Lance. This was one smart guy. Placing one hand above his brows, he shielded himself from the bright stage lights as he scanned the auditorium for the student.

A young man in the third row waved his hand in excitement.

Lance acknowledged him with a nod. "I see you, sir. Let your professor know you deserve some extra credit points for answering this question correctly," he joked. "Yes, in theory, if the machine can bend time, there is no reason why it can't also bend space. Space and time are like conjoined twins; you cannot refer to one without the other.

"So, why am I still working on developing this model? Well, for two purposes. One is purely for the sake of science. For my curiosity. I honestly want to know if time travel is indeed possible. The second purpose? I believe traveling back in time is entirely possible but unethical to ever put into practice; however, with the right refinement, viewing the past without changing anything is a possibility. With the machine model that I'm working on, and with the right calculations, it is possible that we could look into the past as an eyewitness. With such an application, criminal investigations would be a thing of the past because we would be able to look into the machine and see exactly what happened at a given time and place.

"And lastly, a third reason. Oops, so there are three purposes instead of two. Trust me when I say that I'm not the only one interested in this time travel matter. If this type of technology fell into the wrong hands, we could all be in a lot of trouble. Before anyone develops any time travel machine, I want to make sure I fully understand its applications, limitations, and dangers. World leaders can then put proper rules and regulations in place to prevent anyone from doing anything like this that could endanger all of us.

"However, with all that said, there are two things going for us that would prevent anyone from doing anything malicious. One: no one as far as I know is even close to having a working model of such a device. Mine is probably the closest, but it is nowhere near finished. Two: if my theory is correct, if this event were to happen, everything would revert, even our memory and age. This would mean that no one would remember anything that happened in the future. If this machine were to revert ten years into the past, our memory would roll back with it and we would not know anything about the future. We would simply restart at a point where we left off ten years ago. This great time reversal—besides wasting a tremendous amount of energy—would have accomplished nothing because no one would remember anything from the future. With all our previous knowledge and situations unchanged, we would simply remake all our decisions in the same way we had done previously. Absolutely nothing would change, nor would anything be accomplished by traveling back in time. We would in fact all be stuck in a time loop, but no one would ever know."

Lance took a deep breath. "Okay, I think that's enough for one night, wouldn't you say? Thank you so much for your patience and spending your precious evening listening to me talk about my imaginary world. You never know, you might have already heard this a million times; you just don't remember it because we have traveled back in time." He gave a hearty chuckle as the audience rose to their feet and applauded.

Dr. McKenzie returned to the stage and announced it was time for questions. Lance stood underneath the bright lights of the auditorium and looked out at the sea of faces. Several students throughout the room had their hands raised, some with intrigue written on their faces, others with marked skepticism. He looked forward to the Q and A time after each lecture so he could connect with the audience and hear their theories. He was especially excited to hear from young people who were so curious and motivated to learn.

Dr. McKenzie nodded in excitement at the students' enthusiasm. One of the students in the second row had her arm raised straight up with an eager expression on her face. He pointed at her. "What is your question, young lady?"

The student stood up. "Dr. Everett, if one day you could travel back in time, what time would you go back to and why?"

Lance smiled and nodded. *This is the one question I get asked every time.* The answer lay on the tip of his tongue, but he suddenly lost his words. What happened next took him completely by surprise.

An intense fear stirred up within him, causing cold sweat to trickle down his forehead. He doubled over in pain, his chest tight and breathing shallow. Within seconds, his palms became clammy and he had the worst chills running down his back. He felt like a prisoner about to walk into an execution room to face certain death. *What was going on?* He glanced over at Dr. McKenzie, desperately hoping he had an answer for his current state.

Dr. McKenzie immediately walked over and spoke in his ear. "Lance, are you okay?"

Lance caught his breath before he could speak. "No, no, something's wrong." He looked up and saw the female student still standing and waiting for him to reply to her question. *Juliet!* Somehow, he knew in his heart that danger awaited Juliet. He needed to get to her as quickly as possible. He handed the microphone to Dr. McKenzie and leapt off the stage. He gathered up his belongings from his seat and started running.

As Lance made his way toward the exit, an older gentleman sitting along the aisle stepped out in front of him. "Excuse me, Professor," he bellowed in a heavily accented voice.

Lance bumped into the man's outstretched arm and muttered an apology. "Sorry." He picked up his pace without looking back.

Once Lance stepped outside the doors of the auditorium, he reached into his jacket pocket for his phone. He dialed Juliet's number and listened as it rang multiple times with no answer. A feeling of horror came over him so intensely that it left a sour taste in his mouth. As soon as he heard Juliet's voicemail greeting, he hung up and dialed again. He spotted the taxi that had delivered him to the school parked at the curb and ran toward it. The phone continued ringing in his ear. He climbed into the taxi and slammed the door. "Quick, to the airport."

The driver noted Lance's rushed words and started the engine. "Yes, sir."

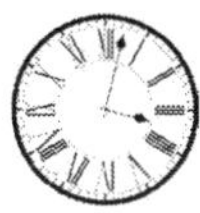

The older gentleman who had interrupted Lance earlier stepped out of the auditorium just as the taxi took off. The man took two steps forward as if to chase after it, but he hesitated.

Instead, he ran a hand through his graying hair then produced a cell phone from his trench coat and spoke into it. He wore a puzzled, yet concerned expression as his eyes trailed the cab down the road.

Chapter Four

Lance felt helpless and on edge during the drive. *Where is she?!* He called Juliet several more times and finally decided to leave a voicemail. "Juliet, call me back when you get this message. Something's wrong, I don't know what, but I have this intense feeling that something is really wrong. Please call me back as soon as you get this message. I'm on my way to the airport now. I'll see you as soon as I get back. Please call me."

Upon hearing Lance's message to Juliet, the taxi driver remarked, "Sir, I'm not sure when your flight is exactly, but business has been very slow, so I came back a bit early to wait for you. It has only been a little over an hour since I dropped you off."

Lance's heart rate sped up at the driver's words. He had originally planned for at least fifteen minutes of Q and A and then another few minutes to catch up with Dr. McKenzie before heading back to the airport. He wouldn't be able to board his plane for at least another hour and half. *This is crazy, I won't be flying for at least another two hours.* Lance cursed under his breath. He picked up his cell phone and called the airline. "My original flight is tonight at ten thirty flying from

LAX to San Jose, but I need an earlier flight back."

A female voice on the other end answered, "Sir, I would be happy to help you. Would you please tell me your name and your flight information?"

Lance clutched the phone in one hand and gestured wildly with the other. He could barely sit still. "My name is Lance Everett and I'm flying out from LAX at ten thirty to San Jose. I need an earlier flight. Whatever you have."

"Thank you, I'm searching in our system now, please give me a moment." After a few seconds, the attendant replied in an apologetic tone. "I'm sorry, sir, but we don't have any flights going back to San Jose earlier than that one. Our only other flight is at one thirty in the morning."

Lance swiped at the beads of sweat on his forehead. "That won't work. I need something earlier."

"I'm sorry sir, but we don't have any earlier flights."

Lance threw his hand up in the air. "That's great."

"Sir, is there anything else I can do for you?"

"No." He lowered the phone from his ear.

The taxi driver called out to him, "Sir, can you fly into San Francisco or Oakland?"

Lance sat up straight as if a jolt of electricity had shot through his body. *Why didn't I think of that?* He placed the phone back to his ear. "Hello, yes, can you check if there are any earlier flights from LAX flying into Oakland or San Francisco?"

"Let me see. One moment, sir." The clicking of a computer keyboard filled the silence. "Yes, there is one flight leaving LAX, arriving in San Francisco. But it leaves at eight thirty."

Lance looked at his watch and took a deep breath. Seven fifteen. *It's going to take a miracle to make it through security and onto this flight.* He had no other choice. He asked the driver, "Can you make it to the airport in thirty minutes?"

"I'll do my best, sir."

Lance replied to the operator, "Please book that ticket for me. I'll be there in time."

"Okay, no problem. I'll book the flight for you. Sir, please understand that there is no refund for this type of ticket nor can it be transferred to..."

Before the operator could finish listing the disclaimers for the ticket, Lance interrupted her. "Yes, yes, I got it, just book the flight for me. I'm in a rush."

"Yes, no problem, sir. It will take a few seconds." She took down Lance's credit card information. "Mr. Everett, your flight has been booked. Thank you for flying..."

As soon as he heard the confirmation number, he hung up and immediately dialed Juliet again. Her voicemail greeting played again in his ear. *Can't answer your call right now. Leave a message and I'll think about giving you a call back!* Hearing her bright and cheerful voice both comforted him and left an ache in his heart.

"Babe, please call me when you get this message. I-I don't know how I know, but I feel in my gut that something is wrong or going to go wrong. Please give me a call. I love you."

Lance suddenly remembered Juliet had been scheduled for the midday shift at the hospital and could be working late. He dialed her work number.

"Stanford pediatrics department," a woman answered. "How may I direct your call?"

"Is Dr. Bradley there?" He whispered a prayer under his breath. *Please let her be there.* "Is she still there?"

"Lance? This is Tricia. Juliet left for the day already."

"Tricia, what time did she leave? She's not picking up her cell phone."

"Um, about twenty minutes ago." The concern in her voice matched Lance's anxious tone. "Is everything okay?"

"I'm just trying to reach her." Lance closed his eyes in frustration. "If she calls or returns, please ask her to call me."

He looked up as the taxi slowed down. The driver had done his best, and against all odds, they had made it to the airport under thirty minutes. He grabbed his wallet, took out a hundred-dollar bill, and handed it to the driver. "Keep the change." He gathered his backpack and stepped out of the taxi like a trapped bird freed from its cage.

Lance dashed inside the terminal with adrenaline pumping through his veins. He saw the line for the security checkpoint and decided to make things as simple as possible for himself. He dumped his backpack in the trash can without a second thought, then rushed over to the electronic ticketing machine and retrieved his ticket. He glanced at his watch and felt his heart rate pick up. *I must make this flight.* His eyes frantically searched for a faster way through the security line.

A uniformed security officer noticed Lance's frenzied behavior and walked over. "Sir, are you okay? Is there something I can help you with?"

Lance waved his ticket. "I need to catch a flight that's leaving in thirty minutes. They should be boarding now. Is there any way I can get through? Please, I have to make this flight."

The security officer looked over Lance's ticket and then back at him. "Okay, come this way."

Lance picked up his pace and followed the officer to the front of the line. He thought quickly and took off his belt and removed any change from his pockets and dumped them into a trash container. Left with a wallet and cell phone, he deposited them into a plastic bin for scanning. He stood before the full body scanner for his turn.

The security officer reminded him, "Sir, sir, your shoes. You need to take off your shoes."

Lance hit himself on the forehead and cursed under his breath. He stepped back, removed his dark brown sneakers, and threw them into a bin. He returned to the body scanner and stepped in as the female worker shot him an impatient glare. Once she cleared him, he grabbed his belongings and took off for the gate. He arrived as the flight attendant began to rope off the walkway to the plane. She waved him over, checked his ticket, and allowed him to board.

He found his seat and pulled out his phone. Standing before him in the aisle, the flight attendants reviewed the safety instructions and prepared for take-off. He glanced at the time on his phone. Eight twenty-nine. He attempted to call Juliet one last time when an attendant walked up to him.

"Sir, we need you to turn off all electronic devices. We are taking off right now." She spoke with such a firm tone that Lance knew it was pointless to argue. He put his phone in his pocket. "Sir, please put on your seat belt."

Lance buckled himself in, feeling like a prisoner strapped to the execution chair. His sense of urgency had not subsided since he boarded the plane; rather, it had intensified tenfold. Sitting powerless and still for an hour was the last thing he wanted to do. He checked his watch and willed the hands to move faster. An immense feeling of helplessness gnawed at his core and left him feeling raw.

He had no idea how he passed the time, but an hour later, he felt the plane touching ground in San Francisco. Although he would normally allow other passengers to exit first, he threw courtesy aside and pushed his way off the plane. When he reached the corridor, he turned on his phone to call Juliet again. He breathed a sigh of relief when he saw she had left a voicemail. He played the message and waited anxiously to hear her voice.

"Hi, Lance, sorry, I was in the shower. Are you okay? What's going on? You sounded freaked out. I hope the Caltech kids didn't give you a hard time." He could see her sweet face in his mind, her red hair flowing around her shoulders. A rush of joy filled his heart before fear seized it once again. "Oh hey, someone's at the door. I'll call you back." Juliet rushed her words before the message ended.

"No! No, no, no, no, no. Don't open the door, Juliet!" Lance's instincts told him he needed to protect Juliet from whoever was at the door. The hairs on his arms stood up and he felt even more alarmed. He checked the time of Juliet's voicemail. Eight thirty. His watch read ten after ten. The phone showed no new voicemails from Juliet. He called her again, waiting anxiously to hear her voice. Any hope he had began to fade with each ring of the phone.

His feet pounded the pavement as he ran to the taxi line and hopped into the first vehicle. "Stanford Villa in Palo Alto. Please drive as fast as you can."

The taxi driver started the meter and stepped on the gas. To Lance's relief, the freeway was clear so there were no delays during the drive. He tried several more times to reach Juliet, but with no success. By now, he knew something was horribly wrong. It was so unlike her to miss his calls. She had said she would call him back, but too much time had passed.

As the taxi driver neared Juliet's apartment complex,

Lance heard the wail of a siren in the distance. He gasped and searched through the window for the flashing lights of an ambulance. *No, no!* As they turned onto the cross street, the sound of the siren grew louder. He desperately prayed for a miracle. *This is not happening.* He hoped beyond hope that exhaustion from too many sleepless nights had his brain playing tricks on him.

He remembered being at Juliet's home just two nights ago. They had eaten Chinese take-out in front of the TV and then taken a moonlit walk around the grounds, stopping to kiss at the circular fountain below her second-story apartment. That evening had been peaceful and quiet, with the sounds of an occasional car driving by.

Tonight, however, the scene before Lance looked like one from a Hollywood set. As he stepped out of the taxi, he noticed several police cars parked on the street with their red and blue lights flashing. Half a dozen uniformed officers walked around on the manicured lawn. Lance looked up at Juliet's apartment and saw his worst fears realized. Several more police officers stood outside her open door. They wore grim expressions on their faces as they spoke to her neighbors.

Lance took a hesitant step toward the complex. He knew something was wrong; every nerve in his body told him so. But a small part of him wondered if he would wake up from this nightmare. He had to find out what had happened. He raised his head and gathered the last bit of resolve within him. As he ran toward the apartment building, one of the police officers noticed him approaching and stopped him.

"Sir, do you live here? There is a police investigation going on right now. Unless you live here, we ask that you not enter at this time."

Lance's voice faltered as he spoke with tears in his eyes. "My fiancée lives in apartment 214. Is she—is she okay?"

The officer's eyes widened in surprise. He turned away from Lance and spoke into the radio clipped on his shoulder strap. "Chief Williams, the fiancé of the victim is here. Do you want to speak to him?"

Lance heard the words and knew the death sentence had been handed down. He couldn't move. He stood paralyzed as everything before him blurred. A gust of wind hit his cold, sweat-drenched body, causing him to shake.

A male voice broke through the haze clouding his mind. "Sir, are you all right? Sir, are you okay?"

Lance turned to see the officer staring at him with concern in his young eyes. Suddenly, the only desire he had was to see Juliet. "I want to see her. I have to see her."

He pushed his way past the officer and began running toward the staircase. He had taken only a couple of steps before two officers grabbed his arms and held him back. He tried to shake them off, but he had no strength left. Even as he pushed the officers away, he found himself leaning on them for support. His vision blurred as his legs buckled beneath him.

A plainclothes man holding a black notepad approached them. "I'm Detective Marks. Are you all right?"

"I need to see my fiancée. Please, let me see her." Lance's voice cracked under the weight of his anguish.

The detective sighed and shook his silver-streaked head. "Son, I can't let you do that. It is a crime scene now. Your fiancée lived in apartment 214?"

At this point, Lance lost his composure and fell to his knees. "Yes." He held his head in his hands as his body shook uncontrollably.

Detective Marks knelt beside Lance and placed one hand firmly on his shoulder. "I'm sorry. The occupant in 214 was pronounced dead when the paramedics arrived on scene."

Lance looked up, his face damp with tears. "Can I see her? Please, I want to see her."

"Son, that's not a good idea."

Lance slowly rose to his feet. He cleared his throat and wiped at his eyes. He tried to pull himself together for a chance to see Juliet. "Please, please, I can do it. I'm okay. Please let me see her."

A figure approached at that moment, casting a shadow near Lance's feet. The sorrow on the older woman's face added lines to her already wrinkled features. "Lance, I'm so sorry. I don't understand. Why would anybody do such a horrible thing to Juliet?"

Lance looked over to see Annette, Juliet's next-door neighbor, clutching the edge of her sweater with trembling hands. The words she had spoken didn't ring true in his ears yet. He returned his focus to the detective. "Please, I need to see her. Please."

"Are you sure you're okay?"

He fought to keep his voice even. "Yes, yes, I'm fine."

The detective sighed. "Okay, son, we'll go up together, but please understand this is a crime scene. I cannot have you touching anything. Is that clear?"

Lance nodded and followed the detective upstairs. Gripping the cold metal handrail for support, he dragged his feet up each step. He paused midway, surprised at the tremendous effort it took to do such a simple task. When they reached the second floor, the officers stationed there stepped aside. Detective Marks opened the door to Juliet's apartment and walked through.

From the doorway, Lance saw her hand first. It was her left hand, still wearing the engagement ring that he had given her, the diamond ring surrounded by two colored stones. As he stepped closer and saw her lying on the floor, he lost all sense of reason. He bolted toward her, propelled by disbelief. The detective barked orders for the deputies to hold him back, but Lance was already in motion. His strength had suddenly returned to him, and he pushed away anyone standing in his way.

Juliet's body lay a few feet from the door. A single bullet wound marred her blue cotton pajama shirt, piercing her heart. A rich, crimson pool gathered around her body, leaving a dark trail in the cream-colored carpet.

Lance fell to his knees beside her, his nostrils overwhelmed by the metallic scent of blood. He grabbed her hand, shock riding through him as he noticed how limply it rested in his palm. He screamed, his voice ragged with emotion. "Juliet, Juliet, I'm here. I'm here. I came as fast as I could." He looked in her blue eyes but saw nothing. The light had gone out from them, like a darkened sky void of stars.

Two officers reached down to pull Lance back, but the detective held them off, telling them they would further contaminate the crime scene.

Lance began sobbing uncontrollably.

Detective Marks came up behind Lance and whispered in his ear, "Son, I'm sorry, but you have to let go now."

Lance's eyes darted about the room in search of some medical personnel. He spotted three paramedics in the corner of the room and screamed at them, "Please, please do something." Sensing their hesitation, Lance pleaded, "Try CPR, use the defibrillator. Don't just stand there. Do something."

One of the senior paramedics spoke up, "Sir, I'm sorry, but she bled out even before we got here. The bullet went through her heart. When we arrived, she had no pulse or any blood pressure." He paused for a second then continued, "We tried everything. I'm sorry."

Lance however wouldn't give up. "Please try something else. There has to be something else you can do."

The same paramedic shook his head. "Sir, we tried everything. I'm sorry, but there is no hope here." He looked over at the detective, signaling for him to do something.

Detective Marks spoke, his voice louder and firmer than before. "Son, you have to go now. You are contaminating the crime scene. If you want to help us find whoever did this to your fiancée, you must let go. Now."

Lance gripped Juliet's hand, noting with dread how quickly it was losing its warmth. He lifted it to his lips and placed a kiss on her soft skin, then gazed at her face. Her complexion had grown so pale as if all her blood had been drained from her, but her features were still lovely and perfect. He longed to memorize every detail he saw, from the smooth curve of her cheekbones to her full mouth. It was the woman he loved, but only a shell of her remained.

She was gone. Deep down in his soul, Lance knew she was gone.

Detective Marks placed one hand gently on his shoulder. "Son, you need to go now."

Lance gave Juliet's hand one last squeeze and let go.

CHAPTER FIVE

Lance looked out the windows of the black limousine as it neared Skylawn Memorial Park in San Mateo. He and Juliet's family had chosen to have her laid to rest at a place overlooking the Peninsula, the area she had come to call home in recent years. He looked around the car at the grim faces of Juliet's loved ones. Her parents sat leaning against each other, their shoulders hunched and heads down. Her brothers, Chris and Nick, surrounded Aunt Liz, one on each side of her.

Lance inhaled deeply and smoothed the pants of his black suit and adjusted his tie. His throat constricted and his eyes burned from the tears he held back. How he had made it through the last six days, he didn't know. Juliet had come into his life out of the blue, then departed it, only to reappear for a mere two years. Even though the time they had spent together was short, her love had already rooted itself deep in his heart. Lance considered how difficult it had been to deal with Juliet's departure the first time around; he was not sure he would survive this second time.

As illogical as it was, he questioned in his heart why Juliet would do this to him. Her absence brought him so much pain.

Yet, he couldn't imagine a life not having known her. Without meeting Juliet, his life would have been meaningless. But still, it hurt so much. The pain of her death was so real, he literally sensed a sharp pain in his chest.

He had glimpsed the same pain in Aunt Liz's eyes this week. Though she herself was grieving, she tried to keep her act together and stay positive for everyone else. The night before the funeral, she had the whole family over at her home. She wanted to give people a chance to celebrate Juliet. Though her life was cut short, she had touched so many. Aunt Liz encouraged people to remember how Juliet lived, not how she died. Knowing that Lance wasn't doing well on his own, she got him involved whenever possible in planning the gathering. He was secretly thankful to her for keeping him so busy this week, otherwise he would not have been able to bear his grief.

It should have been a great get-together, if it were not for the occasion of the gathering. But Aunt Liz did what she could, despite the circumstances. She had invited Lance and his parents, as well as Juliet's parents and brothers. Both families finally met for the first time, unfortunately a few months earlier than expected. They had been planning to meet for a wedding, not a funeral. Everyone present could not help but think of the could-have-beens, what a wonderful couple Lance and Juliet could have made and the adorable children they could have had.

For Lance, this was his third time meeting Juliet's parents. He had met them for the first time when he flew down to San Diego before he proposed to Juliet. He was an old-fashioned kind of guy and had wanted to get their blessing. He still recalled the conversation he had with Aunt Liz when he asked for their phone number.

Lance had stopped by Aunt Liz's house one afternoon while Juliet was at work. "Hey, Aunt Liz, how's it going?"

Aunt Liz welcomed him in with a tub of yogurt in one hand and a spoon in the other. "Good, good, things are good. Sparkle is not doing so well though, that poor dog. She just came back from the vet and they said she has arthritis. Thankfully, it's only in the early stages so it's not too bad yet. Exercise will keep her in good shape, so I'm gonna be doing more walking from now on. Maybe it will help me stay in shape too, you know. Say, how's the time machine?"

Lance chuckled at her youthful energy. "The time machine? Well, I'm still working on it." He really had no intentions of chatting with Aunt Liz about technology; he only had one thing on his mind. "Hey, Aunt Liz, can I have Juliet's parents' phone number?"

Upon hearing Lance's question, Aunt Liz almost stopped breathing, her spoon still in her mouth. Her face turned as pink as the strawberry yogurt on her lips. She grabbed Lance and hugged him tightly. "Oh my, what are you doing to me? You're gonna propose to Juliet, aren't you? What—oh, I'm terrible at keeping secrets. When are you gonna do it? I hope you are proposing tonight. There is no freaking way I can keep this from her for more than a day. This is so exciting. When, when?"

Aunt Liz's excitement added to Lance's own, causing the joy in his heart to bubble up like a fountain. He couldn't stop smiling. He had not planned on telling Aunt Liz he was going to propose, but she had obviously figured it out. "Juliet doesn't know anything yet, so I would appreciate it if you kept this a secret."

"Are you sure about that? She's a sharp girl, you know. She

might already know, but doesn't want to ruin your surprise."

"I certainly hope not. I really want it to be a surprise."

"You know, I could find out for you. I could say something in a really roundabout way and see if she has any clue that you're about to propose."

Lance shook his head adamantly. "No, no, no, I don't think that will be necessary. Just keep it a secret, please. I only need a few more days."

Aunt Liz's voice ascended an octave in anticipation. "How many days? I really can't keep this from her for long. When I see her, I just know I'm gonna get so excited I'll want to tell her."

"Please, Aunt Liz, you'll have to stop yourself. Maybe it would be better if you didn't see her for a few days. I really need you to keep it a secret."

She sighed in disappointment, the sound of her breath coming out like a punctured balloon. "This is going to be hard to do."

Lance smiled. "You can do it. I'm sure you can do it. Keep yourself busy for a few days."

"Oh, I'll really need to find something to do for a few days. Are you sure I can't tell Juliet?"

"No, please don't. It's just a few days."

"Just how many days exactly? When are you going to propose?"

"Two weeks."

Aunt Liz threw her hands up in the air. "Two weeks? Why are you telling me so early? This is gonna be torture keeping a secret from Juliet for two weeks."

"I know, I'm sorry. I wasn't going to tell you until much later, but I need to talk to Juliet's parents first before I officially propose. I think it's important that I do that. I want to make sure they know I respect them."

Aunt Liz nodded. "Good, good. Tom will appreciate that." She gave Lance the number and hugged him again. "I'll keep my big mouth shut, I promise."

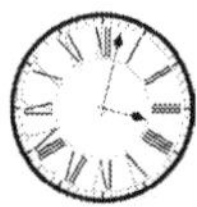

That day at Aunt Liz's seemed like it was just yesterday. How could things have changed so quickly?

When Lance greeted Tom and Cheryl at the gathering last night, he instinctively wanted to say, "It's great to see you again." But in his heart, he knew the circumstances were anything but great. Even as he met Juliet's brothers for the first time and exchanged a polite, "Nice to meet you," it all felt wrong. So wrong. It wasn't supposed to be like this. They should be meeting a few months from now, happily celebrating their wedding day. Everyone should be hugging and cheering, not mourning. It was not supposed to be like this.

As Aunt Liz brought everyone together in one room, she tried to focus on happier times. Instead of avoiding the topic of Juliet, she started talking about how Juliet would have been so happy to see everyone there. She spoke about how happy she had been recently preparing for her marriage to Lance. She then asked others to share their memories as well. For a while the family had a bit of a reprieve as the conversation took on a more lighthearted tone.

Chris, Juliet's older brother, spoke up on his turn. "Do you guys remember when Jules was in first or second grade and there was this kid who always picked on her and her friend?

What was her friend's name…?"

Juliet's younger brother Nick remembered. "Little Kristy."

Chris continued with a big smile on his face. "Little Kristy, yeah. That boy picked on Jules and her friend every day. And one day Jules just had it. She was like half a head shorter than him, but she decided to go after him anyway. She totally beat that kid up. We were all surprised how Jules, this tiny little thing, could go up against this big kid. The kid ended up crying and went looking for his friends to back him up. That kid came back with a few more kids, but luckily Nick and I got there just in time. The look on their faces was priceless. I was so proud to be Jules's big brother." He turned to Nick with a smirk. "Didn't that girl Kristy have a crush on you? I heard you guys kissed."

Nick's cheeks reddened. "Dude, shut up, I was like nine at the time." People in the room all laughed at his embarrassed demeanor.

Tom joined in next. "You guys might think it's funny now, but did you know your mom and I used to worry about Jules all the time. She was always a bit of a tomboy when she was growing up. We were worried that with her following the two of you around, doing all the boy stuff that you guys did, that she wouldn't be able to find a nice man when she got older. Man, but did she change when she turned thirteen. She went from being a tomboy to putting on a fashion show every morning before school. Our phone bill went crazy at that point. She was suddenly hanging out with her girlfriends all the time and talking about boys. Your mom and I, we literally switched from worrying about her being a tomboy to worrying about her bringing a boy home when she was only fifteen. You know Jules was outgoing, too, and quite popular in high school. She certainly gave us a few gray hairs."

Nick jumped in, "Well, that's why you had me protect her. Wherever she went, I went, too. I was always keeping tabs on her."

Aunt Liz added with a grin, "What great brothers you both are. Those were fun times."

As the night went on, Aunt Liz even brought out some old videos of Juliet. Everyone thoroughly enjoyed watching them. The evening ended with the video of Lance proposing to Juliet. That clip touched people the most; there wasn't a dry eye in the room. It was a bittersweet reminder of what should have been, but was no longer.

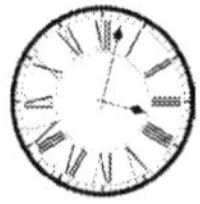

The limousine parked at the cemetery, bringing Lance's thoughts back to the present. He still had a hard time believing the reality of the situation. Today, Juliet would be laid to rest.

Many guests were already seated on the well-manicured lawn, a sea of black umbrellas open above them. Lance drew in a breath as he stepped out of the limousine and prepared to greet everyone. *So many people showed up for you, Juliet.* He saw many of her coworkers from the hospital, her neighbors, including Annette, as well as some old classmates from Cal.

Greg, who had become a mutual friend since the Big Game incident years ago, stepped forward first to shake Lance's hand. "I'm so sorry, man." He shook his head in disbelief.

"Thanks for coming, Greg." Lance managed a small smile. "Juliet would have appreciated it."

Lance approached the front row of seats where his family was sitting. His dad stood up to embrace him, his face somber.

For a former Army Ranger, he appeared strangely frail. "Son, you can sit here."

Lance sat down next to his mom who was crying uncontrollably. "Mom…it's okay." He put his arm around her shoulder and held her close.

"It's not right, Lance. Just not right." His mom shook her head and spoke through tears. "Juliet was so young. How could this happen?"

"I don't know, Mom. I don't know." Lance didn't have any words left in him. His sister, Jessica, sat down next to him. She gently rubbed his back, bringing him comfort with each one of his labored breaths.

The service began with several eulogies delivered by Juliet's family members. Aunt Liz had asked Lance if he wanted to say anything, but he opted not to. He honestly had no words left, and even if he had, he didn't have the energy to speak them.

Lance listened to the heartfelt speeches, many of which moved him to tears. The memories people spoke of brought to mind his own times with Juliet. If he allowed himself to dwell in those moments, he felt peace. If only he could remain in a state of remembering and never wake up.

At the end of the service, the funeral director announced it was time for the final viewing.

Jessica glanced at him. "Lance, are you ready?"

Lance appreciated his sister's support and sensitivity. He took a deep breath and nodded.

Together they walked forward. Warring emotions raged within him as he approached the casket; he wished to cherish this last time he would be able to see Juliet, yet he knew the person lying there looked nothing like his fiancée. He saw her body only, an empty shell. Juliet's spirit was long gone.

Lance eyes lingered on the engagement ring on Juliet's hand. They'd been so close to getting married and living happily ever after. The diamond setting, surrounded by a blue and red stone on each side, not only symbolized their school colors, but their future. Lance had hoped they could one day represent their children, a boy and a girl. How life would've been so perfect with their own family. But now, the hope of that reality existed no more.

Looking at Juliet's body, he poured out his heart to her in his thoughts. *I'm not sure why the big guy upstairs let you and I meet, only to keep us apart. As if the first twelve years we were apart were not enough, it looks like we will be separated for a bit longer this time. If I never see you again, I still thank you for the last two years. In these last two years, you brought me so much joy, so much happiness. If I had to do it all over again knowing that it would hurt so much at the end, I would still do it in a heartbeat. Being with you was that good.* He grasped the edge of the velvet-lined casket as his emotions brought him to his knees. *Juliet, I miss you so, so much. I would give anything just to see you again, just to see your smile and to hear your voice. Oh, how I would give everything just to see you again, even for one second. Juliet, I love you. Goodbye for now, baby.*

When Lance finally stood up on shaky legs, Jessica held tightly onto his arm. They walked to where Juliet's family stood greeting the departing guests. Lance took his place next to Chris and Nick, as Tom directed him to do. Lance was grateful for this gesture. Even though Juliet and Lance had not married, her family had already accepted him.

Dozens of people came up to shake their hands and offer them hugs. It took every ounce of strength within Lance to not break down. He kept his head low and repeated the same words, "Thank you for coming," his voice void of emotion.

After the final guest had left, it was decided that the family would head back to Aunt Liz's house.

Aunt Liz came over to Lance and asked, "Are you coming? Everyone's heading over now."

"Thanks, but I'm going to stay here for a bit and then go home. I'm pretty tired."

"Are you sure?" Aunt Liz's eyes clouded with concern. "Will you be okay by yourself?"

"Yeah. Yeah, don't worry, I'll be fine."

"Okay, please don't think too much. Call me if you want to chat."

"Sure. Thanks, Aunt Liz, you've been great."

Aunt Liz gave him a long hug before taking off.

Meanwhile, Lance walked over to his family. "Hey, I'm going to stay here for a bit. Why don't you guys go home first. I'll head home soon and get some rest, too." He could tell from their faces that they didn't want to leave him alone. But since they were all staying at his apartment, they would know if he didn't return.

His parents nodded. "Okay, we'll see you in a little bit, son."

After a while, Lance was the only person left at Juliet's gravesite. He stood there motionless, soaking in all his loneliness. He just wanted to be there with Juliet and no one else. His solitude, however, was cut short after only a few minutes. Much to his surprise, an older gentleman of South Asian descent appeared and approached him. He wore a black suit and walked with a slight limp to compensate for legs of different lengths. At first glance, Lance sensed a familiarity about him, but he couldn't quite place his face or recall where he might have met him. He figured this man was a friend of Juliet's family who had attended the funeral service.

The man reached him and bowed his head low. "Hello, Dr. Everett. I'm truly sorry for your loss. Please accept my deepest condolences."

Lance nodded and met his eyes for a moment. "Thank you. I'm sorry, but are you a colleague of Juliet's?"

"No, I'm not." He paused. "I'm here because of you."

Lance thought he had heard him wrong. "For me?" This was not his funeral; what did the man mean?

"Dr. Everett, we actually met before during several of your speaking engagements. My name is Krishna Singh."

Lance was in no mood to entertain a science buff. "Mr. Singh, I'm not really in the mood to talk about physics now."

"I completely understand. I wasn't thinking of bothering you, but just now I saw you standing here by yourself. I thought I would come by and say hi." Mr. Singh clasped his hands together. "You see, I too know what it is like to lose someone dear in your life. But I also believe in the saying that *Time heals all wounds*." He reached into the pocket of his suit jacket and pulled out a business card. "Dr. Everett, I think you are extremely talented. I believe I can help you realize your dream and possibly even heal your broken heart."

Lance clenched his fists tightly at Mr. Singh's words. No one would ever be able to restore his broken heart. If this was some businessman with an idea to sell, this was neither the time nor place to make a sale. He crossed his arms against his chest and replied in a brash tone, "Mr. Singh, I obviously have a lot going on here. If you don't mind, excuse me." Lance proceeded to leave.

Mr. Singh reached out his hand. "Please, take my card. I

can truly help you heal. Give me a call when you are ready. I just want to talk."

Lance snatched the business card and took a quick glance at it. The cream-colored card was well-designed with a clean feel. Across the front, black script read *Krishna Singh, President, Singh Enterprises.* He jammed the card into his pants pocket and walked away, unaware of the beguiling smile lingering on the man behind him.

Chapter Six

After Juliet's passing, Lance called his boss Professor Edward Ehrlich, the dean of physics, and told him he would not be back to work for a couple of weeks.

A few weeks, however, turned into months.

Months of visiting Juliet every day, sitting at her gravesite until the sun set, took their toll. Lance was caught in a cycle of depression, spiraling deeper and deeper into it, until he had reached rock bottom. He realized if he didn't return to living a somewhat normal life again, he might never make it back.

He attempted to go to work one late spring day, but memories of Juliet assaulted him everywhere he walked on the Stanford campus. There was the corner not far from his lab where they had bumped into each other for the second time around. The view from his office reminded him of the many times they had picnicked on the large grass lawn below. He lingered on these memories until he could no longer bear to think of them. Emotions overwhelmed him to the point where he didn't know what he felt anymore, other than anger. He was mad at the world, mad at God. Why had He given him the chance to meet Juliet then taken her away? It made no sense.

The mental anguish he'd been grappling with for so long cut at his heart, leaving him raw and unrestrained. His emotions suddenly rose to the surface and took over his body. He stood up, and in a burst of rage, shoved everything off his desk. All the items—papers, pens, even a glass mug Juliet had given him—went flying. Broken pieces of glass hit the time machine sitting in the middle of the lab, producing a loud noise. The sound vibrated long and loud in his ear like that of a tuning fork at work.

He turned and his gaze landed on the jagged pieces of glass on the floor. His heart pounded hard as he took in the sight. The time machine. It had taken the last piece of Juliet from him.

He reached for the only thing remaining on his desk, a lamp. With all his might, he hurled it at the machine. The incandescent tube shattered on impact as metal crushed against metal. The resulting sound was decibels louder than the one caused by the mug. The entire room now reverberated with the high-pitched echoes of a hundred tuning forks.

Lance placed his hands over his ears and willed the irritating noise to stop. Anger rose in him even more as his head began to throb. In his rage, he looked around for something else to throw at the machine. Seeing nothing but his desk, he bent down to pick it up. Just as he was about to lift it, a voice called out to him.

"Lance!" Professor Edward Ehrlich stood in the doorway of the lab.

Lance immediately released his hold on the desk. He dropped his shoulders and took a long, deep breath. "Professor."

"Lance, I take it you are not ready to come back to work yet?"

Even though his boss's tone sounded grave, Lance found his remark laughable. He scoffed. "You've sure got that right."

Professor Ehrlich sighed then gestured for him to follow. "Lance, come on. Let's go have a talk."

Lance dragged his feet down the hall toward the professor's office. Once inside, he slumped into a chair as his boss took a seat at his large cherrywood desk.

"Lance." Professor Ehrlich paused to clear his throat. "We've worked together many years now. You—you and Juliet both—are like family to me. I'm so sorry for what happened. I was so looking forward to your wedding…I know how hard this must be for you."

Lance avoided his gaze and instead looked around the office. Pictures of the university's sponsors hung on a wall over a small bookshelf of business and scientific journals. A silver-framed photo of the dean's wife and their two children sat on the desk. Anger rose in him as he stared at the dean's picture-perfect family. Clenching his fists, he lashed out, "You have no idea what it's like. You have everything you want. I have nothing. There's nothing left for me." He shot out of his chair and headed for the door. "I don't want this anymore. I quit."

Professor Ehrlich waved his hands in protest. "Wait, wait!"

Lance paused in the doorway.

"Let's not make any rash decisions here. Lance, I really like you, and I really appreciate all the work you've done here. Why don't you take a break? In fact, take a long break, go somewhere and let yourself heal. And when you're ready to come back, give me a call. How about that?"

Lance stood still and silent.

Professor Ehrlich continued in earnest, "Come on, Lance, give yourself some time. There's no hurry. You know, you've never taken a sabbatical before. Why don't you use this opportunity to take one? I can use the school's budget to send you somewhere for research purposes. Come on, this is what you love to do. Think about it, will you?"

Lance stuffed his hands in his pockets. Hanging his head in defeat, he walked out.

Professor Ehrlich hurried after him. "I'll take that as a yes. Unless I receive a written resignation from you, you are still a professor at this university."

That was the only time Lance attempted to go back to work. He did not have much outside contact afterward for a very long time.

Lance returned to the safety net of his previous routine. Morning after morning, he drove to the cemetery and stayed there until darkness fell.

Today was no different. With his head down and hands in his pockets, he made his way across the well-watered lawn, navigating a path that had become familiar enough to walk with his eyes closed. When he reached Juliet's grave, he lay down on the stone bench next to it.

As Lance lay there, he did what he did every day. With eyes closed, he conjured up every memory of Juliet that he could remember. He relived each moment he had with her from the very first day they met to their chance reunion, and then each sweet moment they shared during the following two years.

Unfortunately, the flashbacks always ended with the day she was murdered.

Lance's tears began at this point, a silent flow that streamed down his stoic face. He lay still, allowing his sorrow to consume him at the core of his being. To him, loss was the worst kind of pain imaginable. He existed in a space devoid of solace. Some people had told him to snap out of it and move on. But they didn't understand. Moving on would mean forgetting about Juliet. He would never do that. He would rather choose sorrow than forget about her. Somehow, he reasoned, if he continued to feel the pain, Juliet was still with him.

The last tears fell as darkness began to envelop him. Lance gathered his strength and sat up, ready to return home for the day.

As he turned away from Juliet's grave, a man walked straight toward him. It didn't take long for Lance to recognize him. The man was dressed again in a suit, this time in navy. He leaned upon a cane to compensate for his limp. It was the man who had approached him at the funeral with some kind of business deal to sell.

In an instant, rage replaced Lance's sorrow. How dare this man return to the cemetery? How dare he disturb him, not once, but twice in his private place with Juliet?

Before the man could speak, Lance blurted out, "It's Mr. Singh, isn't it? I don't know what you're trying to sell, but whatever it is, I'm not interested. Please do not come here anymore or any other place for that matter to look for me. I don't want whatever it is you have to sell."

The older gentleman looked up, his face calm and gracious, despite Lance's coarse outburst. "Mr. Everett, I certainly didn't mean to disrupt your peace and quiet. I'm visiting my daughter's grave. You see, I also lost someone close to me."

Lance swallowed hard. He suddenly felt like the biggest jerk in the world. He had been so irritated at seeing Mr. Singh again, believing he was there to sell him something, that he had failed to notice his driver walking behind him with a bouquet of flowers. Tulips likely meant for his daughter. His anger retreated. "I'm sorry." Although his earlier outburst was certainly not polite, he wasn't about to make a long apology. Stepping aside, he began to walk away.

Mr. Singh's voice rose in volume as he continued speaking in Lance's direction, "My daughter also passed at a very young age. She was still in her twenties when she was killed in cold blood." He paused and called out to Lance, "Mr. Everett, would you mind listening to this old man for a few moments and hear how my daughter died?"

Lance turned around. Although he wasn't all that interested in Mr. Singh's story, he considered hearing him out for the sake of courtesy. Who knew, perhaps he could learn something that would help with Juliet's case.

Mr. Singh offered a smile of appreciation. "Lance, I hope you don't mind me calling you Lance."

Lance moved his head slightly, gesturing that he didn't mind and prompting him to go on.

Motioning with his free hand, Mr. Singh dismissed his driver. "You see, I am a successful businessman. Everything that I want I can buy for myself. But the one thing I truly loved and cared for—it doesn't matter how much money I have, I can't see her again for even one second. If I could, I would trade everything I have just to be with her for one more day. Out of all the people in this world, I think you, Lance, would understand what I'm talking about."

That was exactly how Lance felt about Juliet. Nothing mattered anymore. Even if he won the Nobel Prize one day, it would mean nothing without her by his side. The tension in his shoulders fell away, along with his feelings of annoyance. It seemed they had more in common than he could have imagined.

"I don't mean to compare whose story is more tragic. Tragedies are all horrible." Mr. Singh hung his head as he rubbed his hand down his weathered face. "About a year ago, I lost both my daughter and my grandson on the same day."

Lance inhaled sharply. He couldn't fathom the anguish Mr. Singh must be experiencing to have lost two of his loved ones.

"We were supposed to have dinner in San Francisco that night. She was eight months pregnant at the time. She was walking out of the parking garage when some thug thought she would be an easy target and robbed her at gunpoint. According to the police, she didn't struggle and just handed her purse over, but the robber was probably too nervous and ended up shooting her anyway. I was seated about a block away waiting for her to arrive. To this day, I have no idea who killed her. My daughter and my grandson gone, just like that."

During the last couple of months, many people had expressed their condolences to Lance. He appreciated their intentions, but thought what they said had little to no effect in helping him cope with his sorrow. Now hearing this tragic story about Mr. Singh's daughter, he realized how limited words were when it came to responding to someone's grief. He said the only thing he could, "I'm very sorry for your loss."

"Thank you." Mr. Singh nodded then sighed. "The police have absolutely no clue who the perpetrator was. I have spent a lot of money hiring private investigators and paying off some policemen, even setting up a reward, but it has all amounted to nothing."

What Lance heard caused him to panic. The police had no leads on Juliet's murderer either. They had found nothing of significance that could be traced to a suspect. He feared that, as more time passed, the case would grow cold and he would never find out what had happened. Even if he could never get her back, he desperately wanted to find the perpetrator, wanted him to pay for his crime. Most of all, Lance needed to know why Juliet had been targeted.

Mr. Singh's eyes narrowed as he pointed a crooked finger at Lance. "Lance, do you want to find out who killed Juliet?"

Lance couldn't believe his ears. Obviously, Mr. Singh was asking a rhetorical question, but he didn't quite know what he was getting at. Could it be that he was offering to help finance a private investigation of Juliet's case? However, considering the fact that he couldn't solve his own daughter's case, why would he even contemplate looking into another one? With no better response, he answered, "Of course."

"What if I told you I could help you find Juliet's killer, but it would require you to help as well, would you consider it?"

Mr. Singh's offer intrigued Lance. "Sure, but what exactly do you have in mind?"

He smiled. "In the last twelve months, I've established a team of top-notch scientists," he boasted, "to create a time machine."

Lance immediately understood why Mr. Singh had attended his scientific talks, as well as Juliet's funeral. He wanted him to help create a time machine to find out exactly who had pulled the trigger and killed his daughter. While Lance had built his entire career researching the theories of time travel, the actual act of traveling back in time was something entirely different. He didn't mean to insult Mr. Singh in any way, especially after he had just shared the tragic story of his daughter's passing, but he couldn't help laughing. "You can't be serious."

Mr. Singh's countenance hardened as he challenged him. "Lance, your own theory says it can work."

"Mr. Singh, the energy, resources, and money required to build or even to consider building a real time machine are astronomical. And there is absolutely no guarantee that it would work. In fact, the chances of failure are about 99.999 percent."

With a wave of his hand, Mr. Singh countered, "You let me worry about that. Feel free to Google how much I'm worth. Again, I'm willing to lose everything I have just to see my daughter one more time. Only when I find out who killed her will I be able to die in peace."

Hearing the determination in his voice, Lance realized he was serious. He was serious about building a time machine. He blinked quickly as the reality of the situation began cementing in his mind.

Mr. Singh continued nonchalantly despite the complex matter at hand. "In fact, I believe you know one of the top-notch scientists who is actively working on my project, Dr. Rostov."

Lance was shocked to hear Dr. Rostov's name. He had been his role model during college and was now the current authority on time dilation studies. The many papers he had written on the subject remained unchallenged to this day. If Lance's memory served him right, he had heard that Dr. Rostov had joined some large corporation as Chief Scientist. That corporation was, without a doubt, Singh Enterprises. Lance's eyes widened as he realized Mr. Singh would try to bring his plan to fruition with or without him. "Do you understand what you're doing?"

"I absolutely do."

"But do you understand there is only a .001 percent chance that you will be able to build a functional time machine? And assuming you do succeed, if you made even the smallest of mistakes somewhere along the way," Lance warned, "it could mean the end of the world?"

"That is why I need you. I need the world's foremost expert on this matter," he asserted eagerly. "I assure you that we will take the most extreme precautions. We cannot be afraid of the unknown or we will never progress."

"But, Mr. Singh, you don't understand—"

Mr. Singh cut him off. "Lance, we don't actually need to reverse time. As your own theory states, when the right energy is applied we can get a glimpse into the past without reversing time. All I'm asking is to look into the past. I want to see my daughter one more time and find the person who killed her. Mr. Everett, do you not want to do the same? You could see Juliet one more time and find the person who killed her! Don't you at least owe it to her to find the person responsible for her murder?"

Of course he did. Lance remained silent, gritting his teeth as faith and doubt warred within him. Despite his years of research, he didn't have enough to go on. "Mr. Singh, you don't understand. Theories are what we scientists live by, but at the same time, theories are just theories. Until we have better tests and evidence to prove that these ideas can become reality, they are still theories. No one has ever attempted to time travel, at least not in a serious manner."

Mr. Singh laughed. "Really? How would you know, Lance? If someone has already attempted to time travel and succeeded," Mr. Singh challenged, "you certainly wouldn't know, would you?"

Lance's shoulders tensed. Mr. Singh was right; how would he know if someone had attempted it? But who could do such a thing? Who would have the resources? Who else besides him understood so much about time travel? Perhaps Mr. Singh was saying these things simply to entice Lance into helping him. But the thought intrigued him. He hadn't thought about his time travel research since Juliet's passing. Mr. Singh's proposal rekindled a fire inside of him, with a new desire to search for Juliet's killer.

Lance wanted to say something, but he couldn't quite make up his mind. Understanding time travel and building a time machine had been his dream since childhood. Now that someone was offering him the chance to rekindle this dream, he was afraid. He had studied time travel for so long, but no one had expected him to invent a time machine. At most, it was a good talking piece and something so grandiose, no one believed it would ever be accomplished, at least not in the next decade or two. Now that Mr. Singh's proposal required him to believe that such a thing could be possible, Lance was quite stunned and unsure of what to do. He considered asking for more time to think, but Mr. Singh spoke up first.

"I'm an old man, but I have been waiting for you for over a year now. A few more days won't hurt me. I look forward to speaking with you soon." With that statement, he stretched out his hand.

Lance reached out as well, and they shook hands.

"Lance, it is really nice to finally meet you. This is my card.

Please take as much time as you need, and call me when you have made your decision."

Lance nodded and watched the older man limp toward his waiting car. He failed to hear the exchange between Mr. Singh and his driver who held the car door open for him.

"Sir, do you want me to follow up with Mr. Everett in a few days?"

"No need. He has already agreed to help. He just doesn't know it yet."

Chapter Seven

Peaceful sleep had eluded Lance since Juliet's death and even more so the past few nights. Following his conversation with Mr. Singh, his mind simply could not stop thinking. As usual, he had woken up early to streaks of red and orange coloring the dark sky. A cool breeze blew in through the patio door, lifting the curtains halfway up. Seeing the scene from his living room couch reminded him of a similar day just a year ago. Back then he had been eagerly looking forward to meeting Juliet to go over their engagement pictures. Today, however, he looked forward to finding her killer.

Even though he had not promised Mr. Singh anything regarding his proposal, Lance knew his quiet days of mourning were over. His mind was like an old record player stuck in a loop, analyzing the possibilities over and over again. What if a time machine could indeed be a reality? Could he revisit the past and witness the exact moment when Juliet was killed? The more Lance considered the proposal, the more excited he became.

Yet, just when he was ready to commit and say yes, doubt caused him to reject the possibilities. Building a time machine was not possible. It might be a great topic to throw at new students and to inspire them to major in the sciences, but no one believed it was possible. Honestly, Lance didn't think his own boss, Dr. Ehrlich, believed he would ever build a time machine. No one did. But just when he was about to give up on the whole idea, he remembered a conversation he once had with Juliet.

One summer she had visited him at work on a particularly hot morning. They usually met in his office or in the lobby before they made their way somewhere, but on that day, she had arrived early and stopped by the lab where he was finishing something up. Juliet had sat in the viewing room next to his office and watched him work through the large double-paned window. He had been frantically typing away on a tablet he held with one hand, while squinting at a large monitor as massive amounts of data ran across the screen.

Minutes passed before he was aware of her presence, and only after his lab assistant tapped his shoulder and pointed to the window. It was then that he remembered their lunch date. He hit himself on the forehead with the palm of his hand, feeling foolish that he had lost track of time. He proceeded to remove his protective headset, but his entire body jumped when the loud racket of the machine shocked his senses. He immediately dropped the headset, and it fell back over his ears.

Juliet placed her face up to the window and mouthed the words, "Are you okay?"

He smiled sheepishly and mouthed back, "I'm okay." Pointing to the door, he gestured for them to meet in the hallway.

Juliet winced when she saw him. "Can you hear me?"

Lance poked his index fingers into both ears, tilted his head to one side and moved his fingers in and out a few times.

"I think so. Good thing I have a lot of earwax. I think it saved my eardrums."

Shaking her head, she replied, "You are so silly."

They both laughed for a few seconds, then Juliet reached out to give his earlobe a gentle tug. "You need to be more careful when you work with these giant machines. Even though I'm a doctor, there are some things I can't fix."

"I know, Dr. Bradley. Thank you so much for your concern. I will be your best patient and follow whatever you say."

"Good. It's always in your best interests to follow the doctor's orders." Juliet smiled and placed one hand lovingly on his face, her thumb caressing his cheek.

His spirits immediately lifted in Juliet's presence. Any time he spent with Juliet was a welcome change of pace compared to the complex and uncertain aspects of his job. "You know, sometimes, I really don't know why I work so hard on this thing. No one believes I'll make any new progress aside from what Einstein discovered ages ago. Now, that man was smart. What he discovered was decades beyond his time. I don't think I can even reach a third of what he accomplished."

The playful look on Juliet's face faded and her voice took on an intense tone. "Lance, don't be discouraged. You are the most brilliant person I've ever met and with the kindest heart. If anyone will find a breakthrough in this field, it will be you. I don't doubt that one bit. The only thing I worry about is that people might take advantage of your discovery and use it to benefit themselves financially."

He had been so appreciative of Juliet's words, but moreover of the belief behind them. The idea that she believed in him was such a stark contrast to what he was used to in the scientific world. In his competitive field, having faith in someone was such a foreign concept. No one believed anyone else unless there were hard facts to prove their theories and hypotheses. He nodded appreciatively. "You really believe I will have a breakthrough one day? Maybe even create a time machine?"

Juliet smiled. "Yes, I do. Just make sure that one day when you're rich and famous, you won't find a younger girlfriend and forget about me!"

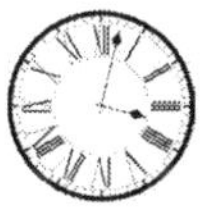

Thinking about that moment made his chest tighten. He had once experienced such happiness with Juliet. It was only a year ago, but time had changed everything. Now Lance was left on his own.

Remembering their conversation, Lance found the motivation he needed to join Mr. Singh in his scientific venture. He didn't care about making a name for himself or about being rich; he was spurred on by Juliet's love and faith in him. If for nothing else, he owed it to her to at least try to make good on what she believed he could do. He needed to find out who killed her and why. Why would anyone harm his Juliet, someone who cared about nothing but helping people? If he could find the killer, he could begin to make things right. He had to make things right. This was his new purpose in life.

He switched his attention to a lightweight computer sitting on the corner of his coffee table, both of which were covered in a fine layer of dust. Picking up the laptop, he blew off the dust then wiped his hands on his jeans as he sat down on the couch. He lifted the cover and pressed the power button, surprised to find some battery left in the system. The laptop booted after a few seconds, then the login prompt appeared. So much time had passed since he had logged in that he couldn't remember his password. After a moment of hesitation, his muscle memory took over. As if they had a mind of their own, his fingers hovered over the keyboard and typed in his password correctly on the first try. His eyes widened and he chuckled to himself. "Ah…that's what it is."

Countless files appeared on the home screen, creating a montage of white squares and rectangles. To most people it looked messy, but this was exactly how he liked it. He reached for the laptop's power cord and plugged it in, just as the low battery warning popped up. As his eyes scanned the screen, flashes of the past began coming back to him. Memories of his previous studies crossed his mind, as well as the difficult challenges he had faced in his last few lab experiments. This information revived his passion for the sciences and made him eager to dive back into his studies.

But there was one thing he needed to do first.

He pulled out a business card and typed in a basic search for Krishna Singh. Soon, he busied himself scanning page after page of information on the man he knew nothing about. Many of the immediate results pulled up articles about his success in business, particularly as a stock investor. Some magazines even compared him to Warren Buffett, the Oracle of Omaha, and called Mr. Singh the Prophet of Silicon Valley. As the president of Singh Enterprises, a privately held investment company, he managed funds of well over a billion dollars.

A further search led Lance to a couple of articles about Sashi Singh, his daughter. Her murder hadn't made many of the headlines, possibly because San Francisco had a high crime. Unless it was a sensationalized story, many cases lost their appeal as time went on. Since Mr. Singh was only a businessman and not a celebrity, his daughter's death had made it to some local newsgroups, but there was nothing on the national scale.

In one article that did highlight the murder, the story itself was barely three paragraphs long. It was a short factual report about the location and time of the crime, how police were investigating the robbery, and how the murder victim was the daughter of a wealthy Bay Area businessman. Lance tried to find out more, but there simply was no more information related to the murder or any new leads on the case. He could understand why Mr. Singh would want to spend his own money to further the investigation.

He felt sorry for the old man whose only child had been taken away from him for no apparent reason. Just like Juliet had been taken away from him. He decided he would take on Mr. Singh's project, for the sake of his daughter, as well as for Juliet.

He would contact Mr. Singh, but before he dove into a busy research schedule, he needed to tend to some tasks first. He had neglected many things over the past year, his health being one of them. He decided to go for a run to refresh his body and mind. Running in the mountains always helped him feel better, and he was long overdue for some exercise. Then he planned on visiting Aunt Liz. Months had passed since he had talked to anyone. It would be good to reconnect with her and ask if the police had any new leads on Juliet's case. He also needed to buy groceries and stock up his empty fridge.

Lance dressed for his run and made his way downstairs to the ground floor of the apartment building. Darkness covered the parking garage, except for some dim lighting from a couple of fluorescent bulbs overhead. From outside the garage, light peeked in as the sky began turning blue.

Lance got to his car, pointed the remote at it, and clicked. To his surprise, instead of the usual *beep beep*, he heard a much softer, single *beep* as the taillights flickered. He had only driven the car a day ago, and the remote had worked perfectly. He pressed the remote again, but this time the car didn't even sound. *Must be something wrong with the battery.*

He decided to investigate the problem himself. He was a scientist after all, used to critical thinking and troubleshooting on a daily basis—or he once had been. Diagnosing this car problem would be a good exercise to get his brain warmed up before going back to work. In a matter of seconds, he had popped the hood open and spotted the problem. *What a lousy design.* The clutch fluid reservoir was located directly above the alternator and, probably due to normal wear and tear, it was leaking and dripping fluid onto the alternator. With a malfunctioned alternator, the battery would not charge.

Fixing the alternator would likely take two to three hours. He checked his watch. 5:35 a.m. If he hurried, he could still get in his run, though it would be a little delayed. Lance jogged back to his apartment, grabbed his tool box, and returned to start on his little project. He quickly located the leak coming from a tube below the reservoir and patched it up. Next, he removed the alternator, took it apart, and gave it a thorough cleaning. To be safe, he soaked the electric coil in a cleaning agent and used an ultrasonic cleaner to remove all traces of oil. Lastly, he dried all the parts before putting them back into the car.

He checked his watch again and noted not even three hours had passed. *Not bad.* Now for the moment of truth. He hooked up a charger to the dead battery, put his key into the ignition, and turned on the car. The engine turned over without any issues. *So far, so good.* He unplugged the charger and placed a voltage meter to the battery to check the alternator. When he was sure everything was working, he put his tools in the trunk and walked to the front of the car.

Just as he was about to close the hood, he noticed a black box that he had never seen before sitting near the driver's side tire. A perfect cube, it was two inches by two inches in size. He wondered if it was some kind of GPS remote control device that the manufacturer had installed. Being short on time, he decided to check it out later. If he hurried, he could still squeeze in that run he had been looking forward to and meet up with Aunt Liz for lunch.

He closed the hood and opened the car door. As he slid into the driver's seat, the rev of a car engine sounded to his right. He turned in its direction, surprised to find someone else in the garage. During the last three hours, he hadn't noticed anyone coming or going in the vicinity. A couple of cars had entered and exited the lot, but they had been a good thirty to forty vehicles away from where he was parked. The car in question was located directly behind his on the other side of the aisle. Lance glanced in his rearview mirror and spotted two men wearing dark shades sitting inside the vehicle. *Have they been there the whole time?* He turned on his own engine, backed up the car, and headed down the ramp toward the exit.

The black car pulled out of its space and proceeded behind him. Taking the same path that Lance had driven, it followed him from a distance. Lance considered stepping on the brakes to get a clearer look at their faces but laughed as soon as the thought crossed his mind. *Who would follow me?* He took one last look in the mirror as he made a right turn out of the garage, wondering if the car would turn that direction as well. The sunlight reflected off the hood of the American-made car as the driver made a left. *So much for that.* Shrugging his shoulders, Lance put the car out of his mind and drove to his old running trail.

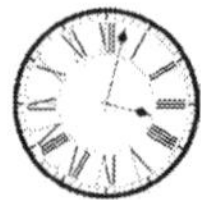

The morning had worked out well. After his run, Lance had gone back to his apartment to shower and was now ready to surprise Aunt Liz for lunch. Walking up the driveway to her house, Lance paused to catch his breath. The drive over had already brought back so many memories, but being in this place completely overwhelmed his senses. Everything about the brick path and the surrounding trees reminded him of the first time he had driven Juliet here. He could almost hear her laughter in the air and feel the tight hug she gave him when they parted ways the morning after the football game. The memories, though bittersweet, gave him strength to pick up his feet and walk up the steps leading to the door. As Lance raised his hand to ring the doorbell, the door swung wide open.

Aunt Liz regarded him like an old friend who had just returned from a long trip. "Lance! What brings you over?"

Lance smiled, happy to be greeted with such enthusiasm. Before he could speak, Aunt Liz pulled him close and gave him a warm hug.

"Come in, come in." Closing the door behind them, she held onto his arm and led him to the kitchen. "It's been so long since you visited me. You have no idea how bored I've been these days. Without you and Juliet coming around, I just don't have much to do."

Lance remained silent, surprised to hear Aunt Liz's matter-of-fact tone. It seemed she had accepted Juliet's passing so much better than he had.

She pointed to a wooden chair at the small table. "Sit. Would you like some tea? I just got a rose tea from the local market that is quite flavorful."

"Sure, tea sounds good."

Aunt Liz busied herself at the sink, filling a stainless-steel kettle with water. She set it on the gas stove and sat down across from Lance. "I'm so glad to see you. I was just going to make a pot of tea and was thinking to myself, it will take me such a long while to drink it all by myself, when I heard your car." She tilted her head to study his face. "I see you're feeling better. I knew you would come around; you just needed some time."

"I guess I did," Lance replied, surprised at Aunt Liz's belief in him. Up until the last few days, he himself hadn't thought he would ever turn around. His despair had been so great that he had at one time considered taking his own life. He appreciated the fact that she had not given up on him. "Well, thanks for the faith you had in me."

She grinned, her lips curving up in mischief. "Oh no, not faith in you. I had faith in Juliet. I knew the guy she picked would do better than flip over and play dead at the first sign of trouble. The man she picked would be strong enough to face tough times."

"Well, thanks, Aunt Liz." He chuckled at her wry sense of humor. "I can tell you're my biggest fan."

She gave him a teary smile. "Lance, I'm so glad to see you

smile again. I know Juliet would be very happy, too."

Lance glanced down, a wave of sadness washing over him at the mention of Juliet's name.

Aunt Liz wiped at her eyes and took a deep breath. "Well, we both know Juliet never liked lazy bums. Are you going back to work soon?"

"Actually, I am, but I'll be working for a different boss. The work should be pretty exciting."

"Oh, that's great." Aunt Liz rushed out of her seat as the kettle whistled. She filled two mugs with tea and set one down before Lance. "A new place and new project sound like a good idea. I must say, the stuff you were doing before sounded fun and all, but it was a bit extreme. Did anyone ever expect you to actually build a time machine?" Pausing to take a sip of tea, she asked, "What will you be doing at this new place? Something a bit more relaxing? Anything a commoner like me would understand?"

"You're going to love my answer," he replied, trying to keep a straight face. "I'm going to be building a time machine."

"What? You're kidding me. You know it was that kind of crazy work that gave Einstein his crazy hair. You don't know the meaning of relaxing, do you?"

"I'm sure most people would think I'm crazy for even attempting it," he stated with a shrug, "but I think Juliet would be proud of me for trying. I think I'm going to succeed one day."

Aunt Liz reached over to touch Lance's hand. She looked him in the eye and nodded, her usual cheery demeanor turning serious. "Juliet is proud of you. I know she would be happy, so long as you are happy."

"You know..." he began then paused as he debated whether

to tell Aunt Liz about his personal quest to peek into the past. He was sure she would also want to find out who killed Juliet and why, but at this point it was too early to say anything. Not wanting to give her any false hope, he changed the topic. "Have the police contacted you about the investigation?"

Her cheeks flushed as she rolled her eyes in frustration. "Those so-called officers must be the most incompetent people out there. After all this time, they still have no new leads on Juliet's case. I chatted with Detective Marks a couple of weeks ago. He seems about as incompetent as they come; he had absolutely no new information. His theory is that it was a case of mistaken identity." She rolled her eyes again and shook her head. "I asked how they knew it was a case of mistaken identity. You know what he told me?"

Lance shook his head, any hopes he had for new information on the case diminishing by the second.

"He said they didn't find any evidence that proved otherwise. What kind of stupid logic is that?"

His jaw dropped. "You're kidding me."

"I pressed the guy many times to give me something concrete, but the best he could tell me was that based on their investigation into Juliet's lifestyle, hobbies, occupation, and friends, nothing warranted someone wanting to murder her. There was no motive from any angle whatsoever." She sighed loudly. "I got so frustrated with him and his conflicting theories that I told him to call me back when he gets his story straight."

Lance closed his eyes as Aunt Liz talked, trying to recall the details of that night. The open apartment door. A pool of blood on the carpet. The bullet shells. He remembered seeing two shells scattered on the floor just a few feet away from the front door. Something about those shells tugged at his mind. What was it? He focused on the memory and drew in a breath. Bullet shells were generally made of brass and copper in color. The shells he saw in Juliet's apartment were silver. "Did Detective Marks say anything about the bullet shells?"

"The bullet shells? No, I don't remember him saying anything about them. Why? Was there something special about them?"

"I think so." He hesitated and added, "I'm not sure." Could he have remembered it wrong? But in his mind, he could clearly see the silver shells. "I'm going to set up a time to chat with the detective. I have a few questions I want to ask him."

For the first time in a long time, Lance sensed a bit of hope in his circumstances. His conversation with Aunt Liz, coupled with his new memory of the crime scene, reinvigorated his mind and heart. He even welcomed the twinge of pain in his stomach as it let out a soft rumble. He took another drink from his mug and set it down. "That was some good tea, but I think I'm ready to eat. Aunt Liz, would you like to go grab some lunch?"

"I thought you'd never ask."

Lance chuckled, thankful to be feeling like his old self again. His appetite for food and, more importantly, life was returning. Along with that was also a deep hunger to find more answers to Juliet's murder.

CHAPTER EIGHT

Lance turned the business card over in his hands. For several hours, he'd sat at the kitchen table, giving himself a chance to come up with any reasons not to move forward with the time machine project. His mind wavered between the pros and cons. Ultimately, only one reason prevented him from committing: fear.

A fear of failure, that nothing worthwhile would come out of the project. Fear that should he succeed, the time machine would fall into the wrong hands. And fear that he himself would misuse the machine.

Fear taunted him to give up everything again, to return to his hermit days and live an isolated life. But fear was never a good reason to do or not do something.

Ever since Lance was a young man, he had learned to take risks. His successes so far resulted from his willingness to take risks and to commit. This however was one of the biggest decisions Lance had ever considered. The bigger the decision, the more was at stake. Along the same vein, the bigger the risk, the stronger the commitment would need to be.

After much thought, Lance knew there was no better time

than now to take a risk and to commit.

He picked up his cell phone and dialed Mr. Singh's number.

After three rings, Mr. Singh answered.

"I'm surprised you don't have someone to pick up your calls," Lance remarked.

Mr. Singh chuckled. "Lance, I've been waiting for you to call since we last spoke. I told my secretary to transfer your call directly to me. Caller ID has been invented for some time now."

Lance smiled. "We should talk about your project."

Mr. Singh quickly corrected Lance. "No, it is our project. I absolutely cannot do this without you."

Lance was flattered. "Do you want to talk on the phone or meet up somewhere?"

"I will have my driver pick you up in fifteen minutes. Why don't we meet up in my office in San Francisco? We can show you around our facility. Perhaps that will increase your interest in our project."

"Sure, we can meet at your office, but no need to send your driver. I can drive myself."

"Trust me," Mr. Singh cut in, "it would be much easier for my driver to pick you up. It is extremely difficult to find parking in the city. Of course, we have our own parking structure, but it will take anyone an extra half an hour just to go through our security checkpoint. My driver is precleared for all security checks. Let him drive you this time, and next time, you can drive yourself. Besides," he added, "he is already on his way."

Lance was surprised at his insistence but assumed he treated all his clients this way. A successful businessman like himself knew how to establish relationships. "Okay. That's fine." Just as he finished replying, his doorbell rang.

"That's my driver at your door."

"What?"

"You have no idea how badly I need you on this project. I've had my driver waiting for you for days now. I will see you in a little while."

Lance was almost speechless. "Okay." He opened the door, and sure enough, it was the same driver he remembered from the cemetery.

"Mr. Everett, we may leave whenever you are ready."

"I'm ready, let's go."

They walked downstairs to where the car was waiting in a no-parking zone in front of the building.

Lance smirked. "I guess you're not worried about getting a ticket or getting towed."

The driver replied with a smile. "Absolutely not. Mr. Singh always says customer satisfaction is our first priority. Besides, this car has been modified. It cannot be towed by a normal tow truck. The chassis of the car can be lowered to almost touch the ground. All the windows are bulletproof, and every side of the car has been reinforced with steel plates, including the bottom."

Lance took a closer look at the vehicle. Indeed, the windshield and windows were significantly thicker and the car sat very low to the ground.

The driver reiterated as he opened the back door for Lance, "Normal tow truck companies wouldn't attempt to tow this car."

"Thank you, but next time I'll get the door myself."

"Certainly."

The inside of the vehicle looked exactly like what Lance expected of a luxury car. He sat down on the leather seat and spotted some expensive bottles of liquor—wine and scotch—as well as a flat screen TV, across from him.

"Mr. Everett, please feel free to help yourself to any of the amenities."

"I'm good, thanks." In an effort to start a conversation, Lance asked, "By the way, what's your name?"

The driver replied from the front seat, "I appreciate you asking, but just call me Driver. It is more appropriate that way."

Lance cocked his head in amusement, grasping onto the armrest as the car picked up speed. Even though the car was heavy with its steel plate modifications, it was speedy and responsive.

The driver remained silent the rest of the ride as he drove along the roads with a sense of ease and familiarity. He made many turns and shortcuts through San Francisco until they arrived in front of a very tall, cylindrical building with glass on all sides.

Mr. Singh wasn't kidding about their security. Armed guards stood outside the building and at the multiple checkpoints inside the parking structure.

The driver made more turns inside the parking lot and came to rest at a reserved parking space. "Mr. Everett, we are here."

Lance exited the car and followed the driver through an open double-sided glass door. On the other side stood none other than Mr. Singh.

Mr. Singh reached out to greet him. "Lance, it is so good to see you."

Lance extended his hand with caution. He still didn't know much about the man standing before him other than what he had learned on the internet.

"Let me you show you around our facilities. I think you will really like what you see."

They headed toward an elevator where Mr. Singh pressed the highest button on the panel. "You have no idea what we had to do to the building to accommodate this project. We literally took the roof off and redid the entire top floor."

The elevator *dinged* when they reached the 58th floor.

With a pleased smile, Mr. Singh turned to Lance. "Allow me to present to you…"

Lance wondered what waited for them behind those elevator doors. When they opened, he blinked, unable to believe his eyes.

"…the time machine!" Mr. Singh announced.

Thick glass windows surrounded a giant machine that sat in the middle of a full-sized lab. The machine looked exactly like the model he had at Stanford, but about three times bigger. It was the size he imagined a fully functional time machine would need to be.

Lance found himself mesmerized by the odd-looking tubes poking out from the top to the bottom. A mixture of various metals made up the spherical and octagonal shapes throughout the machine, including the four large posts at its four corners. It was so stunning, he couldn't help but be drawn to it. He lost sight of the people working in the facility and even of Mr. Singh as he approached the machine. The only thing that stopped him from walking closer was literally the glass that blocked his way.

He reached out and put both hands on the window, wishing he could examine every part of the machine. As soon as he touched the cool pane, he jumped back. *Could it be?* He placed a hand back on the glass and felt a slight tremor. There was no doubt about it. The machine was on. The high speeds of the atoms traveling inside the machine's tubes were causing the vibrations.

Lance turned around, speechless. "How…?"

Mr. Singh nodded. "Lance, you can take a closer look if you like, but let me first introduce you to the person who put your design together."

Lance noticed someone standing next to Mr. Singh. He immediately recognized the round-faced older gentleman with the receding hairline as Dr. Rostov. The brilliant scientist already had several commercially successful patents under his name. Lance recalled his medical breakthroughs included the core technology for an advanced brain scanner, MRI machines, as well as the 3D mapping and projection of the human body for diagnostic purposes. His ability to transform his research into working models made him the perfect candidate to bring the time machine to life.

"Dr. Rostov," Lance stated as they shook hands, "what an honor to meet you. I've admired your work for a long time now."

"Dr. Everett, the honor is all mine. The design of your time machine design is absolutely mind-boggling. When Mr. Singh first introduced me to this project, I thought he was mad."

That makes two of us. Lance chuckled to himself.

Dr. Rostov continued, "When I reviewed all the documentation and the work that you already did on the design, I simply couldn't believe that this could be real. To be honest with you, every scientist, including myself, likes to think they can do it better, but your design is flawless. Your calculation is so absolute that any slight deviation could jeopardize the functionality of the whole machine. Some of the parts took us a long time to make because not many manufacturers can produce the precision that the machine requires." Dr. Rostov paused and reiterated, "Lance, it is truly an honor to meet the man behind this creation."

Lance lowered his head humbly. "But I never did put together a working time machine. All my research is useless unless it actually works." He gestured at the machine and asked, "Does it actually work?"

"I wish the machine was fully functional." Dr. Rostov smiled. "We are still collecting data and testing how fast we can get the machine to push the molecules."

Lance breathed a sigh of relief. He absolutely wished to see his research pan out, but having a fully functional time machine was a very scary thought.

Dr. Rostov's tone turned serious. "Dr. Everett, we are not able to get the last few steps needed to turn this machine into a functional one. You are the only one who can make that happen."

"Dr. Rostov," Mr. Singh interrupted, "let's not give Lance any pressure. He has yet to agree to be part of this project."

"Really?" Dr. Rostov's eyebrows rose. "But why not! We have state-of-the-art equipment here. Our researchers are top scientists from all around the world. This is the place to be for a scientist like you."

Lance couldn't disagree. This lab was as the brilliant scientist stated. He imagined it must have taken many millions just to build the place.

"Let me introduce you to another critical member of our team." Mr. Singh motioned for Dr. Rostov to step aside.

To their right, Lance saw a giant table, with a large piece of glass positioned vertically on it. Before he could confirm his suspicions of what it was, he saw the screen light up.

Dr. Rostov stood in front of it, commenting, "Albert, please meet Dr. Lance Everett."

A digitally created human face appeared on the screen and responded, "Pleased to meet you, Dr. Everett."

Lance stood frozen in place. Although he had heard about supercomputers with built-in artificial intelligence, he had never been face-to-face with one before.

"Go ahead," Dr. Rostov encouraged. "Feel free to talk to Albert like you would talk to any person. By the way, we of course named him after Albert Einstein."

Smiling, Lance approached the computer. "Albert, how close are we to creating a functional time machine?"

The computerized voice spoke, "It depends on your definition of close. The machine itself is functional. It can accelerate a particle to an extremely fast velocity. Dr. Rostov and the team have been able to accelerate particles that have significant mass to near light speed, which has never been done in human history. For that, you should be very proud. However, even reaching the speed of light does not satisfy the true purpose of this machine. The final equation to push past the speed of light is needed to fulfill the goal of this project. Discovering that final equation is not something that can easily be measured as close or not close."

Lance smirked. This was certainly not the textbook answer he'd expected. It would take much longer to determine if this machine truly possessed AI, but at the very least, it was capable of complex interpretations and analyses.

"If Albert can't help us with our current project," Dr. Rostov smirked, "he'll at least do well in the field of philosophy."

Albert replied, "Thank you, Dr. Rostov, I appreciate your compliment."

Everyone laughed at Albert's oblivious understanding of sarcasm.

Dr. Rostov gestured to the supercomputer. "Dr. Everett, take as much time as you like with Albert or with any of our staff members. Please do let me know how I can assist you in making your decision. It should be obvious that we all would love the opportunity to work with the creator of this machine."

Flattered, but aware of the seriousness of the situation, Lance pressed the scientist for more information. "While we understand there is good that can be done with a time machine, there are also a million reasons why it is a dangerous project to undertake. Have you thought about the safety of this project?"

"Most certainly. As you can see, Mr. Singh has provided us with one of the most secure facilities in the world. It is easier to get into the White House than it is to get in here—"

Before Dr. Rostov could finish, Lance interrupted, "But what about ourselves?"

Dr. Rostov and Mr. Singh exchanged surprised glances.

Dr. Rostov replied with obvious hesitation, "Well, that is a legitimate concern, but we have to trust ourselves. Both you and I have been in the scientific field long enough that we understand the strict ethical code we adhere to."

Lance nodded, but he was certainly not satisfied with his answer.

Mr. Singh broke the silence first. "Lance, do you have a suggestion in mind?"

Lance quickly replied, "I do. I suggest we set up a three-way authorization, where each one of us has our own key. And only with all three keys available can we can access key components of the formula and turn the machine on for testing."

Mr. Singh quickly agreed. "This is a very serious project with potentially disastrous outcomes. Taking the right precautions is not only prudent but absolutely necessary. We should set up a three-way authorization as Lance suggests."

"I don't disagree with the method," Dr. Rostov cut in, "however, this could slow us down drastically in terms of our progress."

Lance held up a hand. "But we cannot trade safety for progress. We simply cannot rush this project."

Dr. Rostov stole a glance at Mr. Singh who closed his eyes briefly and nodded.

"We don't have proof yet," Dr. Rostov began, "but we believe there is a very high possibility that another group is doing exactly what we are doing. Someone else out there is building a time machine as we speak. There is a very real reason why we have to rush."

Lance narrowed his eyes, not believing what he was hearing. He looked over at Mr. Singh for confirmation. Who else would have the knowledge and audacity to even attempt such a thing—and why? Yet, even as he asked himself these questions, he realized the answers.

The how was not difficult; Mr. Singh and Dr. Rostov had gotten as far as they had without his involvement. The why was just as simple. If any government agency in the world possessed such a machine, the applications would be endless. Time travel would provide the means to fulfill every selfish gain known to man.

Lance immediately inquired, "How did you get—"

Mr. Singh replied with a knowing smile. "I bought your research legally from Stanford. They were happy to sell all of your life's work to me for the cost of a new wing on campus."

He softened his voice. "They didn't believe in you. They didn't think your research and study was of any value. It was just an intriguing subject to attract new students and funding for the school. I didn't have to do much negotiation to buy all the patents and rights to your study. I did however bar them from selling your research to anyone else," he added.

Lance placed his hands on his hips and hung his head. This was shocking news, not to mention a blow to his ego.

"Dr. Everett, we need to move as quickly as we can on this project," Dr. Rostov attempted to convince him. "Can you imagine what would happen if this technology fell into the wrong hands?"

As he processed the urgency of the situation, Lance suddenly remembered the black car in his apartment garage from a couple of days ago. Could those men have anything to do with this race to create a time machine? He had no proof, only a hunch, that they were involved.

"Lance?" Mr. Singh asked, "what are you thinking about?"

"Nothing. What makes you think someone out there is also trying to put a time machine together?"

"Much of the material, equipment, and parts that Mr. Singh and I acquired for this project are completely unique; no manufacturers should have ever seen or produced them before. However, it appears we are not the only ones buying these exact same tools."

Mr. Singh chimed in. "Ever since we found out someone else was looking for similar parts and materials, we have been very careful to not let our vendors know who we are. We have gone through lengthy efforts to pay in cash and use multiple contracting firms."

Dr. Rostov crossed his arms and, in a grave tone, remarked,

"The most worrisome part of all is that in the recent months, up to about a year ago, we detected some very strong energy waves traveling in the atmosphere consistent to the values that a time machine would generate!"

Lance let out a long breath. He understood the implications of this detection. Based on his previous calculations, the time machine would require a tremendous amount of energy to be ready for time travel, and as a side effect, it would also emit a huge amount of energy. Such an amount would need to be released into the atmosphere to dissipate. "Do we know where these energy waves are coming from?"

"Unfortunately, no." Dr. Rostov shook his head. "We were not looking for these energy waves, we simply noticed them because our highly sensitive equipment picked them up. Those waves caused our readings to be off and we had to rerun many of our tests. We assumed at first we were having problems with our own equipment, but then we realized they couldn't all be having problems at the same time. We started to consider external factors, if something in the atmosphere could have caused the misreadings. That's how we discovered these waves. The wave patterns are also similar to the energy that our own time machine emits, but on a much, much larger scale. We do believe whoever these people are, they are running their machine from within the country."

"I understand. We need to get on this as soon as possible, but safety is still safety," Lance reiterated. "We must establish a three-way authorization, otherwise I will not participate in this project."

"Agreed," Dr. Rostov answered. "Let's get the encryption going."

Once the decision was made, it didn't take long to set up

the encryption. They also agreed that Albert would control the activation and deactivation of the time machine, as well as all the testing and results.

Happy with the outcome, Lance followed Mr. Singh to a corner office on the same floor as the time machine. A modern tempered glass desk with a black leather swivel chair sat in the middle of the large room with a view of the San Francisco skyline behind it. Another wall looked out into the entire laboratory.

"This is for you, Lance."

Lance balked at the well-furnished room. "I don't need such a fancy office."

"All our offices are the same." Mr. Singh smiled. "Besides, this is the only other office, besides Dr. Rostov's, that has a direct terminal connection to the supercomputer. In here, you have direct access to Albert, which will help you do your work slightly faster. In the time crunch we are facing, every little bit helps."

Lance nodded in agreement. He walked over to peer through the glass into the lab. Feelings of pride and astonishment coursed through his body as he looked upon the time machine. His creation, although very familiar to him, appeared strangely mysterious as well. It offered him hope, and he hoped one day soon, it would also give him the answers he was searching for.

Chapter Nine

Life suddenly turned hectic for Lance. Just a few days ago, he was living in isolation and biding time. Now he held a full-time job and a new purpose. While he was eager to work on the time machine, he couldn't forget his recent conversation with Aunt Liz. He called Detective Marks to follow up on Juliet's case. The detective returned his call four days later and, at Lance's insistence, agreed to a meeting.

He arrived at the Palo Alto police station and took a seat in the waiting room. The interior of the modern building resembled a hotel lobby with plush chairs and complimentary coffee and water. If not for the uniformed officers, one would hardly recognize it as a government building. Lance only hoped the police spent as much of their resources on their investigations as they did on their facility.

A white-haired man in his late fifties or early sixties walked out to greet him. "Mr. Everett?"

Considering the circumstances of their first meeting, Lance didn't have a strong memory of Detective Marks. He seemed older than he remembered and much more tired. The smile on his weathered face lasted a second before it faded.

Lance reached out his hand. "Detective Marks, thanks for meeting me."

"How can I help you?" he asked in a gruff voice as he shook Lance's hand.

Sensing disinterest in the detective's blank expression, Lance got straight to the point. "I've been in recovery mode for some time so I wasn't able to contribute much to solving my fiancée's case. I wanted to come down and see if there's anything I could help with. I also want to go over some of the case details with you."

Detective Marks drew his brows together and shrugged. "I've already told the aunt everything I know. But if you want me to go over the case with you, I can do that."

Lance ignored the annoyance in the detective's tone. "Great. Thanks for your time."

Detective Marks squeezed out another smile, one that lasted half a second. "Follow me."

Once they were in his office, the detective sat down behind a cluttered desk and leaned back in his chair. The afternoon sun shone from behind him, casting a shadow upon his serious face.

Lance took a seat across from him and glanced around. A common laptop computer and one framed photo stood out among piles of manila folders. Based on the physical similarities of the two teenage girls in the picture, they looked to be sisters. Attempting to lighten the mood and connect with the detective, he commented, "Are those your daughters?"

"Yes, they're in their junior year of high school. Fraternal twins."

"Any plans for college yet? I know a couple of the deans at Stanford. I would be more than happy to make some calls for you."

Almost immediately, Detective Marks's countenance changed. He leaned forward and nodded eagerly. "You're serious? You can help my daughters get into Stanford?"

Lance couldn't believe he had caught the detective's attention. "Sure, but you need to first make sure your daughters want to attend Stanford."

Detective Marks couldn't respond fast enough. "Who in their right mind wouldn't want to go to such a fine school? I would really appreciate it if you could help them. I've been thinking about this for months. I want to make sure my girls go to a good school and somewhere close so I can keep an eye on them. Their mother and I are divorced; she lives out in Texas. The last thing I want is for them to move there. They are both good students and have decent GPAs." He lowered his voice as he added, "Do they really stand a chance of getting in?"

Suddenly the tables were turned, and Lance's shoulders relaxed. Now Detective Marks was asking him for a favor. "I can't promise you anything at this moment, but again, I do know a few deans at the school. I would be happy to send in letters of recommendation for your daughters."

"You have no idea what a relief it is to hear this. Thank you, Mr. Everett."

"Call me Lance," he answered with a smile. "Detective Marks, let me put it this way, getting them into Stanford is not the difficult part, but ensuring that they stay and graduate, that's the hard part. That will be up to you and your daughters."

Detective Marks nodded. "Right, of course. I've raised them right. They just need a little help getting in, but I'll make sure they do a good job once they're in." He leaned over the desk to shake Lance's hand. "Lance, thank you so much. If you need help with anything, don't hesitate to let me know."

"No problem." Lance cleared his throat, thinking that this was a good time to get to the real reason he was there. "Regarding Juliet's case…"

Detective Marks's cheeks reddened. "Right, your fiancée, Miss Bentley."

"Bradley, Juliet Bradley."

The detective shifted in his seat and opened a desk drawer. He took out a pack of cigarettes and tapped it against his palm. "Do you mind?"

"No, go ahead." Lance looked up and noticed a smoke detector above them that had been covered up with duct tape. He smirked at the detective's workaround.

Detective Marks lit the cigarette and leaned back again in his chair. He inhaled, and the amber light at the end of the cylinder grew bright. When he exhaled, smoke clouded the room and hid his somber expression for a moment. "I wish I had more information for you, but after months of investigating, we have no major breaks in the case. We didn't have too many leads to begin with. The crime didn't make a whole lot of sense. Palo Alto is a wealthy neighborhood with a very low crime rate; homicides are especially rare in this city. Your fiancée does not in any way fit the usual profile of a murder victim." He took a long drag of his cigarette. "I bet you didn't know there are profiles for murder victims. Most of the time it's someone who gambles and owes a lot of money or a drug addict who's looking for the next fix. Or it could be an innocent party who didn't do anything wrong, but they had bad luck and a couple of greedy family members who wanted them dead so they could collect on their insurance policies. People don't just get killed out of the blue. Random killings by crazy people are very rare. As I said, she didn't fit any of these profiles. She had some money saved up, but by no means was she wealthy enough that someone would want to kill her to get rich. And you—we already checked you out. No offense, but we do have to check out all potential suspects."

Lance quickly nodded. "Of course."

"We checked out her neighbors, too; all of them had alibis. With no motive and no suspects, we had absolutely nothing to go on. We concluded it was a case of mistaken identity."

As Aunt Liz had warned him, talking to Detective Marks was of no use. Disappointment and frustration set in, but Lance knew he needed to keep a level head. He still needed the detective's help. "Do you mind telling me what evidence was collected at Juliet's apartment?"

Detective Marks raised his eyebrows. "Evidence? There wasn't much of it. The perpetrator didn't leave anything behind. The apartment was completely undisturbed. Nothing was taken, nothing was removed. The only things we found were two bullet shells."

Lance leaned forward. "Did you check the shells for fingerprints?"

"Of course we did. But bullet shells are so small, you can never get a full print from them. We couldn't even find a partial print. The shells were clean."

"What about the next-door neighbor? Did Annette hear anything?"

"The old lady said she heard what sounded like two shots, which is consistent with the gunshot wounds. Said they sounded like compressed air being released from an air pump."

"An air pump?"

"Her husband was a mechanic who showed her once how an air pump works." He paused as he flexed a jaw muscle. "I believe we're looking at a pistol with a silencer."

"So, Juliet was shot twice?"

"Yes, twice to the heart." He winced as he continued, "If it's any comfort, she likely lost consciousness before she even hit the ground. It happened so fast she probably didn't know what hit her."

Hearing this gave Lance some consolation, yet it also confirmed a growing suspicion. "You said there were two shots to the heart?"

"Yes, with perfect aim."

As Lance pieced together the facts, he grew more alarmed at the conclusion he was coming to. "Could this have been the work of a professional killer?"

Detective Marks crushed his cigarette stub against a glass ashtray, using more force than was necessary. "Lance." He sighed. "I'm not going to lie to you. That certainly crossed our minds. But it's a farfetched hypothesis. You have to match up the circumstances with the evidence. And the evidence points to the fact that there is no legitimate reason why anyone would hire a contract killer to murder her. She wasn't a high-powered executive or wealthy by any stretch of the imagination. She wasn't involved in any kind of organized crime or an extramarital affair. There was no reason for anyone to harm her, let alone hire a contract killer to kill her." Detective Marks looked Lance in the eye. "We can only assume this was a case of mistaken identity. Your fiancée was in the wrong place at the wrong time."

For a second, the detective's reasoning made sense. However, the longer Lance thought, the more preposterous his logic sounded. The contract killer was good enough at his job that he risked going to a populated apartment building in the early evening when most of the residents were still awake and active. He was skilled enough that he committed a murder without being seen. How was it that someone so professional could mistake the person that he was supposed to kill? It was inconceivable!

He felt Detective Marks's eyes on him, observing the disbelief that was surely showing on his face. There had to be something to go on in this case. He was sure his next question would be out of the ordinary, but he was desperate. "Can I see the bullet shells?"

The detective's eyes widened. "We don't show evid—"

"Please," Lance cut in. "It would mean a lot to me." He shifted his gaze to the photo on the desk and smiled politely. It was clear the detective cared a great deal about getting his daughters into Stanford, and he would use that card to his advantage.

Detective Marks's eyes flickered to the photo as well. He nodded eagerly and stood up. There was even a hint of a smile on his face as he agreed, "Sure. The shells are downstairs in the evidence room. I can take you there right now."

"That would be great."

The clerk manning the storage room handed Detective Marks a brown cardboard box. He placed it on a nearby table and removed the cover, careful to block the box and shield it from any onlookers' view.

Lance looked inside and was surprised to find several of Juliet's personal items placed in clear evidence bags. He took out a framed photo of them taken on the day of his proposal. Underneath it was a floorboard from the apartment with a piece of bloodstained carpet attached to it.

Detective Marks reached into the box and pulled out two small plastic bags, each holding a metal casing. "We collected a lot of things in the beginning of the case, but the only things we found useful were these."

Lance swallowed hard at the sight of the shells that had contained the bullets that killed Juliet. He carefully took one of the bags and held it up to inspect. "These shells are silver," he remarked in surprise. "They're not like the copper ones you normally find. My dad was in the military, so he's taken me shooting before. We've used anything from handguns to automatic rifles, but I've never seen anything like this before."

Detective Marks shrugged. "Yes, but they're really nickel-plated casings. It's rare to see silver shells, but it's not entirely uncommon. You can easily buy these on the internet."

"I'm aware you can buy bullet casings and make your own bullets, but this means the perpetrator made his own bullets."

Detective Marks rubbed the stubble along his jawline. "Well, we do believe the perpetrator was likely a professional, so yes, he could have made his own bullets. But again, it was more than likely a case of mistaken identity."

Lance decided to get a closer look at the shells instead of arguing with the detective. He proceeded to open the bag but stopped when he heard a grunt.

"I'm not worried you will smear any fingerprints on the bullet shells, as there are none. However, you do not want to accidentally leave your prints on them. You would have a hard time explaining to the judge why your prints are on these shells," Detective Marks warned in a stern tone.

Lance nodded and switched his grip on the bag. He slowly flipped it upside down, careful to hold the bullet shell in place, then let the shell slip from the bag onto the table's edge. He did the same with the other bag. Squatting, he leaned close to examine the smooth casings. Other than their silver color, they looked like any other shells he had seen before.

"Detective, do you see this?" His eyes suddenly picked up on a semicircle imprinted on the metal. It was small, around two millimeters in length.

"What is it?" the older man drawled.

"Did you notice these semicircles on the shells?"

Detective Marks looked over, his eyebrow twitching slightly. "Hm, I never noticed them. It's possible they're some kind of manufacturing defect."

Too excited to care about the detective's apathetic response, Lance took out his smartphone and turned it on. He knelt and focused the camera lens on the shells.

The detective opened his mouth to speak then waved his hand for Lance to proceed. "I didn't see this," he muttered under his breath.

Lance began taking shots from all angles. The special macro lens he had bought to take close-range photos in his lab worked well for this task. He smiled at the sharp images appearing on his phone screen.

"Wow, I need one of those," Detective Marks remarked over his shoulder.

Satisfied with the photos, Lance stood up and shook hands with the detective. "Thanks for your time today. I appreciate your help." He turned to leave then added, "Give me a call when your daughters apply to Stanford. I'll arrange a visit for them and introduce them to the deans."

Detective Marks nodded enthusiastically. "I'll do that. Hopefully I answered all your questions."

Lance smirked. That couldn't be farther from the truth. He was leaving the police station with more questions than he came with, but he hoped the evidence in his photos would give him some answers.

Chapter Ten

On his way home, Lance decided to make a quick stop at the market. Thanks to his recent sixteen- to eighteen-hour work days, he didn't have time to restock his refrigerator. He chose the store nearest his apartment, one that he and Juliet used to frequent.

He wandered from one aisle to the next, feeling overwhelmed at the selection of colorful produce. He truly was at a loss for what to buy. During the past months, he hadn't cared about eating for reasons other than survival. If it was up to him, he would eat at Happy Donut every day. Juliet was always the one who would sneak healthy foods into the shopping cart when he wasn't looking.

Thinking about those times with her helped him. He suddenly recalled some simple recipes she had taught him and the ingredients he would need. With a smile on his face, he walked with purpose, placing items into his shopping basket.

Perhaps it had also been too long since he did anything outside of his home. As he shopped, he couldn't help feeling out of place, even a little uncomfortable. The hairs on his arms stood up, and for a moment he questioned if someone was watching him. He glanced around and laughed at himself for having such a foolish thought. Around him were regular folks minding their own business.

One customer intrigued him. The young child looked to be around five or six years old. Her blond pigtails bounced up and down as she followed her mom in the baked goods aisle. He smiled at her and she smiled back, revealing a gaping hole on her upper gum.

Her mother noticed Lance glancing their way and nodded in greeting.

Lance remarked, "Your daughter reminds me of my niece Chloe. It's cute when kids lose their front teeth."

The little girl hid behind her mom's skirt with her eyes peeking out to look up at Lance. Upon hearing his comment, she covered her mouth.

Her mother chuckled. "Oh, don't mention that, she already feels self-conscious about it."

Lance approached the girl and squatted to her eye level. He pointed to his own mouth and grinned. "I lost my two front teeth before, but don't worry, they grow back quickly." At her enthusiastic nod, he continued, "Make sure you put any teeth that fall out under your pillow, so the tooth fairy will leave you something special."

"Oh, she knows," her mother reassured. "She already spent her money on candy."

"What a smart girl," Lance mused.

"Okay, it's time for us to go. Say goodbye." The little girl and her mother both waved as they walked away.

Lance proceeded to stand up, but a strange sight stopped him in his tracks. At first glance, there was nothing unusual about the area fifteen feet in front of him. Next to the bakery was a small coffee shop with a few wooden tables and chairs for customers to use. One particular table however caught Lance's attention. The patron sitting there looked ordinary enough, reading a newspaper and drinking from a mug. Approximately in his early forties, the man wore casual clothes, jeans, and a sweatshirt with the words *I Love San Francisco* written across the front. He sat at a ninety-degree angle to Lance so only his profile was visible. His right ankle rested on his left knee, which shook rhythmically from the incessant tapping of his foot. It was his right foot that piqued Lance's interest, specifically the object attached to the top of his sneaker. The object appeared to be a camera. Its body was black and small, but it boasted a relatively large lens for its size. The lens resembled a dime and was likely big enough to capture images in low light.

Lance squinted and inhaled sharply. The camera was pointed at him. If he had been standing, there was no way he would have seen it. But because he had lowered himself to chat with the little girl, he saw more than enough to alarm him.

The man suddenly peered over the side of the newspaper and set it on the table. The moment his eyes met Lance's, he reached down and then stood up and walked away.

Squinting, Lance tried to spot the camera on the man's shoe, but it was nowhere to be seen. How had he grabbed it so quickly, and where had he put it? His skills were as smooth as a magician's.

Dropping his basket of groceries, Lance bolted to his feet and ran after the customer. He spotted an earpiece on the man's left ear, which from a distance looked like an ordinary Bluetooth. However, at close range he could see a clear cord attached to the device that trailed down the man's neck and disappeared into his shirt.

Reaching out his arm, Lance attempted to flag down the man as he walked through the automatic doors. He followed him outside the supermarket and glanced around the parking lot. The man was nowhere in sight. How could that be?

Lance ran his hand down his face and wondered if his eyes were playing tricks on him. The man and his camera and earpiece all didn't make sense. Why would someone be taking pictures or videos of him? Why would anyone want to follow him?

Flashes of the recent early morning episode in his apartment garage crossed his mind. Could this man be related to the two men who had been parked in the black car?

Lance gave up on finding the man and returned to the store. He began walking back to get his basket but decided to stop by the table where the man had been sitting. Only a cup of black coffee remained.

He swallowed slowly as a wild idea took shape in his head. With his fingers gripping the mug's rim, he picked it up and set it on the palm of his other hand. He found a trash bin and poured out its contents. Glancing around to make sure no one was looking, he walked out of the supermarket.

Though he had been planning to go home, he took the road back to work. He wanted to find answers. As he thought through the recent incidents, he started seeing them through a lens of suspicion. He remembered the small black box he found inside his car and wondered if it had been placed there by someone other than the manufacturer.

Once he arrived at the office, he parked and popped open the car hood. He located the box and gave it a tug. To his surprise, the object came off easily. He turned it over in his hands and guessed it had been held in place by a magnet.

Chills ran down his back. At this point, Lance had no doubt he was being followed. Instead of being worried or fearful, however, he felt a strange thrill. Someone was watching him for a purpose, and perhaps the reason was tied to his recent efforts. Either they were involved in Juliet's murder or they were interested in the time machine.

Lance couldn't wait to analyze the three puzzle pieces he had acquired that day. He placed the box in his jacket pocket and carefully removed the coffee mug from his car before heading up to his office.

"Good evening, Dr. Everett."

"Hey, Albert," Lance responded to the computerized voice. "I need you to run something for me.

"Certainly."

He took out his phone and hooked it up to the supercomputer. Although Albert was meant to analyze mass quantities of data and calculations, he could also use his connections to online cloud databases to process other subjects. "I need you to analyze these photos. Anything you can find out about the markings on the bullet shells will be useful."

Lance turned his attention to the coffee mug. He had never lifted fingerprints before, but he had watched enough crime shows to understand the science behind it.

First, he took a similar-looking mug from his desk to practice on. He grasped the mug with his fingers, released them, and examined the fingerprints left on the smooth surface. Next, his eyes searched around for a fine, powdery substance. Unable to find anything usable in the office, he went down the hall to the break room and returned with a container of organic cocoa powder.

He sprinkled the dark powder over the oil marking left

by his skin. The distinctive arches and whorls of a fingerprint appeared on the smooth surface. He gently blew over the mug to get rid of the excess powder, and the sweet aroma of cocoa filled his nostrils. He took a piece of transparent tape and slowly covered the print. With great care, he lifted the tape and evaluated it. Success.

He performed the same steps on the coffee mug from the supermarket. In a matter of minutes, he had lifted three complete and one partial fingerprints, taken pictures of them, and uploaded them onto the supercomputer.

"Albert, do you have access to any databases that cross-check fingerprints?"

"Yes, Dr. Everett," the image on the screen answered, "due to the high security of our lab, we complete our own background checks."

"Great. Please run these fingerprints for me."

While Albert worked on the two tasks given to him, Lance moved on to the next puzzle piece, the little black box found in his car.

He popped the lid off with little effort. As suspected, he found a tracking device inside. He took it apart and inspected it piece by piece. The GPS sensor was unlike any he had seen before. To begin with, there was no brand name nor serial number on the parts, making it virtually untraceable. From what Lance could tell, it was not a consumer product.

He assumed the wireless GPS would need a master device to contact it in order to pull its data. If it had been pulled recently, whoever was tracking him knew he worked in this building with Mr. Singh.

Noticing how quiet the place was, he glanced at his watch. Nine thirty. Several hours had passed since he arrived, and the lab was all but empty.

A computerized voice spoke up, breaking the eerie silence. "Dr. Everett, I found no match for the fingerprint in the database."

Lance sighed. "Thanks for checking, Albert."

Another dead end. It was a far stretch to assume Albert would be able to find a match. After all, the computer only had low-level access to criminal databases. The result only confirmed the man at the supermarket had never been arrested. If he wanted to cross-reference the fingerprint with other databases, he would need to find another way.

Lance tapped his fingers on the table then sat up straight. Perhaps he had one. He picked up his phone. "Hello, Detective Marks, this is Lance Everett."

"Mr. Everett? How can I help you?"

Given the fact that the detective had gone so far as to give him his personal number, Lance figured it was worth a shot to call him. "Listen, I have a favor to ask." He relayed the incident from the supermarket and his suspicions of being followed. "I need you to run the fingerprints for me. I think that man may have something to do with Juliet's murder."

"Send it over and I'll see what I can do."

Lance thanked Detective Marks and emailed the print to him.

Next, he turned his attention to the supercomputer's giant glass display. "Albert, have you found anything on the bullet shells?"

"Yes, Dr. Everett." Photos of the shells appeared on the display, along with text. "They are 9mm bullet shell casings, one of the most popular calibers for handguns. These shell casings are distinct from other more commonly used shells."

"Are you referring to their color?"

"Yes," Albert continued. "These are silver in color while generic bullet shells are made of brass. Assuming the colors of these photos are accurate, these shells were likely plated with nickel. There is another detail that makes them unique. They bear a semicircle signature not seen on other shells."

Lance's eyebrow twitched. "Albert, why do you call the semicircle a signature? Couldn't it be some kind of manufacturer defect?"

"They are unlikely to be defects from the manufacturing process. The semicircles look to be marks added after the fact."

"How did you come to that conclusion?"

"Silver-colored bullet shells are in general plated with nickel. Bullet shells are typically not made with solid nickel as nickel is a brittle metal. During the stretching process of making the shell, nickel would crack. Brass, however, is soft and can be stretched and molded. For those who want to make silver-colored shells, they would apply the nickel plating process to add the color. The semicircle on this shell is so small and precise that if they were introduced during the stretching process of the brass bullet shells, they would have been covered up during the nickel plating process."

"That makes sense."

"As with any plating process there is a smooth surface on the object being plated. You would not leave marks such as these semicircles. Therefore, these semicircles were added intentionally after the bullets were assembled."

Lance nodded. "But why do you call it a signature?"

"It is not uncommon for gun enthusiasts to mark their bullets with their own signature. These signatures can include a letter of the alphabet or a symbol. These two signatures are represented as semicircles, and from first glance, they appear identical." The photo on the display zoomed in on one of the semicircles. "However, with ten times the magnification, you will notice that the pressure applied to make these semicircles was not consistent. These marks were created by human application. Since these semicircles serve no purpose in how the bullets perform, there is a ninety-nine percent probability these were meant to be signatures."

"Good work."

"Thank you, Dr. Everett."

Suddenly a thought popped into Lance's head. "Albert, I'm guessing you didn't find a match for these signatures. Have they been used anywhere else?"

"You are correct. I was not able to find any historical record of anyone using bullets with this signature."

"Understood. Thanks, Albert."

Lance suddenly noticed movement out of the corner of his eye. He turned and found Mr. Singh leaning on his cane with a wide-eyed look on his face.

"You are working late, Lance," Mr. Singh said with a tight smile. "I thought I would drop by and see how things are going with you. I'm curious, how does the study of bullets help move our time machine project forward?"

"Mr. Singh, I'm glad you stopped by. We might have a problem."

The older man's eyes flickered from the giant display to Lance. "Oh, do tell."

Lance lowered his voice as he confided, "I believe I'm being followed. Someone put a very sophisticated tracking device in my car. And I believe whoever killed Juliet was a professional contract killer."

A sharp line formed between Mr. Singh's brows and his brown complexion paled slightly along the edges of his mouth.

Reading the shock on his employer's face, Lance explained in further detail. "Whoever killed her could very well be after me now. There is a good chance they know I'm working for you and that I work in this building."

Mr. Singh shook his head adamantly. "Lance, we must take precautions. It is not safe for you to use your car. For the time being, my driver will take you around. I would advise you to also stay in our corporate apartment instead of going home. I will have the apartment ready in an hour." Reaching out his hand, he continued, "Lance, please give me your car key. I'll have someone take it somewhere far away from here."

"Thank you, but that's not necessary. Losing the car might tip off whoever's following me that I'm on to him. Let me drive it back to my apartment. I can pick up a few things while I'm there."

"The apartment is fully furnished and stocked with supplies. You will have everything you need there. You must not put yourself in harm's way." Gesturing to the pieces on the table, Mr. Singh asked, "Is that the tracking device? I think it's best if you reassemble it so we can put it back in your car. I'll have someone drive it back to your apartment."

"I can drive myself."

Mr. Singh sighed. "Lance, what if whoever is following you is after the time machine?"

Lance ran his hands through his hair as he contemplated the possibilities. Lance couldn't believe the situation had gotten so chaotic, so quickly. He had only begun working on this project a couple of days ago. He couldn't have anticipated any of what had happened. But one thing was for sure, if it were not for his knowledge of the time machine, he would be of little value to anyone. "That's very possible. I am the time machine; the time machine is me."

He handed over his car key and felt any semblance of control he thought he had leave his grasp.

Chapter Eleven

In the darkness, Lance stared up at the ceiling, allowing the plush king-size mattress to cradle his body. The bed at the corporate housing was likely the most expensive one he had ever slept on. To call this temporary home an apartment would be an insult; the place was more like an executive penthouse.

His new home occupied the top three floors of a San Francisco high-rise. Each floor exhibited its own style and decor. Walking from one to the next made him feel like he was entering a different season with its blend of colors. The top floor had its own gym, including an infinity swimming pool overlooking the entire city skyline. A fully-equipped kitchen, plus an expansive living room with a small theater to entertain guests, occupied the second floor. His bedroom on the bottom floor had a walk-in closet and a luxurious marble bathroom.

Though his body was tired, he couldn't stop thinking. So much had happened in the past few days, and his mind was now catching up. He closed his eyes, but sleep eluded him. Instead, he decided to start his day.

He sat up and swung his feet over to rest on the plush

carpet. Without hesitation, he reached to the side of the bed and pressed a button. The electric blinds on the other side of the room began rolling up, revealing a large window. The morning sun streamed in, and Lance squinted as his eyes adjusted to the light. A strange feeling overcame him and he glanced again at the switch. Mr. Singh's driver had given him a quick tour of the place yesterday, but he hadn't mentioned where the controls were for the blinds. *How did I know it was there?*

The odd sensation followed Lance out of the bedroom and upstairs into the kitchen. Almost as if on automatic pilot, his feet led him to a cabinet in search of coffee. Wanting a cup of coffee wasn't the strange part; knowing exactly where the coffee beans were located was. Even more disconcerting, he had a feeling he knew exactly what brand of coffee beans was behind the stainless-steel door. The name of a cafe he used to frequent near the Stanford campus came to mind. He remembered the store's logo well; it was the same vivid shade of blue as the sky on a clear summer's day. The same beautiful azure color of Juliet's eyes. The last thought made him swallow hard. He exhaled and opened the cabinet. His jaw dropped. A bag with an image of a blue bottle sat on the shelf.

He didn't know how to explain it, but he felt certain he had been in this apartment before.

If Lance ever considered believing in déjà vu, it would be now. He recalled reading before that little glitches in the brain caused this type of phenomenon. The result was that a person's new experience became stored in the brain's long-term memory instead of the short-term one, thus tricking the person into thinking they had experienced it before. The theory was strange and had neither been proven nor disproven, but it was plausible. The inexplicable sense of knowing that he had experienced twice that morning made it seem even more plausible.

Moreover, Lance had no memories of the surrounding neighborhood. When he arrived last night, the street didn't look familiar, and neither did the building. He glanced around the kitchen slowly; the marble countertop, stainless-steel appliances, and dark hardwood floors all appeared new to him. The strange feeling he had earlier left. No doubt his sleepless nights were playing tricks on his mind. He laughed at himself and turned his attention to brewing coffee.

A rich aroma soon filled the room, awakening his senses. Lance decided to go for a morning swim before starting work. He was sure Mr. Singh would be getting in touch with him soon regarding their next steps.

An hour later, he was showered and changed, resting comfortably on the leather couch with a fresh cup of coffee. As he picked up the TV remote, his phone rang.

"Lance, I hope I didn't wake you," Mr. Singh said. "Dr. Rostov and I would like to come over in the next fifteen minutes to talk."

Lance agreed and hung up. He proceeded to turn on the TV to check out the news. After flipping through several morning talk shows, he found a local channel that caught his attention.

"We turn our attention now to a story that you may have heard of before," the anchorwoman announced, "the Déjà Vu Phenomenon. With us today is an expert in the field of neuroscience, Dr. Martin. Dr. Martin, thank you for joining us today."

A gray-haired gentleman showed up next to the woman on a split screen. He adjusted his earpiece and stared off to the side of the camera, visibly uncomfortable being on the air. "Thank you," he responded in a hoarse smoker's voice.

"There have been reports in recent months of a significant increase in the number of people experiencing this phenomenon. You know, I've been on this show for fifteen years and every now and then when I walk up to this chair, I have a feeling that I was just here yesterday," the anchorwoman joked. "Might I be experiencing déjà vu, too?"

Dr. Martin smiled awkwardly. "Ah, not exactly. Déjà vu is a feeling that one has when he or she is in fact doing something new, but they feel like they have done this exact thing before. The feeling can be about a location or a task or even a thing. For example, the subject may be visiting a place for the very first time, but somehow, he has a familiar feeling that he has been there before. Or there may be some task that the subject has never done before, but he has a familiar feeling that he has done that task before."

That's exactly what happened to me. Lance had never used the remote control to open the bedroom blinds or made coffee in this penthouse, but he felt like he had done both before.

The anchorwoman continued, "I've heard stories that an old lady in France claims she was a princess in her past life. She remembers living in a castle and can recall great details of things inside the castle even though she has never been there. Would that also not qualify as déjà vu?"

Dr. Martin nodded. "That's correct. I have heard of that French lady's story as well, but you are correct, that is not related to déjà vu. Déjà vu is not related to the theory of past lives. Generally speaking, most people who experience déjà vu describe it as a feeling of having done something they are certain they have never done before. But none of the subjects that I've met claim these feelings come from a past life. They experience these feelings as a part of themselves."

"Now that you've explained it, I do recall having these kinds of feelings myself, but I don't remember now what I was doing. In your opinion, is there any harm per se of having such feelings?"

The doctor's face brightened. "That is not surprising. It is a very common experience. I would say that I myself am a frequent sufferer of déjà vu; in fact, that's why I chose this subject for my doctoral thesis many years ago. I wanted to find an explanation of why people experience such a phenomenon. I used to write down in as much detail as possible each time I experienced a déjà vu, but studying oneself can cause the results to be a bit subjective. That's when I switched to studying other people instead." He gave a small smile and continued, "As to answer your question, for those who experience an occasional déjà vu, there are no serious medical problems. Most people have what you described, a temporary feeling that may last a few seconds. However, there are some with more severe cases, like the few subjects that I work with at my school. These people suffer from recurring déjà vu. Their feelings of déjà vu are so strong and so frequent that at times they become confused over what they have done and what are new experiences. Some of them are actually on disability and cannot function normally."

The woman let out a sharp gasp. "I didn't know it could be so serious."

"But these serious cases are very rare," Mr. Martin assured. "If you only experience déjà vu once in a blue moon and the feeling does not last for more than a few seconds, there is nothing to be alarmed about."

"But according to your studies the phenomenon seems to be on the rise."

Dr. Martin cleared his throat. "Yes, however, déjà vu is not something that is frequently reported in general. The phenomenon has probably been happening since the beginning of time, but no one cared to study it until a couple of centuries ago. Not until the early 1800s were there formally documented cases of déjà vu. Even then, not many scientists have taken this subject seriously. It is true that we are now receiving more reports of déjà vu, but that could simply be because healthcare is more available to the masses, especially mental health services."

"Most of these cases have been documented by mental health practitioners, not so much by medical doctors?"

"That's correct."

"Well, thank you very much for spending some time with us, Dr. Martin. For anyone interested in your study, how can they contact you?"

Dr. Martin concluded, "They can visit our website to find out more." The website address flashed across the bottom of the TV screen.

Intrigued by his earlier experiences and the interview, Lance made a mental note of the website so he could look at it later. It was then that he realized he had left the lab so quickly he'd forgotten his computer there. There had to be a computer in this penthouse somewhere; he just needed to look for it. That thought made him laugh and proved again that he had likely never been there before.

Before Lance could search, the doorbell rang. Mr. Singh and Dr. Rostov stood at the door with the driver a few steps behind them.

"Good morning," Mr. Singh greeted Lance, "I hope you were able to catch a few hours of sleep."

Lance gestured for them to enter. "Not really, but certainly not because of the place. This is an amazing penthouse. I just couldn't fall asleep with all the recent activities."

Mr. Singh and Dr. Rostov walked in, while the driver closed the door and stayed outside.

"I made coffee if anyone wants some," Lance offered.

Dr. Rostov smiled. "Sure, I love Blue Bottle coffee. I'll take a cup, Dr. Everett."

Lance raised his eyebrows. "How did you know..."

"It's not the first time we've had coffee here. That's my favorite brand. I'm so used to drinking it, I'd recognize the aroma anywhere."

"Not the first time? I've never had coffee with you in this apartment."

Dr. Rostov frowned for a second then chuckled. "I must have been thinking about our times at the lab and got confused." Before Lance could comment further, Dr. Rostov turned to Mr. Singh. "Would you like a cup as well?"

"Why, yes, I will," Mr. Singh replied with a tight-lipped smile. "Thank you, Lance."

"Sure thing." Lance walked to the kitchen and poured two cups of coffee, all the while thinking over the awkward exchange in his mind. Dr. Rostov's words were even stranger considering Lance's recent bouts with déjà vu. Perhaps the older scientist just experienced an episode himself.

Lance brought the cups to the living room, and they all took a seat on the leather couches. He turned off the TV before Mr. Singh began speaking.

"Lance, for your safety and the safety of our project, it is my recommendation that you stay here for the remainder of the project. I know that is a huge ask, but we don't know who these people are that are following you. Who knows what they would do if you were to return to your apartment."

Lance was afraid Mr. Singh would make that recommendation. Even though the penthouse was amazing, there was no place like home. But for the project, as well as his own safety, he agreed. "I understand. I certainly don't want to compromise our project. For now, I'll stay here."

Mr. Singh breathed a sigh of relief. "Great. I know this is a huge inconvenience, but feel free to let the driver know what you need and he will get it for you. Just let him know whatever you need or wherever you need to go. He will take good care of you."

"Thanks for the gesture, but I don't need a driver. I can take care of myself. There's public transit just about everywhere in the city."

"I know you like to do everything yourself, but until we know exactly what is going on, I think it is safer to have the driver drive you. This way, at the very least, I know no one would put a tracker on our car."

Lance reluctantly agreed. "I'll do it for the time being. But we need to figure out who these people are and what they want."

Dr. Rostov spoke up. "Mr. Singh said you ran into someone at a supermarket who was recording you? I'm guessing that person didn't look familiar to you."

Lance shook his head. "I didn't get a good look at him. When I saw he had a camera pointed at me, I walked toward him to talk, but he got away before I could reach him. But I did get a hold of his fingerprints." Seeing the confused look on

Mr. Rostov's face, he explained, "I took the coffee cup he was drinking out of."

"We can use Albert to analyze the prints—"

Lance smiled and interrupted him, "Already done. I'm one step ahead of you. Albert checked all the known criminal databases, but nothing turned up. But I reached out to a police friend that I know. Let's hope he finds something."

Dr. Rostov and Mr. Singh exchanged surprised glances.

Mr. Singh exclaimed, "You work fast. If you don't mind sharing, send me the fingerprints; I know a few people as well."

"Sure, the prints are with Albert in the documents folder. Just pull them out from there. I'm very eager to find out who this guy is. Whatever you find, please let me know."

"Of course," Mr. Singh replied. "Whatever I find out, you will know immediately." He paused then continued, "We will also be increasing our security at the lab. I'm going to double the number of guards and have undercover officers patrol a three-block radius around our building at all hours."

Lance nodded. "That sounds like a prudent idea. I'm sorry for causing so much trouble. I just started working there a few days ago and now everyone has to deal with safety concerns."

"Don't worry about it. But I do appreciate you laying low for a while until we can ensure everyone's safety. In the meantime," he paused to make a quick call on his phone, "we have a computer for you to use here at the apartment."

Mr. Singh directed Mr. Rostov to open the door. The driver brought in a laptop and handed it to Mr. Singh.

"That's why I didn't know where it was," Lance murmured under his breath.

Mr. Singh asked, "Excuse me?"

Lance chuckled. "No, just what you said reminded me of something, that's all."

"You will love this laptop. Not only is it lightweight, it is a direct extension of Albert. You can run everything from here as if you were in the office."

Lance smiled as he took the laptop. Just as Mr. Singh stated, the system weighed little more than a paperback book. The cover was simply a piece of glass with a keyboard below it. He marveled at its advanced technology. "This is great, thank you."

Dr. Rostov nodded. "I will go into the office as frequently as possible to continue our project. Meanwhile you can work from here and not miss a beat. Do let me know if you need anything done at the lab. I would be happy to be your remote hands."

"Dr. Rostov, I really appreciate it. Thank you so much in advance for all your help."

"No problem at all. I was a fan of yours before, but after having seen your work firsthand, I'm a big fan now."

Mr. Singh stood up. "I will let you get familiar with your laptop. Dr. Rostov and I will return to the lab. I hope you don't mind me borrowing your driver to take us back to the office."

"Just don't get used to having a driver drive you around," Lance joked as they all laughed.

As they walked toward the door, Lance decided to pick his fellow scientist's brain. That morning's TV interview, as well as the day's "coincidences," remained on his mind. He turned to Dr. Rostov and inquired, "Dr. Rostov, what do you make of the déjà vu effect?"

Dr. Rostov stopped suddenly and turned. "Déjà vu? I'm guessing you are asking for my professional opinion."

"I'm curious about any opinion you may have. It doesn't have to be any formal study that you might have done before. Really, I'm just curious more than anything. Just before you arrived, I was watching a news story about a surge of déjà vu being experienced by the public."

"Unfortunately, I really don't know too much about this particular subject matter. I have never done any serious research on this subject."

Lance appreciated Dr. Rostov's honesty on the matter. "No problem. Do you happen to know anyone who has studied this subject before?"

"I wish I could be more helpful, but I don't remember coming across anyone who studied the subject of déjà vu or its related subjects."

Lance nodded. "It's certainly not a common field of study. Almost as uncommon as time travel. Thanks anyway." He said goodbye and closed the door.

Alone again, Lance wasted no time in logging into his new laptop.

A computerized voice spoke up, "Dr. Everett, how may I assist you?"

"Can you bring up this website for me, please." Lance relayed the web address to Albert and watched the site appear on the screen.

Lance quickly scrolled through Dr. Martin's website. According to his report, the number of people reporting experiences of déjà vu spiked in recent months, more specifically about a year ago. Most of the reporting came from developed countries, such as the United States and European nations. It was possible that the phenomenon was not happening to people in Asia or non-developing countries, but more than likely the individuals experiencing it there did not have the same level of access to healthcare facilities.

Even more interesting, the subjects who suffered from déjà vu had nothing in common. They were from different parts of the country, were male and female, and were of all age ranges.

However, Dr. Martin did recently find one commonality across the board. With the use of a high-powered brain scan, he discovered all the patients' brains appeared to have some unique wrinkles that he had never seen before. These were not the same kind of wrinkles generally referred to as ridges and crevices; these wrinkles appeared on the ridges of the brain.

Lance studied one of the scan results Dr. Martin posted on the website. The image had been magnified and labeled to show the wrinkles. Lance's jaw dropped. This brain was unlike any he had seen before. The wrinkles appeared far apart from each other, yet evenly spaced out over the brain. Each wrinkle looked like a very thin jagged line going across a ridge of the brain. There even appeared to be some extra blood vessels around these wrinkles.

Lance sat back and clasped his hands behind his head. This subject certainly intrigued him. It's not like he had never heard of déjà vu before, but for some reason, he was very, very curious about it now. He wanted to find out more, and who better to ask than Dr. Martin himself?

"Albert, please call Dr. Martin's office."

"Certainly."

Within seconds, Lance's laptop started ringing. It rang a few times until an answering machine picked up. "You have reached Dr. Martin of the Neuroscience Institute at UC Berkeley. I specialize in the study of déjà vu. If you suffer from frequent feelings of déjà vu, please be sure to leave me your contact information. I would love to sit down and chat with you. For everyone else, don't bother leaving a message."

Lance smiled, amused at the doctor's passionate but curt recording. "Dr. Martin, my name is Lance Everett. I'm a quantum physics researcher at Stanford University." Lance paused for a second, remembering that he no longer worked there. The odds were low that the doctor would return his call, so he decided not to correct himself. "I came across your study on the déjà vu effect and browsed through your website. Your research and data are all very intriguing. I would like to meet with you and discuss your study further. You can reach me at 555-340-3420. I look forward to speaking with you."

Lance ended the call just as his cell phone rang. "Detective Marks, how are you?"

"Lance, where exactly did you get those fingerprints from?" The detective's voice was gruff and serious.

"I got them off a mug like I told you yesterday. Did you find something?"

Detective Marks lowered his voice. "I don't know exactly what I have." He paused for a second and continued, "These prints appear to belong to someone in the military. Probably someone high up."

"How do you know that?"

"I don't know for sure. A match was found, but it was stated as classified. That usually means the prints belong to someone working for the government."

What could the government possibly want with him? Did they know about his research? If so, they could be after the time machine. Or did they know something about Juliet's murder? Worse yet, were they involved in it?

Detective Marks broke the silence. "Lance, are you still there?"

"Yes, I'm here."

"I don't know how you got involved with this person, but you should be careful. You don't want to mess with the government, especially not the military."

Lance thanked the detective and hung up more confused than ever. Even though he had found another piece of the puzzle, it only deepened the mystery.

Chapter Twelve

This was a day like no other. The noise inside the lab was louder than anything Lance had ever heard. He could only equate it to the reverberating roar of a car speeding down the highway with one window open, except a thousand times worse. Even from the comfort of the corporate penthouse, he sensed the enormous power of the time machine. He was certain those in the lab not only heard the booming noise, but also sensed it vibrating through their bodies.

Dr. Rostov and the entire team wore advanced headsets to communicate with each other. Aside from the discomfort of the overwhelming noise, Lance could read one emotion on everyone's faces: exhilaration. He felt the excitement himself at the thought of achieving a feat no one else had ever accomplished. The target for today's experiment involved speeding up a particle to the speed of light.

A particle able to reach light speed would also increase exponentially in mass. So far no scientist had found one that could do the job. However, through extensive research, he and Dr. Rostov had fine-tuned the time machine and modified its equation to accommodate the latest particle, the Higgs Boson. This extremely lightweight particle could be a game changer in the world of quantum physics.

At the moment there were four Higgs Boson particles swirling inside the time machine at a high frequency. Four were needed to balance the force caused by the acceleration in the tubes and to prevent the machine from bursting into pieces. Even with the particles in perfect balance between north to south and east to west, the machine still shook violently. Lance could tell from the way the image oscillated on his laptop screen that the whole building was humming from the vibrations. He fixed his eyes on the time machine's measurements to ensure the readings were within the tolerance level.

"Lance, I think we should go for it!" Dr. Rostov's face appeared on the screen for a split second as he yelled into the microphone.

Lance held up one hand to acknowledge the scientist's words. He took a deep breath. Would the time machine be able to handle the next move? He quickly analyzed the three numbers displayed on the supercomputer's giant screen. The first number, the speed of the particle, climbed steadily as the momentum inside the machine continued to rise. The goal was 299792458 m/s. The second number reflected the energy remaining in the four tanks that powered the particles. Once the tanks ran out of power, the experiment would be over. It was crucial that there was enough energy to speed up the particles, as well as slow them down. Without a proper spin-down, the particles could break through the machine and cause catastrophic damages. The last number on the screen gauged the machine's pressure as the particles gained speed and momentum.

Many more parameters flashed across the screen, numbers which most of the people in the lab didn't comprehend. Only Dr. Rostov and Lance understood their implications, but Lance understood them the best. He was the one who wrote the equations and came up with all the critical measurements.

After making some calculations, Lance spoke into the communications system. "Agreed. Let's make the push for it."

Everyone in the room cheered at his go-ahead. Some of the technicians couldn't help but shout for joy.

Lance calmly stated, "Prepare the photon injection on my mark."

Several technicians replied in unison, "Preparing photon injection," as they typed in commands on their keyboards.

Within a couple of seconds, one of the technicians announced, "Tank one photon injection ready."

Another technician confirmed, "Tank two photon injection ready."

A third technician also stated, "Tank three photon injection ready."

Lastly, the fourth technician informed the team, "Tank four photon injection ready."

Lance nodded and narrowed his eyes on the screen. "Albert, start the countdown."

Albert spoke up. "Photon injection starting in…five… four…three…two…photon injection commencing."

The image on Lance's screen jumped, and several people in the lab yelped in response to the strong jolt the machine produced. The vibrations continued, increasing in strength and frequency to the point that the machine blurred. Lance blinked quickly to make sure his eyes weren't playing tricks on him. As if he needed more evidence of the machine's movement, he noted several objects in the lab starting to tremble as well.

Lance stared in awe at the display. The machine's energy level plummeted while the speedometer climbed at a rapid pace. His heart raced as the number neared the speed of light.

People in the room began screaming as the situation grew chaotic. Lance could see tension and fear etched in the lines on the technicians' faces.

"One more digit to go," Lance thought out loud.

Just as the words left his mouth, the tolerance meter redlined. Lance immediately screamed into the mic, "Begin power down sequence."

Before the technicians could respond, Dr. Rostov commanded, "Do not power down. I repeat, do not power down."

The technicians stared at each other, unsure of what to do.

Lance repeated himself, this time with more force. "We need to power down. Dr. Rostov, the machine is vibrating too much; it is no longer safe. We must power down. Now."

Dr. Rostov's voice rose in excitement. "One more second. Just one more second."

"Dr. Rostov, we don't have another second," Lance reiterated. Beads of cold sweat broke out on his forehead as he watched the pressure meter continue to climb. "The machine's not stable."

With their fingers hovering over the keyboards, the four technicians looked from one scientist to the other, awaiting instructions.

Lance opened his mouth to give the order to power down, but right at that moment, the particles reached light speed.

Dr. Rostov gestured wildly and screamed, "Shut it down! Begin power down sequence now!"

The technicians complied, and Albert followed their keystrokes with a verbal confirmation. "Power down sequence has begun."

The intense vibration and noise inside the lab suddenly decreased, and the whole room seemed to exhale in relief.

Lance unclenched his jaw. They had just made history by successfully pushing a particle to the speed of light and safely powering it down, but at what cost? How could Dr. Rostov have disregarded his call?

The older scientist, typically calm in demeanor, could barely contain his excitement. He shouted into the comm system, "We made history!"

Though Lance was not in the room, Albert projected his image onto the giant screen, as well as the image of the lab onto the wall of the penthouse. At the sight of the whole lab cheering in celebration, Lance smiled as well. They had done something great. He leaned back in his chair and exclaimed, "We have made history today. You guys are amazing."

As everyone continued celebrating, however, Lance began to worry. He didn't quite know what was happening, but an unsettled feeling overcame him. It was almost like a sixth sense telling him something bad was coming, like the foreboding he experienced about Juliet's death. He decided he needed to take a closer look at the data collected from today's test and determine his next steps.

Dr. Rostov had regained his composure now and spoke into the comm, specifically addressing Lance. "Dr. Everett, a quick word with you, please."

Lance refocused his thoughts and answered, "Sure, I'll call your office."

Dr. Rostov acknowledged his reply with a nod and walked

out of the lab.

Upon answering the phone, Dr. Rostov exclaimed, "Lance, congratulations. You did it!"

"Thanks, but you should take the credit. You led the team to get us here. I only joined recently."

"Don't be so humble. We couldn't have done it without you. Your formulas got us here in the first place."

Shaking his head, Lance knew the success of the test didn't outweigh the concern weighing on his shoulders. "Thank you, but, Dr. Rostov, I think we need to slow down on our project."

"What? Slow down? No, no, no. You saw how much progress we made today! We are closer than ever to achieving our goal."

"We don't know what we are getting close to. The machine obviously can't handle any more stress. We were lucky the entire building didn't blow up."

Dr. Rostov paused for a moment. "Lance, you are not upset that I didn't take your power down command seriously, are you?" he sneered. "What happened earlier was nothing new. Before you joined us, we already ran multiple experiments where the machine behaved in a similar fashion. I knew the machine could handle it. I would not jeopardize everyone's safety. I was sure your machine could handle it."

"That's not what I meant."

Dr. Rostov justified himself further. "Lance, I know your machine very well by now. I think we could push the tolerance meter even higher. Come on, you should trust your own design," he touted. "You built a great machine."

"I appreciate the sentiment, but I'm concerned—"

"There is nothing to be concerned about," he interrupted. "Just remember you've done an amazing job on this project. We are so very close to a breakthrough."

Lance raised his voice slightly in frustration. "Dr. Rostov, please hear me out. All I'm saying is that we need some time. I need to study the data we collected today and determine what we have and what our next steps should be."

"Of course, study the data. But we don't have a lot of time," he warned with a hint of irritation in his voice. "You know as well as I do that someone out there is doing the same thing we are. We need to be ahead of the game and figure things out before they do it first."

Lance exhaled deeply, fully aware of the seriousness of the situation. "Let me look at our data, and we can discuss this in more detail in a week or so."

"Fine," Dr. Rostov conceded. "I know you've been working tirelessly on this project. At least take today off and celebrate our progress."

"Sure, thanks. You, too," Lance replied and hung up.

He stood up and strolled to the window. Even from his vantage point, he could not see through the thick fog that blanketed the city. In the same way, a cloud of worry hung over him and blocked the happiness he should be feeling about today's progress. Something just didn't sit right in his mind. He needed to look through the data to confirm his suspicions.

Lance called out to his laptop computer, "Albert, when will the data collected from our test be available for review?"

"The data is available now for your review, Dr. Everett."

"It is?" Lance turned around in surprise. At Stanford, it had taken the computers a couple of days to gather together test data. "You are a supercomputer. Great. Please display the data on the TV. The resolution on that thing should be high enough to see all the numbers."

"Certainly. Will begin streaming data in twenty seconds.

You will see all the standard charts and diagrams lapsed over time from the beginning of the experiment to the end. "

Several charts began appearing on the screen, shrinking and expanding and changing in colors as they represented the pressure inside the time machine. The data revealed any parts of the machine that were not as efficient in speeding up the particles inside or any parts taking on too much pressure. Lance viewed each one carefully, satisfied to see that all the results were positive. The machine was in fact very well built. In theory, the time machine could accelerate the right particle past the speed of light.

That ability, however, presented a serious problem.

Lance realized something he should have considered before. In time travel, it was either go or no-go. There was no in-between. As a particle speeds up to the speed of light, nothing physical to this world would change. Time would not stop because something reached light speed. But as soon as something passed light speed, the power it generated would be so great that time would immediately start to go backward.

The effect was like a cup of water filled to the brim. Due to the water tension, when more water is added to the cup, the water level would rise past the height of the cup, and no water would spill over. However, when the water tension can no longer hold the amount of water being added, it would break, sending the water over the rim to come crashing down until the water returned to an acceptable level.

So it was with time travel. When the energy in the time machine increased to the speed of light, as soon as there is enough energy to push past that threshold, time would revert. When all the pent-up energy is released, the time reversion would stop and time would begin moving forward again at that point. Lance suspected it was impossible to create a window to peek into the past without reverting time.

He had never planned to revert time. Reverting time, no matter how wonderful the purpose may be—even for the potential of saving someone's life—would be unethical. Everyone in the whole world would be dragged backward in the process. And should time move backward, no one would remember anything that supposedly happened in the future. People would make the same decisions, and everything would happen the same way again. There was no point to reverting time.

This was not what Lance hoped to find. He placed his hand on his forehead then ran it down his face. He began pacing the room as he thought. "Albert, can you confirm my calculations."

Albert replied, "Your formula looks accurate."

"This means there is no way we can create a window to peek into the past. We either use enough energy to actually push time backward or we have a very expensive machine that just vibrates?" He faltered in his steps and shook his head in disbelief.

"Yes, the data confirms that. Creating a window to peek into the past is not feasible."

"This is not good," Lance mumbled under his breath. "This is not good."

"Dr. Everett, I am sorry you are disappointed. I understand that based on today's test results, using the Higgs Boson particle, the time machine will never be able to accelerate past the speed of light. However, may I suggest a different element to test which will have a very high chance of speeding past light speed and achieving the project's goal of time travel?"

Lance's jaw dropped in shock. *The project's goal?* Albert had understood all along that their goal was to revert time.

The supercomputer had been trying to achieve that exact purpose. But what was even more shocking was the fact that Albert appeared to know which element could accelerate past the speed of light.

His heart pounding, Lance was fearful and excited at the same time. He wanted to hear Albert's answer, but he was also afraid to find out. He took a deep breath and asked in a serious tone, "Albert, what particle would achieve a speed faster than light?"

The robotic voice answered matter-of-factly, "Dr. Everett, based on the test results and all available elements known to my database, antimatter would be the best fit for our project. Please look at this simulation I just built. Instead of using Higgs Boson, I've substituted antimatter. Based on my calculation, the antimatter will break the speed of light."

Lance stared at the TV screen in silence. A surge of adrenaline shot through his body. It was that old sense of thrill he remembered getting whenever he solved an impossible equation. He was stunned. Albert had solved this puzzle that no one had ever solved, not even himself.

The 3D simulation looked good. The model was nothing fancy; there were mere lines and tubes representing the time machine and little dots representing the particles inside being swirled around in the machine. To Lance, however, the picture was beyond description. With the four pillars of the time machine each carrying some amount of antimatter, it would gain a speed equal to the speed of light. In the final stage when all the antimatter collided with each other in the final chamber and interacted with regular matter, the energy level would be so high that they would move past light speed. Time would thus begin to revert.

This was the answer he had been searching for.

"Dr. Everett, is everything all right?"

At the sound of Albert's voice, Lance jumped, as if he was waking from a dream. "Yes, yes, everything's fine." He paused as the reality of the situation sank in. "Albert, how did you come up with that?"

"I simply substituted all the known elements in my database into the simulation. Antimatter appears to be the one element that works."

Lance grinned. Of course the supercomputer would compare and contrast and run simulations and compare the results of each simulation. Albert's solution was completely logical, but it was absurd to believe the question of time travel had finally been resolved.

His excitement was immediately cut short. He understood the danger of the situation. If this knowledge fell into the wrong hands, there would be no telling what disaster would come from it.

"Albert," Lance urged, "be sure you do not reveal this solution to anyone. Not even to Dr. Rostov or Mr. Singh."

"Dr. Everett, it is not in my program to withhold any information. If anyone with the appropriate level of authority asks me a question, I am programmed to comply. However, this research is incomplete. My model shows that with the use of antimatter, time travel would be achievable, but accommodating antimatter in the time machine requires a special configuration and a new formula. That information I do not possess. With my current programming and computation power, I am unable to come up with that information."

Lance's shoulders fell in relief. A new formula and configuration would be needed to accommodate the use of antimatter.

The formula would have to be drastically different from all the regular elements they had experimented with so far. Antimatter, being unique, behaved nothing like regular matter. However, someone with a deep knowledge in the field of quantum physics who understood the inner workings of the time machine would be able to figure out the formula at some point. Given enough time, Dr. Rostov would be that person.

Thinking quickly, Lance addressed Albert, "I understand you are obliged to give information when you are asked so long as the party requesting it has the proper authority level."

"That is correct."

Lance continued in a firm tone, "Then please record this piece of newfound data. Without a working formula, the potential of using antimatter is pointless and dangerous. Without the use of a precise formula, even running a test could end in disaster, a disaster large enough to take out half the country." If Albert could not lie, at least he would have all the pertinent information recorded in his notes. Should Dr. Rostov or Mr. Singh ask, Albert would give them this warning as well. Satisfied with the progress, Lance decided to log off. "Albert, thank you for your help today. I need to do some thinking. I will call on you if I need additional assistance."

"Of course." The laptop and TV turned off instantaneously.

Lance ran his hands through his hair, making it stand up on end. He couldn't believe he had the missing piece to the time travel puzzle he had been working on all his life. Yet, this breakthrough was the most dangerous scientific discovery he had ever handled. He needed to figure out how to convince Dr. Rostov and Mr. Singh to drop the project. Drop it once and for all and never consider it again.

He thought about the three-way encryption they had in

place, but that only prevented any one of them from running serious tests on the time machine without all three parties giving their approval. He could hold them off from using the time machine for a while, but if Dr. Rostov and Mr. Singh were desperate enough, they could build a new time machine. Mr. Singh certainly had the financial backing to do that. The key therefore was not to convince them to temporarily hold off on this project, but to end it. They needed to understand the potential devastation should the information fall into the wrong hands.

While Lance attempted to come up with a way to convince Mr. Singh and Dr. Rostov to discontinue the project, his thoughts couldn't help but wander. He began thinking about the formula needed to make the whole thing work. The problem tugged at his scientific mind, urging him to solve it. Lance forced himself to think about something else, but sure enough, his thoughts always returned to the formula.

He sat down on the couch and closed his eyes. Stuck in his own thoughts, Lance remained motionless. Suddenly, a phone sounded. Lance's body jerked in surprise as the ringing cut through the silence in the room.

Who could be calling him? Had Dr. Rostov or Mr. Singh found out he knew about the use of antimatter to power the time machine?

CHAPTER THIRTEEN

Lance picked up his phone and checked the display. No caller ID came up, so he assumed it was a spam call. Not wishing to be disturbed from his train of thought, he answered and barked out, "I don't need anything, and no, I do not have time for a survey. Please put me on your do not call list."

A male responded in a low, rough voice. "Dr. Everett, I presume? If this is not a good time for you, perhaps I will call back later."

Though the man sounded slightly different than he had on TV, Lance immediately recognized Dr. Martin's voice. "Wait, wait."

"Yes? I'm still here."

"Is this Dr. Martin?"

"Yes, this is he."

"I'm so sorry. I apologize for my rudeness. I mistook you for a telemarketer."

Dr. Martin chuckled, a wheezing sound punctuating his laugh. "No problem. I can understand. I get those calls occasionally as well and I, too, dislike them. Perhaps next time I will try your method instead of wasting thirty minutes of my time."

"Thank you so much for calling me back. I really appreciate it. If you normally don't mind spending thirty minutes with telemarketers, I hope you won't mind spending some time talking to me about your study on déjà vu."

"Certainly. I can talk about déjà vu for days if you let me."

"Dr. Martin, I am very impressed with your research," Lance began. As a longtime professional in academia, he understood the importance of showing respect to other scientists. "I really appreciate the fact that you posted all your research and results on the internet so everyone can benefit from them."

"Thank you." Dr. Martin's voice took on a slight lilt, revealing his obvious pleasure. "The truth is not too many people even care about the subject I'm researching. My goal is to create more awareness in the public and to provide a resource for those who are suffering from déjà vu. At the very least, I can confirm and validate what they are going through, so they don't feel alone." He paused to clear his throat. "Dr. Everett, on the voicemail you left me, I believe you said you specialize in the study of quantum physics, correct?"

"Yes, that's right." Lance already guessed Dr. Martin's next question. "You're probably wondering why I'm interested in your research."

"I certainly don't have the slightest clue as to what quantum physics is about, or any interest in the subject, for that matter. If you hadn't called me, I don't think I would ever speak with a quantum physics Ph.D."

Lance appreciated the doctor's straightforward manner. "I do specialize in the study of quantum physics, but I'm interested in all things unexplained. When I saw your interview on TV, I immediately wanted to find out more. It was a great interview, by the way."

"Thank you," he remarked with pride. "That was my first TV experience. I really didn't know how I did, so it's good to get some confirmation."

"I'd be happy to give you more feedback. But, if you don't mind, I'd like to find out more about your study."

"Of course, of course. What would you like to know?"

"In your interview, you mentioned there has been a rise in reports of déjà vu in recent months. Why do you think this is the case?"

"Well, we can only say we are getting more reports of incidents happening around the world. For all we know, déjà vu has been happening to people since the beginning of written history. Of course, centuries ago, people didn't have a term for it. But now when you say the words déjà vu, just about everyone knows what you are referring to."

"Right."

Dr. Martin continued, "From the data we collected, the spike started around June of last year. Years ago when I started my research on déjà vu, I realized it wouldn't be easy to find subjects who experience it on a frequent basis. I advertised in our local area, but the response rate was very low. Then David, one of my research assistants, whose wife was studying to be a therapist, happened to have a client who suffered from déjà vu. After meeting with the gentleman and confirming his symptoms, we realized the best way for us to find test subjects would be through mental health professionals. For years now, we've been working with therapists around the world to obtain a steady stream of patients who have given us very valuable information for our studies."

"Hm," Lance murmured, trying to be patient. Scientists

were notorious for being long-winded about their research, himself included. He hoped the good doctor would get to his point quickly.

"However, in recent months, almost a year now, we started getting very frequent reports of people reporting that they were experiencing déjà vu. To give you an example, before June of last year, we were getting maybe one case a month, and that's counting all our partners throughout the world. There were several months where we didn't get any. But starting last June, we began getting three to four cases a month. More recently in the last couple of months, the number climbed to eight to ten cases. It is very alarming. I have such limited funding for my research," Dr. Martin sighed, "we can't even take on all the cases that are coming in. We can only record the subject's basic information, such as gender, age, place of residence, health history, in particular any major medical surgeries, and how frequently they experienced déjà vu symptoms. Unless the information is out of the ordinary, we simply don't have time to consider each case."

Lance rubbed his hand across the stubble on his jawline and stood up. He began pacing the room as he digested the information. From one case a month to three or four cases, and now eight to ten? The cases had increased tenfold. Anyone with half a brain could tell something abnormal was happening. "Dr. Martin, are there any differences between the incidents reported after June versus before?"

"Ah, Dr. Everett, I should recruit you for my research team; you are very insightful," he remarked with a smile in his voice. "Yes, in fact, there have been differences. Individuals who experienced déjà vu before June tended to have milder cases. They described their experiences as interesting and never negative. The more recent cases however have been much more dramatic. These individuals experienced a higher intensity of emotions, particularly negative ones. They reported feeling frightened or sad by their experiences."

"With all these new cases, you must have wondered what caused them?"

"Of course. I took the information back to our board to show them we may be on the cusp of a breakthrough. I needed more money to look into the ultimate root cause. I was over the moon when they granted me additional funding. We found several individuals who suffer from frequent déjà vu, and with the partnership of one of the world's most advanced brain scan scientists, we were able to scan their brains. The results we found were remarkable," he exclaimed. His enthusiasm sparked a coughing fit.

Lance waited for the doctor to catch his breath, eager to hear more.

When Dr. Martin spoke again, his words ran together in excitement. "The brain scans revealed unusual wrinkles. We're not talking about the ridges and crevices you normally see on a brain, but wrinkle-like marks that go over and across those ridges."

Lance stopped abruptly, his bare feet digging into the plush carpet. *Wrinkles?* "That is truly remarkable."

"Naturally, our next step was to..." Dr. Martin's voice rose in pitch, turning his sentence into a question.

Lance took the doctor's pausing as an opportunity to jump in on his little guessing game. "The next step would be to compare those scans with other brain scans taken prior to the time the phenomenon spiked."

"Bingo!"

At this point, Lance felt his stomach drop. He was almost afraid to hear Dr. Martin's next words.

"When we pulled up those brain scans, scans performed by the same exact machine," he emphasized, "none of those results had wrinkles on them."

Lance's phone slipped from his hand, barely missing the glass coffee table as it fell. The soft thud of it hitting the floor jerked him from the thoughts consuming his mind. He grabbed the phone and put it back to his ear, surprised by its warmth against his clammy skin.

"Dr. Everett? Are you there?"

"Yes, yes, sorry," Lance spluttered. "Dr. Martin, there's something I need to do, but I want to continue our conversation. Would it be possible to meet with you in person?"

"Uh, sure, we can meet in person. What do you have in mind?"

"How about tomorrow morning?"

"Tomorrow morning?" Dr. Martin paused. "Tomorrow morning, I'm meeting a patient, actually with a gentleman who suffers the most severe case of déjà vu I've ever seen. But I can reschedule my appointment with him, it's not a problem."

"No, wait," Lance exclaimed. "Would it be possible for me to meet with him as well? I would appreciate the opportunity to hear firsthand from someone who suffers from déjà vu. Could you arrange that, please?"

"I don't see why not. Let me check with him. He is generally very accommodating."

"Great, thank you. How about ten tomorrow morning at La Petite Rouen. It's an outdoor cafe in downtown Palo Alto."

"I'm familiar with that restaurant. Sounds good. I'll see you then."

"Great. Thank you again, Dr. Martin. I'll see you tomorrow."

Upon hanging up, Lance felt an urgency to discover more answers before his meeting with Dr. Martin. He tapped his laptop, and Albert promptly appeared on the screen. "Albert, please place a call to the driver."

"Initiating call to Mr. Singh's driver now."

The phone rang once and a male voice came on the line. "Dr. Everett, what can I do for you?"

"How quickly can you get here?"

"I'm downstairs," he announced. "Is there somewhere you need to go?"

"I need to go to the lab, but I need to stop by a few other places first. Can you take me?"

After a brief pause, he replied, "I can certainly drive you wherever you need to go, but the lab is not accessible at the moment."

Lance's brows shot up in surprise. "What do you mean not accessible?"

"Mr. Singh has requested that no one be allowed in."

"We ran a large experiment earlier today. I just need to go in and review some material."

The driver's tone remained calm but firm. "Dr. Everett, I can drive you to any place other than the lab."

"That won't do. I need to go to the lab, otherwise there is no point in going to the other places."

"If you like, I can place a call to Mr. Singh and make your request known to him."

Lance's face heated in annoyance. This was unexpected. Why was the lab closed, and why did he need to request permission to enter? Something about the situation didn't sit right with him. Now he was even more curious about going to the lab. It was time to take matters into his own hands. Not wanting to alarm the driver or involve Mr. Singh, he decided to back down. "You know what, never mind. If it is really that inconvenient, don't worry about it. I'll have Dr. Rostov run the tests for me another time, and I'll watch them remotely."

"I apologize for the inconvenience. Are you still interested in my services today?"

"No, they won't be necessary."

"If you change your mind, I'll be downstairs."

"Downstairs?" Lance wondered how long the driver had been there and why. Was his presence here for the sake of convenience—or something more? "Have you been downstairs since I moved in?"

"Yes, I'm here in case you need my services. It's part of the job."

"Ah, I see. Thanks."

"Anytime, Dr. Everett," he replied before hanging up.

Lance walked to the window and carefully pushed aside the heavy pleated drapes. Sure enough, he saw the company car parked illegally at the curb. The driver's side door opened, and a man in a dark suit and sunglasses emerged. He faced the building's entrance and leaned against the car with his arms crossed, as if standing guard.

If Lance was unsure of the driver's intent before, it was becoming increasingly clear now. *I'm being watched.* He made up his mind to go to the lab himself. He gathered up his belongings into a black messenger bag and left the apartment. When he exited the elevator on the ground floor, he spotted the driver through the lobby doors. He quickly turned around and headed toward a back entrance. When he reached the sidewalk, he raised his hand to call for a taxi.

A yellow cab approached, and Lance entered. "Please take me to the nearest pet store."

The taxi driver, an older man of Middle Eastern descent, turned around to greet Lance. He answered with a nod. "Yes, sir."

After a few blocks, they arrived at a small shop.

Handing over some cash, he instructed the driver to wait. "Please keep the meter running; I'll be right back."

A musty odor filled Lance's nostrils as he opened the door. He took a quick look around the shop to locate the rodent section. Across from a wall of fish tanks, he found several cages with furry mice, rats, and hamsters running around. He asked a store clerk to pick out a couple of mice for him then grabbed a small plexiglass tank before heading to the checkout line.

The young woman at the register paused as she scanned the items. "Did you forget to get a lid for the tank? We have wire mesh ones that the mice can't chew through."

"Thanks, but I don't need one. This is only a temporary home for them." He took the receipt and returned to the taxi. He settled the box of mice and tank onto the backseat and asked the driver, "Is there a pharmacy nearby?"

The driver nodded and drove down the street to a drugstore. Lance hopped out of the taxi, made his purchase, and returned within a few minutes. He then gave the driver the address to Singh Enterprises.

When they arrived at the lab, the sun was beginning to set. Lance glanced at his watch and hoped most of the employees had left for the day. He paid his bill, gathered up his purchases, and exited the taxi.

Switching the items to his left hand, he swiped his badge to enter the building. The light on the badge reader remained red, signaling the door was still locked. A few more tries yielded the same result. *Great.* How would he enter now? He noticed a security guard sitting at the lobby desk and tapped on the glass door for his attention.

The heavyset guard approached and called out, "Can I help you?"

Lance didn't recognize the man, but it was not surprising, considering he had only been in the lab a handful of times. He held up his badge. "I work here. On the top floor with Dr. Rostov."

The guard narrowed his eyes and glanced from Lance to the badge and back again. He opened the door just wide enough to allow his hand through and motioned for Lance to hand over the badge. "Do you mind if I check your badge?"

"Sure, no problem. Here."

The guard went back to his desk, scanned the badge on a machine, and returned to the door. He cracked it open again and returned the badge to Lance. "Sir, it appears your badge has been disabled. I can't allow you inside."

Disabled? What is going on? Lance shook his head and remarked, "Are you sure? Maybe my card somehow stopped working. You know what, can you check and see whether Dr. Rostov is in? He can vouch for me and grant me access."

"Sure, give me a minute. Your name again?"

"Dr. Everett, Lance Everett."

The guard walked away to make the call and returned to open the door for Lance. "You're clear, Dr. Everett. Come on in. You might want to check with your employer about getting a new badge."

The tension in Lance's shoulders eased. "Great, thanks. I

definitely will." He followed the guard into the lobby, thanked him again for his help, and headed for the elevator.

Once inside the elevator, Lance breathed a sigh of relief. His hands shook as the weight of the bag he held shifted from one side to the other. "Looks like you guys can't wait to get out," he commented to the box containing the mice. He gave a halfhearted smile and held the bag up to eye level. "Let me be the first to thank you for your contribution to science. Mankind thanks you."

The elevator stopped at the top floor and the doors opened. Lance stepped out, surprised to see Dr. Rostov standing behind the double glass doors.

A deep line appeared between the older man's brows as soon as he spotted Lance. "What are you doing here, Dr. Everett?"

"I need to test something; it's very urgent." He walked into the lab and set his purchases on the counter. "By the way, thanks for letting me up. For some reason my badge wasn't working."

Dr. Rostov followed Lance closely, the edge of his lab coat flying up with the momentum of his steps. "What tests? You want to run some tests?"

Lance didn't notice at first, but now that he had a moment to catch his breath, he saw that the room was nearly empty. Large boxes lined the wall, and one that sat open on the table had a monitor sticking out of it. Nearly all the equipment had been packed away. Only the time machine remained intact.

"Are we moving? Why is everything packed up?"

Dr. Rostov cleared his throat. "Yes, Mr. Singh plans to move us to a new location for safety reasons."

"When and where? Why didn't anyone tell me?"

Dr. Rostov's cheeks reddened as he struggled to answer. "Mr. Singh asked me not to tell you. He wanted you to focus on your research and not worry about the move. But we were going to tell you soon."

His flimsy reasoning bothered Lance, especially the lack of information he offered. He didn't have time to think about either however; there were more important things to consider. It was time to focus his attention on the reason why he had come. He quickly removed the box of mice from the bag and set it on the counter, along with the medical supplies he had bought. Over his shoulder, Dr. Rostov watched his every movement.

"Dr. Everett, what are you doing?" he demanded. "What do you need to do that I can't do for you remotely?"

"I need to run an experiment."

"What do you mean? We have everything packed away. Why don't you tell me what you want and I can run the experiment for you when everything is set up again."

"No, no, no," Lance insisted, "we don't have time. I need to see this myself with my own eyes. All I need is the time machine."

Dr. Rostov raised his hands. "What! No! Our team isn't here right now. There's only the two of us. We can't just turn the time machine on."

Lance turned around to face him. "We don't need anyone else. There's you, me, and Albert. That's enough to run the machine. If necessary, I can do it with Albert."

"Dr. Everett, it's not that I don't want to help you, but you have to understand, running the time machine requires planning. We shouldn't turn it on at random."

Lance looked Dr. Rostov in the eye and spoke firmly. "You

don't understand. This test is critical, and we are running out of time. I will explain everything later, but we need to do this now."

"What's the urgency? The test we did today went well. We learned enough to keep this project moving forward."

"Dr. Rostov, let me run the experiment. Trust me, once I'm done with the experiment, I will explain everything." Lance saw Dr. Rostov open his mouth to speak but cut him off with a final statement. "If I can't run this experiment, I will walk away from this project. I will walk away from this project, and you will never hear from me again."

Shaking his head adamantly, Dr. Rostov spat out, "Okay, fine, let's do it. But can you at least tell me what your experiment is about?"

Lance smiled. "Great. Would you prepare the time machine? I'll explain in a minute. I have some things to prepare first."

Dr. Rostov sighed. "Are you absolutely certain you have to run this experiment right now? As you can see, all our lab equipment is in boxes. It would be difficult to analyze any data we collect."

"Yes, I'm certain," Lance reiterated before pulling a mouse out of the box and releasing it into the fish tank.

"Wh-what are you doing with that?"

Noting the older man's obvious discomfort, he chuckled. He pulled out a second squirmy white rodent and held it up. "Just putting them to work. They really are a scientist's best friend."

"I prefer cats," Dr. Rostov muttered as he backed away. "I'll go work with Albert to get the time machine ready."

"Thank you."

Lance placed the second mouse in the tank and watched both mice run around freely. One scurried up to the glass and touched its pointy snout to it. Its beady eyes met Lance's as it raised its long, scaly tail in the air. Lance tapped the glass and spoke softly, "I'm sorry, guys, but this is important. I appreciate you helping me out."

If his suspicions were right, the mice were the key to helping him answer a monumental question. One that had the potential of impacting mankind's future—or confirming if it had already been impacted in an unbelievable way.

He grabbed the bag from the drugstore and began opening the medical supplies he had purchased. In a matter of minutes, he had filled two syringes with a diluted mixture of oral anesthetic. He picked up one of the mice from the tank and set to work.

After an hour, Dr. Rostov reappeared and announced, "Dr. Everett, the machine is ready." He walked over with a wary look on his face and gestured to the metal tray on the counter. "Are they dead?"

"They're just sedated." Lance glanced down at the mice and nodded. He smiled in relief to see their furry chests moving up and down in a steady rhythm. Years had passed since his undergraduate biology classes, but his dissection skills were still fresh in his mind. With precision and care, he had cut open their heads to expose part of their brains. They were now ready for the experiment. "Let's get started."

"What are you doing with them?"

"You'll see."

Lance left one mouse on the tray and put the other one back into the tank. He carried the first mouse to his office down the hall and placed it on the desk. The second mouse, he took into the time machine's glass chamber and set it carefully on the ground. He returned to the viewing room where Dr. Rostov was waiting with his headset on. He put on his own headset and spoke into the mic. "Thanks for getting the machine ready in such a short time. Let's begin."

Dr. Rostov gave commands to Albert to start the countdown sequence. The time machine woke, generating a horribly loud noise. The numbers on the machine increased at a rapid pace as the room began vibrating.

Lance felt the vibration in his feet first, then legs and arms, until a violent humming took over his whole body. He glanced over at Dr. Rostov, expecting to see fear on his face, but the older scientist remained calm. Taking a couple of deep breaths, he gripped onto the edge of the table to steady himself. His last and only experience with the machine was behind a monitor at the corporate apartment. Being here in person was a completely different experience.

The shaking grew stronger and stronger as the machine propelled the particles to the speed of light. When it felt like the walls of the building might start to crack, the time machine began to blur. Right as it seemed to disappear into thin air, Dr. Rostov shut down the machine and the shaking gradually stopped.

As soon as the pounding of his heart settled down, Lance walked into the glass chamber and picked up the tank. The mouse lay there undisturbed in a heavy sleep. Lance took the mouse to his office where the other mouse remained sedated. He placed both mice under two microscopes he had set up in advance on his desk.

He looked in the first eyepiece, then the second one, and back again. It took about a minute for him to verify his findings, but it felt like time had frozen and locked him in a vacuum. Beads of cold sweat broke out on his forehead, and he fell back in his chair, his legs weak. "No! We need to stop!"

Dr. Rostov rushed to the door. "What? What happened?"

"We must stop our project. Immediately."

Lance watched the older man's pasty complexion darken to a furious shade of red. He inhaled deeply and contemplated his next words. Convincing Dr. Rostov would require him to stay calm. Not only because the man was losing his temper, but more so because of what he had just discovered.

Chapter Fourteen

"What are you talking about!" Dr. Rostov exclaimed. "We are making good progress."

"We have to stop our project. Now. I have reason to believe that not only has our technology been stolen, but someone or some group out there has already traveled back in time."

Dr. Rostov faltered in his stance and gripped the doorframe to steady himself. His face paled. "What? What are you talking about?"

Lance gestured for him to approach.

Looking apprehensive, Dr. Rostov walked over to the desk. He crossed his arms as he stole a glance downward. "Are they—"

"Don't worry, they're sedated. Take a look. Please." Lance directed him to the microscopes.

"What am I looking at?"

"The mouse brain is fairly smooth compared to a human brain, which made it the perfect candidate for this experiment. Now, before the experiment, the brains of these two mice looked almost identical. Neither of them had any observable defects."

"Yes, fine, but what am I looking for?"

"The mouse on your right was in my office this whole time. It was never exposed to the time machine's energy field during the experiment. The other mouse, however, was the one I brought into the glass chamber. Look carefully at it. About a third of the way down on its brain, there is a small wrinkle going across the tissue. That wrinkle was not there before we ran the experiment."

Dr. Rostov arched an eyebrow and switched his focus to the microscope on his left. He adjusted the knobs on it, taking time to focus the lens as he studied the mouse's brain. He did the same with the other microscope. "I think I see a line. But what is the problem? So what if the mouse has a wrinkle on its brain. This is probably an unwelcome side effect from being exposed to the time machine's energy field. We—I mean you—could run some tests on it once it's awake and see if its motor functions were affected in some way." He shrugged. "If you have safety concerns, we can do some more animal testing."

"No, no, no, I'm not worried about that." Lance held up both hands and rose to his feet. "Have you heard of the déjà vu effect?"

"Déjà vu? Yes, I've heard of it. You asked me about it the other day."

"Have you heard of a research scientist named Dr. Martin? He studies the effects of déjà vu."

Dr. Rostov paused then shook his head adamantly. "No, I've never heard of such a scientist. What's your point, Dr. Everett?"

"I spoke with him yesterday. He's been researching déjà vu for many years. In the last year, he's noticed a significant increase of cases around the world."

Dr. Rostov's voice took on an impatient edge as he spat out, "Okay, yes, but would you mind getting to the point? What do these mice and déjà vu have to do with our time machine?"

"In his research, he conducted brain scans on his patients who suffered severe déjà vu. In every one of those scans, they showed wrinkles like the wrinkle you see on this mouse on the left."

Lance was relieved to see understanding register on Dr. Rostov's face. The older scientist nodded his head slowly.

"The brain scans he took a year ago didn't have any wrinkles like this one you see on this mouse. Dr. Martin believes something drastic has changed in our environment since then. These cases are not isolated incidents; they've been found all over the world."

Lance motioned for Dr. Rostov to follow him. Once they were in the lab, he turned to the supercomputer. "Albert, please pull up the brain scans you have in your database, the ones prior to June of last year. Show them on the large display, please."

"Certainly. Here are twenty brain scans taken prior to June of last year."

Pointing to the screen, Lance added, "Please enlarge the sample in the upper right corner."

Albert complied. The scan filled the entire screen.

Lance looked to Dr. Rostov standing at his right. "See, there are no wrinkles here that we can see."

"Yes," he agreed.

"Albert, the next sample please. Same resolution."

"Yes, Dr. Everett."

Lance pointed at the screen. "No wrinkles here either." He continued, "Albert, please pull up the next five samples."

"Next five samples being displayed," Albert confirmed.

"As expected, there are no wrinkles on any of these either." He took a deep breath. "Now, Albert, pull up the brain scans from Dr. Martin's website."

"Here are the brain scans from Dr. Martin's website."

Lance gasped when the first image appeared. "Look at them!" He glanced at Dr. Rostov who was silent and still. "Albert, please scroll through all the brain scans on Dr. Martin's website. Put them on slideshow mode with each being displayed for three seconds and do not loop."

"Certainly. Slideshow mode started."

Lance leaned toward the screen, muttering under his breath as the images scrolled past his eyes.

Dr. Rostov finally broke his silence. "What are you doing?"

Lance took a few seconds before answering, his eyes glued to the screen. "I'm counting the number of wrinkles on each brain scan." As he counted to himself, he ran his hands through his hair, clutching the strands between his fingers. He licked his lips and swallowed, attempting to remove the bitter, metallic taste coating his mouth, but to no avail. The shock coursing through his body was so great that he had difficulty standing up. It took all his courage to not collapse at the magnitude of the situation.

The images on the screen stopped scrolling. "The slideshow is complete," Albert concluded.

Lance turned to Dr. Rostov. "Fifteen. I counted fifteen." He staggered over to the older scientist and grabbed him by the shoulders. "Our situation..." He paused and dropped his hands. He had no words. "I believe...based on these images... someone has reverted time fifteen times already."

The lines on Dr. Rostov's forehead deepened. "Are you sure?"

"Don't you see? The déjà vu that Dr. Martin's patients are experiencing is not déjà vu at all. Those people are actually remembering an event that they experienced in the future—their past future!" Lance paced the room as he continued, "I experienced this myself just the other day at the apartment. Even though I had never stayed there before, I felt like I knew the place. I knew exactly where to get the coffee beans and where the coffee maker was to make the coffee." He stopped suddenly as it all made sense to him. "That's why when Juliet passed away, even though I was hundreds of miles away speaking at Caltech, I knew something was wrong. I knew she was in trouble." He closed his eyes for a moment as the sadness of that day washed over him.

When Lance opened his eyes again, he met Dr. Rostov's shocked stare. "We are stuck in a time loop. The entire world is stuck in a vortex that we cannot escape. Based on the test results from this morning, I now know it's impossible to create a window to peek into the past. When time travel is activated, it is not just one person who travels into the past. The energy and momentum created by a single particle traveling faster than the speed of light will drag the entire world back in time. This is the reason why there are déjà vu reports from all over the globe. The entire world has been dragged back in time fifteen times."

The gray-haired scientist looked as frightened as a young boy awakened from a nightmare. "What do we do now? What can we do?"

"I don't know. I don't know." Lance resumed his pacing as he thought aloud. "If my assumption is correct, each time we travel back in time, everything reverts, so we remember nothing of the future. We just get these glimpses, not a foretelling of the future, only déjà vu-like feelings. We relive our lives the exact same way, the same as the last fifteen times, and make the same decisions as the previous fifteen times, which means we will always arrive at the same conclusion. Whoever activated the time machine will always do it again, as he or she will always make the same decision to build a time machine and activate it, causing us to always revert back in time." He stopped in his tracks and cried out in despair. "There is no way out!"

This realization devastated Lance. It was all his fault. If only he had never watched the *Back to the Future* movie that had made time travel sound so great. If only he had never studied physics or dreamed of building a time machine—none of this would've ever happened. There would be no one to steal his research and no one out there who had built a working time machine. They would not be stuck in a time loop.

He owed the entire world an apology…or at least a solution. But this catastrophe was one he couldn't possibly repair.

Dr. Rostov rubbed the white stubble on his chin and sighed. "There must be a way out. We just have to think harder, look at all the angles."

Lance threw up his hands. "No, there is no way out of this. Whatever you might be thinking of doing, you have already done it fifteen times. Whatever new brilliant method or idea you think you can come up with, you have already come up with it fifteen times before. The result is always the same. We are still stuck in a time loop."

"Wait, wait, wait," Dr. Rostov uttered, his voice rising in excitement. "Wait a minute. What if you are wrong?" He continued before Lance could interrupt. "Hold on just a second, let me finish."

Lance didn't think anything the scientist could say would be helpful, but he gestured for him to continue.

"Let's assume that we are in fact stuck in a time loop and we have looped around fifteen times already." Dr. Rostov cupped his chin as he thought. "You're assuming we're stuck because everyone always makes their decisions the same way, every time, and under the same circumstances. Someone somewhere, whoever that person is, will always make the decision to build a time machine and press the button to activate the machine and loop us all back again."

"You're telling me what I already know," Lance reasoned with a sigh.

Dr. Rostov pointed a crooked finger at him. "But that's circular logic."

The words had barely registered in Lance's ears when he slapped his palm against his forehead. What a junior scientific mistake he had made. Dr. Rostov was right. On the surface, what he proposed sounded logical and complete, but it was all a huge assumption.

The reality was that every time they looped around, things had to be slightly different. What if a kid out there playing a game of *Monopoly* rolled a four with his dice during the last time loop, then rolled a seven this time around, and won the game. Or what if someone who bought a losing lottery ticket last time claimed the winnings the next time around. People would make the same decisions when presented with the same circumstances, but what if by chance, the circumstances were different? A decision made based on the differences, however slight they were, could potentially cause the decision to be different.

Delighted with this realization, Lance clapped Dr. Rostov's back. "You're right!"

The older scientist smiled proudly. "You are very welcome."

"You're talking about the Chaos Theory. The Butterfly Effect."

"Yes, butterflies, such beautiful creatures, unlike rodents," he murmured.

Lance couldn't contain his excitement. He rushed on, thinking out loud. "A butterfly flapping its wings on this side of the world could cause a hurricane on the other side. When you roll a dice, you come up with a different number each time. Essentially, it doesn't matter how hard a person tries, it's impossible to roll a dice the same way and cause the same result each time."

Things in this world weren't controlled by human decision, but by chance. There was a good chance that in each of these fifteen time loops, things caused by chance were different every time, which meant that people's decisions could potentially change due to chance happenings. However, in these last fifteen time loops, these random chance happenings had yet to affect the outcome of the time reversal. But no one could say that it wouldn't ultimately one day change by chance as well.

"There is hope," Dr. Rostov piped up.

Lance looked at the hopeful expression on his colleague's face. There was a sense of reassurance, but not enough. "Even still, we cannot continue our project."

"But I," Dr. Rostov exclaimed, "I have put in too many hours to give up now. We are so close!"

"We need to understand what we're up against first," Lance urged. "I'm meeting someone tomorrow who may be able to help us."

"Who? How?"

"This man suffers from major déjà vu. He should be able to

confirm whether his déjà vu experiences always end up with the outcomes he thought would happen. If they do, any hope we have of ever breaking out of this time loop is miniscule. If not, there's a chance we can break out. It's a long shot, but still a possibility."

"Do you want me to come with you tomorrow to meet with this person? I do think we should speak with Mr. Singh first thing in the morning and let him know our latest findings. Perhaps, instead of focusing on this project, I can talk to him about focusing our efforts on finding out who else is trying to build a time machine."

"Good idea. Why don't you talk with Mr. Singh tomorrow, and I'll meet with the man who suffers from déjà vu? Let's meet up in the afternoon and see if we can come up with a better game plan."

Nodding in agreement, Dr. Rostov conceded. "I understand the evidence you present here is very strong, but I hope you're wrong, and somehow there is a natural way to explain all these things that are happening."

Lance furrowed his brows. "Given the present circumstances, I'd rather not further jeopardize mankind's future by continuing our research."

"I know, I know. It's just a shame. What a shame." He sighed. "But what do I tell all the folks who have been working so hard on this project?"

"Let's not say anything yet. I don't want word to get out and cause anyone to panic. Who knows, it might even be one of our own technicians leaking our research."

"You can't be serious. All our technicians went through extensive background checks and have been in the industry for a long time. It's not possible…"

"I hope not," Lance winced, "but we just don't know."

"I guess you can't really trust people these days." Dr. Rostov cleared his throat and nodded. "I won't say anything to the team until we have more information."

"Sounds good. I'm going back to the apartment now to do some homework before my meeting with Dr. Martin and his patient tomorrow. I'll come to the lab as soon as our meeting is over."

"I'll give Mr. Singh a call now. This is a major development; I need to keep him in the loop."

"Thanks." Lance was relieved he didn't have to be the one to break the bad news.

Dr. Rostov walked out with his phone to his ear. He disappeared into his office and closed the door.

Lance rushed to clean up his desk before leaving the building. He couldn't wait for tomorrow's meeting. If he was correct, Dr. Martin's patient would hold the answers they were looking for. Even if he could only confirm one instance of his déjà vu experiences being different from reality, there was hope. However, if they were all completely the same, every single time, then humanity was doomed.

Chapter Fifteen

Lance wiped his forehead and checked the penthouse thermostat. 72 degrees Fahrenheit. The temperature should have been cool and comfortable enough for him, but he didn't feel any relief.

Given the circumstances, he was surprised to be keeping his emotions in check. He hardly slept the previous night, and he woke up drenched in sweat. Even now as he paced the room waiting for the driver to pick him up, beads of sweat broke out over his neck, slowly working their way down his tense shoulders. He breathed in and out, allowing the perspiration to trickle down his back.

This was more pressure than any person should carry, and he was being crushed under the weight of it all. He felt like he was sinking deeper and deeper into a nightmare that he would never wake up from. A dark abyss with no bottom. How did things get so bad so quickly? Never in his life did he fathom his time machine technology would be stolen. But it went from being stolen, to possibly being used, to now affecting the entire world.

Mankind was stuck in a time loop and had been fifteen

times over. Were those patients of Dr. Martin's, who were suffering from severe déjà vu symptoms, suffering because of the time loop? The idea that he was responsible for that—it was unbearable. The sheer magnitude of the time machine's consequences boggled Lance. More than that, the knowledge that he was alone overwhelmed him. There was no one to help him, nor any person he could share this with. No one would understand or believe what he had discovered. Even if anyone did, word would leak out to the media or the government and cause mass hysteria.

The last thing he should do was panic. He needed to calm himself and control the fear taking over his body. To do so, he needed to find out more. He had to get back to the basics and start there, then find out what he needed to do next.

A knock on the door signaled the driver's arrival. On time, as usual.

Lance released a long breath and decided to take control of the situation. He would be proactive and play the cards he had been dealt. Hopefully this morning's meeting would allow him to do just that.

The driver greeted him with a curt nod. "Good morning, Dr. Everett. Ready to go?"

With a heavy heart, Lance replied, "Yes, as ready as I'll ever be."

During the drive, Lance remained silent. He came up with some questions he wanted to ask Dr. Martin's patient, but was careful to word them in a way that wouldn't alarm the man.

After forty-five minutes, they pulled up in front of a busy cafe in downtown Palo Alto. The driver announced, "We are here, Dr. Everett. I'll wait at the corner for you."

Lance stirred from his thoughts and looked out the window

to see a black and white striped awning with the words *La Petite Rouen* printed above. He thanked the driver and exited the car.

This restaurant was one of his favorite places to eat and a welcome change of pace when he had donut cravings. While it was never crowded, there was always a steady stream of customers, especially on a sunny day like today. Several of the tables and brown wicker chairs on the patio were already occupied with people drinking coffee and eating pastries.

Lance recognized one of the customers as Dr. Martin from his website photo. He presumed the much younger man sitting with him to be his patient. He walked up to them and introduced himself.

"Dr. Martin, it's very nice to meet you face-to-face." The scientist was dressed much like himself in a button-down shirt and khakis. His patient however wore jeans and a white T-shirt. It wasn't so much his clothes that made him stand out but the weariness in his face. He looked like he had not slept—or shaved—in months. Even with his stringy blond hair hanging in his eyes, Lance could see his pupils dilated in fear. He immediately switched his attention over to the young man. "I'm Dr. Everett. You can call me Lance. Thanks for agreeing to meet with me on such short notice."

Dr. Martin jumped in. "Jeremy is not feeling too well today, but he too wanted to meet with you."

Jeremy disregarded Lance's outstretched hand and simply jerked his head.

"No problem," Lance replied before taking a seat. He smiled at Jeremy, hoping to put him at ease. He really wanted to ask him some questions immediately, but seeing how distraught he was, he decided to talk to Dr. Martin. "It's my pleasure to meet with you both today. If, you don't mind, I'd like to dive right in and find out more about your research, Dr. Martin."

"Sure, go right ahead."

Even though Lance was confident that the time reversals were causing the episodes of déjà vu and brain wrinkles, he still hoped there was another reason for the phenomenon. "I've done some preliminary research, and from what I understand, chronic déjà vu is not a new thing. Some studies suggest it could be a result of dysfunction in the temporal lobe area. Since the temporal lobe is believed to control memory of past events, if somehow that area of the brain is damaged..." Lance paused as Jeremy flinched and met his eyes briefly. Wrong choice of words. He immediately changed his tone and continued, "If somehow the temporal lobe region sends out a signal that tricks the brain into thinking that the events it experiences are all past events, even those happening in the present, could that cause the déjà vu?"

Dr. Martin smiled. "Well, Dr. Everett, so glad to see you already have some understanding of my research. Yes, it is commonly believed that the temporal lobe might have something to do with the déjà vu effect by somehow tricking the brain into thinking all events are past events. There have been a handful of cases documented well over a year ago; however, those people who suffered from chronic déjà vu did not progress to the deeper level that Jeremy and his fellow patients have evolved to. They experienced feelings of being in a place they had gone before or doing tasks they had done before, as well as a feeling of impending doom. However, none of those patients were able to predict what was about to happen."

Lance's jaw dropped. He had never considered that possibility. His own experiences with déjà vu were limited to having a feeling that something had already happened, but he wasn't able to predict what was to come. Could Jeremy predict events that would occur in the future?

Dr. Martin gave a proud, hearty laugh that soon turned into a hacking cough. He took a sip of coffee before continuing. "That's something you didn't know before. Yes, we have documented at least one time that Jeremy was able to predict what was to come."

Jeremy lifted his head for a moment, a small smile on his lips.

Lance leaned forward, eager to find out more. "How? Please explain."

"It wasn't easy, as you can imagine," Dr. Martin admitted. "We work with many patients, but most do not possess this ability that Jeremy and a few others have. Because these episodes of déjà vu don't occur all the time, and from our studies we've learned they tend to happen during situations of stress or strong emotions, we couldn't artificially produce such an event. Instead, we asked Jeremy and the others to wear a body camera with them at all times. Whenever they had a sense of déjà vu, they would describe it out loud, then the camera would capture the next events. We were able to confirm this way if their predictions were correct."

Sure, it was a good method given the circumstances, but was there enough evidence behind the hypothesis? As the cliché said, even a broken clock tells the correct time twice a day. Lance questioned, "How much proof have you gathered?"

Dr. Martin nodded. "Of course, having caught just one incident is not enough to say definitively that Jeremy is able to predict the future. But you must understand that the parameters we are working with are very narrow." He glanced at the young man who was staring at his hands. "Jeremy has helped us a great deal. We have been able to explore areas that we never even considered before. According to Jeremy, he never knows when déjà vu is about to strike, and when it does, he only has a few seconds to sense the event before the event happens. He has no time to digest or comprehend what he sees in his mind before the event takes place. What makes things even more difficult is that the details are always blurry. Meaning that if he sees a car in his vision, he can usually see the color of the car, but never the license plate. In fact, that's exactly what happened in one incident that we recorded. Jeremy was on his way home after buying groceries at a local market when he was about to cross the street. He suddenly had a vision of a red car speeding out from the corner of his eye and hitting a skateboarder." He lowered his voice and rushed his next words. "He screamed the words 'red car' to warn the teenager, but it was too late. By then, the car was already crossing the intersection."

Jeremy began rocking back and forth, his breath coming out in shallow spurts. He took the glass of water Dr. Martin handed him and downed it.

"We went over the recording of that incident no less than a hundred times," Dr. Martin continued in a somber tone. "The timing of everything that took place was so short, but we knew what we were looking for. To establish that Jeremy could predict the future, however small that window was, we needed to know if Jeremy screamed before the skateboarder or the car came into his peripheral vision. We brought in a team of experts in camera and video technology and we also went on location to study the incident. Our conclusion was that when Jeremy screamed, there was no possibility that the skateboarder or the car was in his field of vision."

Lance listened intently to Dr. Martin's description of the event. It was certainly intriguing. Based on the parameters of how déjà vu occurred, however, it would be difficult to use one of these incidents to prove that Jeremy could predict the future. The scientist in him began poking holes in Dr. Martin's theory. Jeremy may have picked up on the impending danger using his senses. He could have heard the clatter of the skateboard's metal wheels as they hit the sidewalk. Or heard the car's engine as it approached. But it would be difficult to explain how he knew the car was red.

Lance continued to consider whether there was enough proof that Jeremy could see into the future. He hoped to disprove Dr. Martin's theory because acknowledging it as true only confirmed his worst fears. That Jeremy had this ability, not to predict the future, but more accurately, to remember something he had lived and relived fifteen times already. If they were indeed stuck in a time loop, this loop would happen again. Soon it would be the sixteenth time, then the seventeenth, and so forth. At some point in time, everyone in the world, like Jeremy, would suffer the effects of déjà vu.

Lance shook his head to break out of his negative thoughts. He needed to stay positive. "Jeremy," he began with a wry smile, "your ability is incredible."

The young man looked up for a brief second then slumped into his chair.

"Dr. Martin, regarding those brain scans," Lance continued, "are those wrinkles consistent with all of your patients?"

"Dr. Everett, the scans are most interesting. The wrinkles are not consistent in terms of their location on the brain. They appear randomly over the surface, not only in the frontal or temporal lobes. However, the count is consistent. Every person

I've scanned has fifteen wrinkles. This is very strange, especially given the fact that these wrinkles never occurred in brain scans over a year ago."

"You are certain of the accuracy of these scans?"

Dr. Martin nodded. "Oh yes, absolutely certain. I've been working with the authority on brain scans, Dr. Rostov. He invented the brain scan technology that's being used all around the world."

"Wait—what?" Lance exclaimed. "Did you say Dr. Rostov?"

"Yes, that's right."

"When did you work with him?"

"Several months now. He took a special interest in my research, particularly in the study of these brain wrinkles. We spoke recently, about a week or two ago. Why?"

Lance was puzzled, very puzzled. Why had Dr. Rostov played dumb when he asked him about the déjà vu effect? Why hadn't he told him he knew Dr. Martin? More importantly, shouldn't he have made the connection between the brain wrinkles and the time machine? He felt his chest tighten. None of this made sense.

What about Mr. Singh? How did he figure into this?

"Why do you ask, Dr. Everett? Do you know Dr. Rostov?"

Lance realized Dr. Martin was waiting for his answer. Before he could speak, however, several loud gasps filled the air. The young man sitting with them began convulsing. "Jeremy? Are you okay?"

Jeremy's eyes widened, then he burst out with a maniacal laugh. He stared at Lance intently, the pupils of his eyes eclipsing his blue irises.

"Jeremy," Dr. Martin exclaimed, "what's happening?"

Jeremy shot to his feet and screamed, "It's my time, it's my time!" He began staggering about as if in a trance. He swung his arms around violently, knocking into the chairs and tables around him. "Run!" he screamed. "Guns! Guns!"

Panic ensued as people began fleeing the area.

Lance noticed through the commotion of the crowd that there were several individuals charging toward the cafe. One of them wearing a baseball cap looked familiar. Lance made out the words *I Love San Francisco* on his sweatshirt as he neared, and he did a double take. It was the man from the supermarket who had been videotaping him.

He felt a tug and looked to his right. Jeremy's pale fingers were clamped around his elbow. He started to ask what was wrong, but his attention was diverted by some movement from the corner of his left eye, followed by the glint of sunlight against metal.

What happened next was all the evidence Lance needed.

"Lance Everett, you're under arrest. Put your hands up where we can see them."

Lance turned around to see five people with their guns drawn in his direction. Judging from their plainclothes, he assumed they were secret service agents of some kind.

Jeremy tightened his grip and met Lance's gaze, his eyes lucid for a moment. "Guns," he murmured as a satisfied, strangely peaceful smile lit up his face.

A loud squeal of tires sounded from down the road. Mr. Singh's company car spun around, making a sharp U-turn before speeding up onto the curb in front of Lance. Before Lance had time to comprehend what was happening, Jeremy jumped in front of him, chanting under his breath, "It's my time, it's my time."

The driver got out of the car in one swift motion and swung

his arm out, revealing a gun. Without hesitation, he aimed it at the agents and fired. Two shots whizzed through the air.

Lance yelled out as Jeremy collapsed onto the pavement. Blood began pooling around his heart. A serene smile crossed his young face before his eyes turned vacant.

More shots cut through the air.

Lance dropped to his knees and stayed low to the ground as he watched the exchange. The driver wasted no time in firing multiple rounds at the agents who were struggling to take cover. The agents managed to hit the vehicle but missed the driver who had shielded himself behind the car door.

The driver's next shots made contact, one grazing the arm of a female agent and the other flying straight into a male agent's chest. The man immediately fell. His partner dragged him into the store adjacent to the cafe, and they disappeared from Lance's view.

The driver moved to the tail end of the car and fired again over the trunk. The shots meant for the agents hit two bystanders standing next to them. People screamed and clambered to get away, while a few stopped to help the injured.

Lance tore his eyes away from the chaotic scene when he heard his name.

"Dr. Everett! Time to go."

Lance saw the driver holding the back door open, motioning for him to come.

"Dr. Martin, come with me." Lance pulled the older man to his feet and they both made a run for the car. He wondered if they would make it unharmed. He had to duck a few times as bullets flew past them, some clearing his head by a mere inch or two.

Ahead of him, the driver returned the shots, aiming his

gun and firing at five targets in one continuous motion. The bullet shells clattered to the ground like a sudden downpour of rain.

When they reached the car, Lance moved aside to let Dr. Martin enter first.

Seeing that Lance was within arm's reach, the driver returned to his seat. He shifted gears, ready to drive.

Lance was about to jump in when something caught his eye and stopped him cold. A shell glistening against the black asphalt rolled to a stop at his foot. He picked it up then felt his throat constrict. It looked strangely familiar. Silver in color, it was the same caliber as the ones he had examined just weeks ago. It also bore a semicircle marking. The same marking on the bullets that had killed Juliet.

He looked up and locked eyes with the driver. The truth of the situation finally became clear. The menacing look on the assassin's face further confirmed his fate. In a matter of seconds, the man whom he thought had been trying to save him now wanted him dead.

"Dr. Everett, I suggest you get in the car. Now."

"What's happening?" Dr. Martin's jaw dropped as he glanced from the driver to Lance and back again.

Lance stared at the barrel of the gun aimed at his head.

Surprisingly, the emotion driving Lance in that moment was not shock, but anger. As his heart pounded in his chest, his rage grew. He was soon consumed with absolute rage at the deception that surrounded him.

In a split second, he made his decision. He kicked the side of the car, slamming the door shut and propelling himself backward at the same time. Falling onto the ground, he rolled across the road until he was ten feet away from the car.

The driver sped off with Dr. Martin as bullets shattered the back window of the car.

Lance stood up as he spotted the familiar man in the sweatshirt and cap approaching.

The agent returned his gun to his holster and called out to the others, "Stand down." He reached Lance and extended his hand. "Dr. Everett, I'm Navy Commander Ethan Stratford. We need to talk."

The Navy? Detective Marks had been right. The military had been following him. But what could they possibly want?

CHAPTER SIXTEEN

Lance stared at Commander Stratford's outstretched hand and almost laughed. This gesture couldn't have been more out of place given what had just happened. He shook his head in disbelief, not knowing where or how to start processing this turn of events. He could only focus on the rapid beating of his heart and the beads of cold sweat dripping down his neck that assured him he was somehow still alive. But barely.

He knew for certain now the driver was an assassin. He wasn't merely a personal security guard, for no guard would ever be able to shoot with such precision. His fluid movements demonstrated a skill mastered from years of training but more so an instinct to kill. But the most disturbing truth had been revealed in the way the driver fired his gun. For every target he had gone after, he consistently fired a double round. And he had used silver-shelled bullets.

Lance opened his fist and stared at the shell in his hand. A symbol of a crescent moon confirmed what he already knew: the driver had killed Juliet. He was the one who had shot her twice in the heart. Lance now understood the reason for the smirk on the driver's face when their eyes met for a split second before he drove off. It was a look of pity, not for murdering Juliet, but for Lance.

A look that labeled Lance a fool.

He'd been a fool for trusting the driver and for trusting Mr. Singh. He'd obviously been working for the wrong people. And now the Navy was following him. Could he trust them?

Just when Lance was about to speak to the commander, one of his men ran over.

"Ethan, it's Jamison. It doesn't look good."

Lance's ears perked up to hear Commander Stratford addressed by his first name; he obviously had a close relationship with his team.

The commander attempted to maintain his composure, though he was struggling to speak. "Excuse me, Dr. Everett." He then ran over to a jewelry shop where a man was lying on the ground, his body halfway through the open door.

Lance followed a few steps behind, wondering if there was anything he could do to help. As soon as he saw the agent, however, he knew it was too late. The sight of the man's pale complexion and the crimson stain around his heart—it was eerily familiar. Lance dropped his gaze and shut his eyes.

The man spoke up, his voice trembling between gasps for air. "Looks like…this is it…for me."

The commander dropped to his knees and answered him, keeping his tone light. "You don't look so bad, kid."

"Tell my wife…and son…I love them. Semper Fi, Ethan."

"Semper Fi, Josh."

Lance opened his eyes to see the agent breathe his last.

Commander Stratford cleared his throat before he gave orders to the other agents gathered around him. "Levi, take good care of Jamison. I'll deliver the news to his family. But right now, I need to get information from Dr. Everett."

Lance extended a hand toward the commander as he rose. "I'm very sorry for your loss."

Commander Stratford nodded and returned the handshake, his expression grim. "Thank you. My team and I have been together for a long time. We're like family—" He stopped himself and took a deep breath.

Even though it was their first meeting, Lance sensed this man was worthy of his trust. He recalled hearing once that in a man's weakness, you saw his character. This situation couldn't be truer. "How can I help you, Commander?"

"Dr. Everett, I'm sure you're aware that we've been following you. We initially only wanted to chat, but it appears the situation has escalated faster than we anticipated."

"That would be an understatement."

"Do you know who you've been working for?"

"Apparently, not. But it sounds like you do."

Commander Stratford placed one hand on Lance's arm. "If you'll come back with me to headquarters, I'll fill you in. My car's this way."

Lance followed him down the street until they reached a black car, the same black car he remembered seeing the morning he was repairing his car. "You were the one in the parking garage of my apartment?"

Commander Stratford replied without hesitation. "Yes."

"And you were the one watching me at the supermarket."

"Correct."

Lance got into the passenger seat and looked over at the commander as he took the wheel. "Why have you been following me?"

The commander gave him a somber look and pulled the

car away from the curb. "Dr. Everett, would you believe me if I told you you've been working for one of the world's most dangerous terrorist organizations? The man you've been working for, Mr. Singh, is the second most wanted man on the FBI's watch list. He controls the finances for this terrorist ring."

Lance's jaw dropped. "Why haven't you guys arrested him if that's the case? Why are you allowing him to run a company in San Francisco?"

"Things are not that simple. We can't move in and arrest him until we have solid evidence that he is who we think he is. We believe Mr. Singh's real name is Abdul Azeez. We also believe he has undergone plastic surgery to alter his appearance. He likely has taken language lessons as well, as he no longer speaks with an accent. Other than his height and his limp, we have no evidence connecting Mr. Singh to Abdul Azeez. What's worse, because he's so well-connected, there are politicians who will vouch for him that he's a legit businessman. Which is why we haven't made a move on him yet."

"But how do I figure into this? What could he possibly want from me?"

"That's what we're hoping you'll tell us. Abdul Azeez was never this active in the past. He's always been the type of person to stay in the background, away from the spotlight. That is, until now."

"What could have gotten him to come out of hiding?"

Commander Stratford glanced at Lance with a slight smile. "I'm sure you heard about what happened a year ago, our covert operation dubbed Neptune Spear. It was all over the news, how we captured and killed the leader of this terrorist organization. Since then, we've been waiting to see what Azeez would do. As the Art of War says, when you take out a group's leader, you also need to have a plan for their second-in-command."

Suddenly, everything clicked in Lance's mind and all the pieces of this crazy puzzle he'd been handed finally fell into place. He ran his hands through his hair, grabbing onto the ends as a strange chill traveled down his back. The man he'd been working for, the team he'd been working with—he knew exactly what they were trying to do. And it was ludicrous. "There's no way…"

"What is it? Do you have any idea what the second-in-command of a terrorist organization would want with a quantum physicist?"

"It's because I specialize in time travel."

Commander Stratford released a long breath. "That is insane, even for Azeez."

"I'm afraid that's exactly why they wanted me."

"But time travel—it's not possible."

The scenery outside the car window blurred as they sped onto the freeway, mimicking the flow of thoughts rushing through Lance's mind. There was so much to explain to Commander Stratford, but not enough time to do it. "They already have a working time machine. The only thing they lack is the final equation to make it work."

"They—what? How could you have agreed to build a time machine for them?"

Lance's hands clenched into tight fists as he finally saw the bigger picture. It was a set-up from the very beginning. "They knew I would do it to find Juliet's killer. They killed the love of my life to give me a purpose for building the machine."

The commander's tone softened. "I'm sorry, Dr. Everett."

"But I never agreed to build a machine that would actually travel back in time. It was only supposed to create a window to see into the past. During my research, however, I realized that creating a window was not possible, but time travel was. I warned Mr. Singh and Dr. Rostov to stop the project, but they refused."

Commander Stratford's complexion paled. "How close are they to figuring out the final equation?"

"I can't say for sure. Dr. Rostov is a seasoned scientist, but it could take him months. Or it could be a matter of days."

"Do you know the final equation?"

Lance hesitated. If he admitted the truth, his life would never be the same. With so much power at his fingertips, he would become the government's property. But he couldn't keep the information secret any longer. "I do. But I've never written it down or told anyone."

"Good. Let's keep it that way."

"Of course."

"Now I need you to take me to where the time machine is."

"It's at Mr. Singh's headquarters in the city."

Commander Stratford nodded then pressed a call button on the dashboard. The phone rang once before a male voice answered.

"ID and passcode, please."

"This is Commander Stratford, passcode foxtrot, kilo, 7794."

"Identity confirmed. What's the emergency?"

"I need immediate backup for a cease and take down operation. I need a team of twenty or more at Singh Enterprises in San Francisco. ETA in twenty-five minutes."

"This will require the vice admiral's approval."

"Admiral Farragut is aware of the situation. Please escalate this request immediately."

"Affirmative. Will seek authorization now. One moment, please."

By this time, the commander had already changed course to head toward the city. The car surged forward, weaving in and out of traffic in a race against time itself. Lance understood the gravity of the situation, but he wondered if Commander Stratford would try to take down Abdul Azeez without backup. Just as Lance glimpsed the skyline of the city through the dense fog, the operator came back on the line.

"Authorization granted. A team is being assembled now and will be awaiting your command at Singh Enterprises in fifteen minutes."

"Thank you. Please inform the team to stay put in their vehicles until I arrive."

"Roger that, Commander Stratford."

The commander ended the call and turned to Lance. "How many security guards can we expect?"

"A handful, but I don't think they're at the same level as the driver in terms of their skillset."

"I hope you're right about that."

As soon as they arrived at the building, they were met by two black vans parked on the street. Commander Stratford stepped out with Lance close behind. They made their way to the back of the car where the commander pulled out a bulletproof vest and handed it to Lance. "I normally don't allow civilians on our missions, but you're critical in leading us to the time machine. And since you're the only one who knows how to operate it, you're our expert. Make sure you keep up with me. I need you to stay safe and sound."

Lance put the vest on without hesitation, making sure to firmly secure the velcro panels on both sides.

The commander pulled out a bulky, military grade walkie-talkie and barked his orders. "Team, let's move out."

Immediately, the doors to the back of the vans opened and about two dozen agents in combat gear rushed out. They were dressed from head-to-toe in camouflage and fully covered with protective helmets, goggles, gloves, and knee pads. Each one carried an automatic rifle with the confident stance of a marksman.

Commander Stratford led the group across the street and into the high-rise building. A security guard near the front door stood and held his hands up as they approached his station.

The bald, heavyset man had difficulty getting his words out. "I—I don't want any trouble."

"There won't be any as long as you cooperate," Commander Stratford emphasized. "We're taking control of this building."

"Okay. But there's no one here."

"What do you mean there's no one here?"

"Only a few of us guards are left. There were employees here last night, but they were all gone this morning when I got here. No one's come in today."

The commander cursed under his breath. "They knew we were coming."

Lance wasn't giving up yet. "What about the equipment on the top floor?"

The security guard shrugged. "I don't know. If you like, I can bring you guys up there to check."

Commander Stratford called a few of his men over. "Sweep the building. Let me know if you find anything. I'll take Dr. Everett with me."

The guard called the elevator with his keycard and Lance

and the commander followed him in. When they reached the top floor, they exited and made their way down the well-lit hall. Everything appeared to be how Lance remembered it from the previous night until the guard opened the door to the office.

Upon entering, Lance noticed immediately that the time machine was gone. Not only that, the rest of the place was in shambles. Papers and equipment were scattered all over the floor. Chairs had been overturned. It looked like Mr. Singh—Abdul Azeez—had indeed evacuated the building.

The guard rubbed his chin as he looked around. "Looks like they left in a hurry."

The commander's face turned grim. "Dr. Everett, I'm assuming the machine we're looking for is no longer here."

"That's correct. The machine's gone."

Commander Stratford turned to the security guard. "Thank you for your help. We'll look around."

"Sure. I'll be downstairs if you need anything."

As soon as the guard left, Commander Stratford and Lance began discussing their options.

The commander crossed his arms over his vest. "Do you have any idea where they might have taken the time machine?"

"I have no clue. Azeez didn't talk about any other buildings he owned."

"We need something to go on. Anything—"

"Hold on." Lance's gaze landed on a machine still left in the lab, an energy detection machine. "I may have a way to find out where they went, but it's going to take some time. It also may be a bit on the reactive side."

"Go on."

"Running the time machine gives off large amounts of

energy. If I can get access to a satellite, I can program it to look for a specific energy signature. When Azeez turns the machine on, we will see it immediately."

"What if he doesn't turn it on?"

"That's a possibility, but I'm fairly certain he will. He would've had to take it apart to transport it out of here. Whenever it's assembled again, he'll need to turn it on and run a test to ensure it's working properly. Even a short test would generate a large energy surge that a satellite would detect. And if they don't ever turn the machine on…well, that's not a bad thing."

The commander nodded. "How soon can you get the energy detection set up?"

"It all depends on how quickly you can grant me access to a satellite."

"Let's get back to the command center. I'll get you access from there."

"Great." Lance smiled for the first time that day. "Let's go."

The circumstances were serious and not at all child's play. However, Lance couldn't help but feel like a kid on Christmas morning getting the chance to play with a new toy. His toy of the day? A military satellite.

Chapter Seventeen

Time was of the essence. Lance and the commander took the fastest route to Moffet Federal Airfield, the Bay Area's most prominent military airfield. Upon their arrival, they passed through various checkpoints and entered a building with multiple long hallways.

Although Commander Stratford was dressed in civilian clothing, the base's personnel immediately recognized him and saluted him as they passed. Lance followed suit, pausing and greeting people with a respectful nod.

They soon entered a set of white double doors with a sign that read *Satellite Control Center*. The room inside was exactly how Lance envisioned a command post to look like. Three large displays took up the walls while multiple clusters of computer stations filled the remaining area. Dozens of people were busy at work, staring at the numbers and graphs scrolling across their monitors.

An older man with thinning hair looked up as they walked over. His striped shirt and the employee badge hanging from a lanyard around his neck echoed the room's more casual atmosphere. He gave them a smile instead of the customary Navy salute. "Commander Stratford, I heard you need a satellite."

"George, meet Dr. Everett," Commander Stratford announced. "He's the one who needs a satellite."

George's face lit up. "Dr. Everett, the expert in time travel and time dilation?"

"You know who I am?"

"What a pleasure to meet you in person." George extended his hand. "I attended your talks before at Stanford. Your research is truly amazing."

Lance smiled and shook his hand. "It's a pleasure to meet you, too, and thank you in advance for letting me borrow a satellite."

"No problem at all. Commander Stratford already got clearance for it. I'm simply doing what needs to happen. When do you think people will actually be able to time travel?"

George's question seemed harmless enough, but under the circumstances, it was ironic. "It may be much sooner than you think."

"I'll take your word for it." George chuckled. "Now what kind of satellite do you need and what are you looking for?"

"A geostationary one that can be programmed to look for weather patterns."

"I see. I'm pretty sure you're not interested in when California's next rainfall will be. But the real reason you need this is probably above my pay grade." George looked over at the commander with a hopeful expression.

Commander Stratford gave him a small smile. "Sorry, George, you know the drill."

"I know, I know. I just never have any fun around here." He directed his next question at Lance. "So, a geostationary satellite that can be programmed to track weather, huh?"

Lance nodded. "Yes, but I'll need it programmed to track energy patterns."

George raised one eyebrow. "Energy patterns? I'm not sure we have something like that."

"You should. This kind of energy is what creates pressure in the atmosphere. Meteorologists track high and low pressure to predict where clouds will be gathered. However, the energy I want to track is manmade and quite distinct."

George thought for a moment. "Okay, in that case, Titan is probably the satellite you're looking for." He led them across the room to a substation that contained a cluster of computers. A technician greeted them. "Rob, meet Dr. Everett, the current authority on time travel and time dilation. Rob here knows everything there is to know about working with satellites."

"Nice to meet you, Rob. Can you show me how Titan searches for patterns in the atmosphere?"

"Sure thing," Rob answered and proceeded to explain the details to Lance.

A moment later, Commander Stratford interrupted them. "Time is of the essence here. We need to work quickly. How long will it take to reprogram Titan to look for the pattern that Dr. Everett needs?"

Rob's expression turned serious. "Fairly quickly, sir. If we know exactly what we are looking for, I can program Titan in about four hours. That includes the time needed to upload everything and activate the new program."

"Four hours is too long. We need everything done in two. Can you do that?"

Rob rubbed his forehead and exhaled. "I can try, but I can't make any promises."

"I'll let you both get to work then. I'll check back in two

hours." Commander Stratford turned and walked toward the door as he finished his sentence.

Rob looked at Lance with an uneasy smile. "I guess we better start."

"Let's do it."

They began working on programming the Titan. Rob explained the computer language to Lance, which he picked up on quickly. Soon, Lance had rewritten the satellite's code to reflect the pattern he wanted. Rob nodded in appreciation at Lance's progress, even calling George over to show off their progress. At the rate they were going, it would be possible to meet Commander Stratford's deadline.

Exactly two hours later, Commander Stratford returned. "How are we doing?"

Rob glanced up and answered for Lance who was staring intensely at the monitor. "We're doing good, really good. I've never seen anyone program a satellite so quickly. After this last upload is done, we should be ready."

Lance leaned back in his chair and nodded. "That's the plan at least. This satellite has never looked for this pattern before, so we'll have to wait for it to detect something to know if we programmed it correctly. In the event that we didn't, it won't detect anything even if the pattern we're looking for is actually happening."

"That's true—"

"There!" The commander cut Rob off with a wave of his hand. He pointed to a red dot flashing in a steady pattern that had appeared on the screen. "Does this mean the satellite's working?"

"No way." Lance leaned forward, raising his voice to be heard above the noise in the room. "Yes!"

Rob chimed in excitedly, "We've located the pattern we were looking for."

Commander Stratford smiled for the first time that day. "That's great news. What's the location? I can get men on the ground anywhere in the country within an hour."

"I should've known that's where they'd take it. We're going to need a team much sooner than that." Lance stood up and began pacing. "The good news is they're close."

"How close?"

"A few miles away," he answered the commander. "They're at Stanford University."

"Stanford? Why wouldn't they go somewhere farther?"

Pausing in his steps, Lance faced the commander. "No one would guess they'd stay so close to their original base. But the fact of the matter is that we wouldn't have found them unless they wanted to be found. The pattern we're seeing indicates that they've already reassembled the time machine and activated it. We have to stop them."

"I'll head over there right now." Commander Stratford turned to leave the room before adding, "George, bring Dr. Everett to the comm room in case we need his help. We can radio him."

Lance caught up with the commander. "I need to go with you. I'm the only person who knows how to shut the machine down. I doubt if Singh or his assistant will help you."

Hesitation flashed across his face before he replied, "Okay, let's go. George, bring Dr. Everett out front. I'll be there in five."

Lance made it to the building's entrance as four black SUVs pulled up in front of him. The door to the first vehicle opened and Commander Stratford called out, "Get in."

Lance called out a word of thanks to George and hopped

in. The SUV, which had been modified internally, had bench seats on opposite sides. Lance took a seat directly across from the commander who wore a stern expression on his face again.

"Do you know which building Singh will be in?" Commander Stratford asked.

"I have a good idea. There's a new wing being built on campus. It's a building Singh donated to the school, but it's not finished yet, so it's empty. It's the perfect place for a time machine."

Commander Stratford relayed the information to his team over the phone then informed Lance, "We have a satellite image of the campus. We know exactly where this building is."

They arrived at Stanford in a matter of minutes. Nothing could have prepared Lance for the scene before him. Crowds of people were frantically running away from campus, specifically from the area of the unfinished wing. Even with the car windows up, he heard their screams as they fled the area. As the SUV came to a stop, he realized what the commotion was all about. The ground was moving. Having experienced his share of California earthquakes, he knew what one felt like, but this was nothing like it. This shaking was a faster, consistent movement that didn't wane.

Lance and the commander exited their vehicle, followed by several team members from the other cars. They looked at each other in alarm, trying to assess the situation.

The ground continued to shake violently, producing a low frequency humming that resembled the deep bass sound from a subwoofer. The combination of vibrations was so great that it literally shook the surrounding buildings, causing them to crumble. Cracks appeared in the walls, surrounded by clouds of dust that swirled in the air like a sandstorm, unable to settle on the ground due to the shaking.

"What's going on?" Commander Stratford yelled out to Lance. "Is the time machine supposed to be this loud?"

Loud was not the most accurate way to describe the humming. The sound was not actually loud, but its intensity was so strong, it felt like their ears were about to explode. The pulsations were also starting to affect Lance's vision, making his eyes twitch. "Not at all!" He shook his head, raising his voice to be heard. "It's a very well-tuned machine; it shouldn't generate such vibration or noise."

Commander Stratford simply nodded and gestured for his men to follow. "Let's go."

The team made their way forward, keeping their movements calculated and quick. They followed Lance's lead and approached the unfinished building. Their steps slowed as they reached the front door where the vibration and noise were almost unbearable. However, once they got inside, the intensity was surprisingly milder.

Commander Stratford glanced around, assessing the area. "Dr. Everett, are we in the right place? Shouldn't the vibration be stronger inside?"

"I'm certain this is the building where the machine is stored." A realization came to Lance and he added, "We're in the eye of the storm. It's like a hurricane; the center of it is always still and silent. The machine is close by, I'm sure of it."

"All right. Which way do we go?"

Lance spotted a sign on the far wall that read *Auditorium* with an arrow pointing to the left. The time machine would need a large area with enough height for its peripherals. That had to be the room. He motioned in that direction and called out, "Over there."

The men, with their weapons drawn, moved in formation toward the auditorium. When they reached the double doors, the agent at the front proceeded to lean his head against the door to assess the situation inside. Lance immediately jumped forward and pushed him to the ground. The sudden action caused the entire team of Navy members to point their guns at him.

He put his hands up and calmly explained, "The vibration would've knocked him out on contact. If I'm correct, the time machine has been bolted down into the cement floor. This building is now an extension of the machine. It's safe to touch the door with your hands, but not your head."

Commander Stratford nodded in appreciation at Lance then instructed the team to stand down. He directed their focus to the door and pointed to an agent with a scar over his eye. "Sergio, open the door. Slowly."

Sergio grabbed the door handle, wincing as his entire arm shook and his knuckles turned white.

The door opened to reveal a circular auditorium with dozens of seats surrounding the stage and empty spaces for more to be installed. The lighting was dim as not all the fixtures were turned on, but it was enough to highlight the presence of two individuals in the center of the room. Dr. Rostov was busy working on the time machine while Mr. Singh sat nearby keeping an eye on the monitors.

Before Commander Stratford could command his team to move, a voice came over a loudspeaker.

"Welcome, Dr. Everett," Mr. Singh announced, turning toward the door. His face lit up wildly like a madman's. "Commander Stratford, what a pleasure to have you join us."

Commander Stratford and Lance exchanged a quick glance, acknowledging the fact there was no point in hiding now. They began making their way inside, but Mr. Singh stopped them with an abrupt, "Wait! Commander Stratford, you and I go way back. I might look a little bit different now, but you and I both know I'm still the same guy you met years ago in Baghdad. And Lance, you are my newfound friend; without you, literally none of this would be possible." He paused and cackled. "But your friends, I do not know. I must kindly ask them to wait outside while we continue our reunion."

Commander Stratford shook his head, his tone revealing his impatience. "Singh, or I should call you, Abdul Azeez. The game's over. We have this building surrounded. This is an auditorium, not Baghdad. There are no secret underground tunnels you can use to escape like you did last time. Where are you going to go?"

Azeez laughed hysterically. "You still remember the tunnels where many of your team members were hunted down like animals and slaughtered. Oh, but it looks like you got them replaced just fine."

Commander Stratford remained unmoved by his taunts, his only reaction a slight twitch in his jaw.

"Who says I'm going to run? Dr. Everett, please help me explain to Commander Stratford what we are looking at here. I don't believe he is aware that the time machine can also be used as a bomb?"

Lance swallowed, his mouth dry. That's what Azeez was planning. Even though the time machine was not made to be a bomb, the energy that it used—if incorrectly directed—could result in an explosion like that of a small H-bomb.

Azeez smirked. "Allow me to elaborate. The time machine is fully powered and set to yield the maximum explosion. Right now, as it is configured, it has the power to destroy half of this state and to make California uninhabitable for the next 1000 years. It will also create a huge tsunami wave all the way to Asia. Millions upon millions of people will die and the U.S. economy will be crippled." He threw his head back in maniacal laughter. "This is one opportunity I am willing to die for. Why would I run?"

He pointed at a digital clock on one of the monitors. "We have 120 seconds before the time machine explodes. Commander Stratford, I suggest you ask you friends to wait outside. As Dr. Everett can tell you, killing me or Dr. Rostov will not do you any good as we have set a new password on the time machine. I don't care how brilliant Dr. Everett is, he cannot possibly crack the password and shut down the machine in 120 seconds—excuse me, 102 seconds."

Lance called out in a desperate last-minute bid, "Azeez, you don't want to die here. After that much work, you want to travel back in time, don't you? Otherwise, why spend all this time building a time machine? If you wanted to die and kill millions of people, you could've just built a bomb."

"Brilliant, simply brilliant," Azeez commended Lance. "That's the voice of reason I'm familiar with. Commander Stratford, tell your people to wait outside, so we can begin our negotiations, or—" he threw an ominous glance his way "—I will take the second prize of blowing up everyone and everything. You make the choice."

Commander Stratford eyed the clock then gave the command, "Wait outside."

Azeez rubbed his hands together. "That's it. That's how you begin a proper negotiation. Give a little, build some trust, right?" As the team moved out, he waved his crooked fingers at them. "See you in the next life, and don't forget to close the door on your way out."

When the door shut, Azeez's driver approached, pointing a gun in their direction. His voice was calm as he stated, "Please drop your weapons."

Lance and the commander both dropped their weapons.

The driver walked around them, collecting Lance's gun first, then Commander Stratford's.

"Please come. Dr. Everett, look at your magnificent creation which is about to blow itself up and tens of millions of people along with it. Isn't it marvelous?"

With the driver at their backs, Lance and the commander walked to the center of the auditorium. Little time remained on the clock. Lance urgently asked, "What is it you want?"

Azeez's face twisted in annoyance. "You know exactly what I want. I need the formula from you to make this machine functional. As it is, it will not revert time."

Lance couldn't give that information up. "Stop the machine now, Singh. Your plan will never work."

"I'll be the judge of that. Either way you look at it, I'm going to come out winning. If you don't give me the formula, we'll all get blown up. I'll take all of California with me and I'll forever be immortalized as the greatest warrior who ever lived. If I get the formula, I'll revert time and get another chance at this whole thing again. I win either way."

Lance clenched his fists, trying hard to contain the rush of adrenaline in his body. "Even if I give you the formula, you will not remember anything; you will only end up redoing everything all over again. You will end up here, this exact same point again and again. We will all be here again and again. Don't you know we've been stuck in this time loop fifteen times already?"

"Lance, time is running out." Azeez shrugged. "Do you want to give me the formula or do you want to be responsible for the deaths of thirty-eight million people? Your choice. Let me remind you, it does take a bit of time for Dr. Rostov to enter the formula. We don't have much time here."

"But why," Lance pleaded, "why do you want to revert time again?"

"Forty seconds left," Azeez began counting down.

Lance glanced over at Commander Stratford. The grave look on the older man's face said it all. There was no easy way out of the situation.

"Thirty-nine, thirty-eight, thirty-seven."

Commander Stratford grimaced then gave a firm nod. "Give it to him." At Lance's hesitation, he reiterated, "Go on."

A wide grin spread along Azeez's lips.

"Stop the machine," Lance urged, "and I'll give it to you."

"Lance, why do you think you have any authority here? Give me the formula. Now."

"All right," Lance replied through gritted teeth. "Here it is."

Dr. Rostov who had been patiently waiting by the monitors raised his thumb, signaling for Lance to continue.

"The position of the non-interacting particles has to be placed in a linear array with the energy eigenvalue equivalent to the mass inside the chambers to ensure maximum output, yet at the same time, maximum balance. The injection of antimatter must be in the sequence of wave function subdivided by the energy of the particle. The important thing is to separate each chamber to inject antimatter and matter in an alternating order. At the same time, chambers one and three must be in the same sequence and chambers two and four must be in the same sequence. This will create the maximum velocity and balance and generate the energy required to time travel."

Dr. Rostov's fingers flew over the keyboard as he entered the formula into the computer. "Genius!" he exclaimed over his shoulder, his voice bubbling with excitement. "You're a genius." After a moment, he screamed, "The equation is good!"

Azeez's shoulders shook as he crowed in triumph. "Yes!"

"I'm starting a new countdown," Dr. Rostov stated. "One hundred and twenty seconds until time reverses."

Chills traveled down Lance's entire body. How could he have given away the equation for time travel? It was him. His ultimate question had now been answered. He was the one responsible for this unending cycle. He had to stop it. In a desperate attempt, he cried out, "You will not win this. This is only going to make everyone loop in time again. By my count, this will be the sixteenth time we all go back and repeat everything we've done for the past year."

Azeez scoffed. "This is where you are wrong, Dr. Everett. After fifteen times, I thought you would've grown a little smarter, but you're dumber than I thought."

What was he talking about? Lance shook his head in confusion. No one could remember anything once time reversed.

"How do you think I got so rich?" Azeez questioned him. "Do you think I'm that good at predicting how the stock market will raise and fall?"

Lance raised his brows. Obviously, he understood where Azeez was going. He hinted that he could remember things from previous time loops—but how?

Azeez gave him a pointed look. "Yes, I can remember things even after time reverts back."

"H-how is that possible? No one is able to remember anything."

"How?" He laughed, with a hint of pity in his tone. "Lance, doesn't it intrigue you why some people like Jeremy have these déjà vu feelings? The thing is, even though time reverts, the timeline did happen. The brain picks up something in the ether. Once I realized that, all I had to do was work with people who understand how the brain functions. With the help of Dr. Martin, we developed a serum. It didn't work so well in the beginning—a couple of the subjects didn't survive—but over the course of fifteen live trials, we saw the effectiveness increase. Dr. Rostov and I have remembered more and more each time we reverted time. How else do you think we were able to build a time machine in less than one year's time?"

Lance's jaw dropped. The thought never crossed his mind, but what Azeez said was true. Regardless of how smart or rich one was, they wouldn't have been able to accomplish so much in such a short amount of time. It was possible only if they had practiced this repeatedly.

Dr. Rostov flashed a haughty smile at Lance as if to say, how could you not have figured this out sooner?

Azeez laced his hands, tapping the tips of his index fingers together. "Is it starting to make sense now? Yes, I remember more and more things each time. I remember when the stock market rises and falls. I also remember exactly how to avoid Commander Stratford and his team from finding the evidence they need to track me down.

"Lance, I'll let you in on a little secret. You know how you fear being stuck in a time loop and everything happens the same way every time? Well, that's where you're wrong. Even though I remember a lot of things from each timeline, I can tell you that every time something always changes. At first, it took me years to build the time machine. A few time reversals ago, I didn't go see your boss, Dr. Ehrlich, at Stanford until months later. You know how quickly I went to see him this time? The day after I found out that the Navy barbarically killed my supreme leader. Your boss was surprised to see me, but I already knew exactly what I needed to do to get him to sell all your research to me. You Americans are so greedy. When I promised him a new wing, he couldn't say yes fast enough.

"Lance, this will be the last time that I revert time. I will save my supreme leader. And this time around, as soon as I know our leader is safe, I will kill you." He paused, one side of his lips curved up smugly. "I will save Juliet for myself to enjoy. How does that sound, Dr. Everett? Oh, yes, in case, you haven't figured it out, I was the one who killed your fiancée. I realized killing her would be the easiest way for me to get you to help me with the time machine."

Lance's entire body stiffened. A popping sound filled the air as he squeezed his fists so tightly they cracked. He felt Commander Stratford's hand on his arm, holding him back. He needed to stay calm if they were to defeat the enemy.

The commander spoke up, "Abdul Azeez, you will not win. The United States Navy will not let you succeed."

Upon hearing those words, Abdul Azeez laughed louder than ever. "Commander, entertain me if you will, but how do you plan on stopping me? As soon as time reverses, you will remember nothing about this day. All this will literally become a figment of your imagination, or maybe if you are lucky, you will get a little déjà vu, but you will not remember a thing."

"Don't be so sure. Let me remind you that we killed your supreme leader. My team took him down a year ago. That is a fact. We did it a year ago, and if time reverts, we will do it again."

Abdul Azeez waved his hand in annoyance.

Dr. Rostov spoke into the comm system and announced, "It is time."

"Commander Stratford," Azeez called out, "as soon as time reverts, I will have my supreme leader relocated to Pakistan. You found him in a southern part of Waziristan last time, but next time he will be in Pakistan. I will buy him the biggest house there next to some government buildings in the crowded city instead of the mountain ridges. You will never suspect his hiding place. Then I will accumulate so much wealth so quickly that I will literally buy an island and place him there where you guys will never, ever find him. He will live like a king somewhere in the Philippines right under your noses. You moronic Americans believe you are the superpower of the world. Just you wait." Azeez spit on the ground in a display of disgust.

The commander set his jaw. "We will find you. One way or another, we will find you."

Dr. Rostov nodded to the clock which read ten seconds on the display. "Mr. Azeez, it really is time."

Azeez picked up a suitcase that was on the floor beside him. "It looks like it is time for us to say goodbye. It is unfortunate you will remember none of this—" he patted the suitcase "—without the serum." He then approached the time machine and waved his driver over.

Smirking, the driver trained his gun on Commander Stratford and joined Azeez.

Azeez opened the suitcase and produced a syringe. Lance spotted two other syringes inside, presumably for Dr. Rostov and the driver.

Commander Stratford's eyes flitted from one person to the

other, seeming to assess the situation. When the driver turned his attention to Azeez for a split second, he jumped to action. He dove for the gun, grabbed the barrel, and pressed it firmly to his stomach. Holding it tightly in place, he urged Lance to move.

Lance heeded his order and rushed to the glass cage. Just as he neared it, a shot rang out. Commander Stratford! Lance started to turn back, but the commander screamed for him to go. Within a second's time, he was at Dr. Rostov's side, grabbing the last syringe from the suitcase.

Azeez injected the serum into his neck, immediately collapsing on the ground in convulsions.

Seeing Azeez's reaction, Dr. Rostov paused for a moment before injecting it into his own neck. While he was still halfway through the injection, however, Lance instinctively kicked him in the stomach, causing the doctor to promptly fall onto the time machine.

The time machine was already entering its final phase of time travel. It vibrated so quickly, it seemed transparent, like a mirage appearing and disappearing. As soon as Dr. Rostov landed on the machine, the vibrations caused his clothes to catch on fire. It wasn't just one part of his clothing that burst into flames; all the clothes on his body caught on fire at the same time. Dr. Rostov was suddenly consumed in flames.

It was an unexpected sight for Lance, but seeing that the clock only had a couple of seconds left, he knew he had to make a move. With Commander Stratford still holding onto the driver's gun, it was all up to him. The only chance he had of catching Azeez would be to inject himself with the serum. There was no time to hesitate. He held the syringe to his neck and pushed it in, wincing at the sharp pain. He eased every drop into his body. Suddenly, everything around him blurred. Was this the beginning of time travel?

Lance watched everything slow down around him, including his hand that held onto the syringe at his neck. He tried to pull the needle out—an action that should have taken a split second—but the act of doing so seemed to last an eternity. Even the flames engulfing Dr. Rostov had stilled. Worse yet, so had Lance's mind. His thoughts didn't seem to be flowing. He couldn't process or remember anything.

In the next instant, everything stopped. Fire, light, dust, bodies—everything froze.

Time essentially stopped…until it violently exploded into motion, sucking them all into the past.

Chapter Eighteen

Lance stared out the patio door of his apartment. A gentle breeze blew in through the slightly open door, bringing with it a sense of calm. He closed his eyes, allowing the golden rays from the setting sun to warm his face. Only the soft fluttering sound of the blinds moving registered in his mind. Other than that, he didn't have a care in the world.

As quickly as the peacefulness had fallen on him, it suddenly disappeared. He felt so groundless, without a sense of purpose. He couldn't even remember why he was in this room. Opening his eyes, he glanced around. Everything from his bed to his nightstand and dresser looked familiar, yet he had no memories of buying those items or placing them there.

In fact, he had no idea what time it was. Even the date and the year escaped him. What did he do for a living? He racked his brain for answers. His mind was so blank he didn't even know his own name! Did he have any family? Who were his friends? While he understood the concept of relationships, he couldn't remember if he had any. No faces came to mind, neither did voices.

Was he alone in this world?

He rubbed his forehead, straining hard to remember something—anything.

Perhaps if he recalled one small detail, he would remember more. But as soon as he tried, his head began to throb. It ached so badly, he collapsed onto the floor, writhing in pain. If only he could knock himself out and stop the torture. His brain ached like it was being manipulated and forced to accept foreign matter. Except that the information being shoved into the recesses of his mind seemed…familiar. Images from his childhood. The faces of his parents. Memories of him building a time machine. Scenes from his life flashed through his mind at a blindingly high speed.

He held his head with both hands, clutching his hair as the sudden download of information consumed him. He didn't understand how this could be happening. But what was stranger was that he saw multiple versions of himself building the time machine. Each instance played out differently with different lab techs and laboratories. The length of time needed to build the machine varied from memory to memory. Even though he knew these were all his memories, he felt like he was watching a movie from a third person's perspective. How was it possible for him to have multiple memories of the same period in his life?

The pain in his head finally subsided, leaving Lance with a dull ache. Taking a deep breath, he uncurled his body and stretched out. He had no idea how long he'd been lying on the floor, drenched in cold sweat. He stared at the ceiling and tried to make sense of what had happened.

Outside, the sky was already dark. Pale moonlight shone through the patio door. Lance glanced at the digital clock on the wall. April 30, 2011. 11:14 p.m.

Slowly, his brain began to sort through the multiple sets of memories. From working with Mr. Singh and Dr. Rostov on the time machine, to the fallout that happened each time after the machine was built…to the inevitable time reversal. He shot up to a sitting position. He suddenly realized the horror of the situation. He carefully recounted the times he had built the time machine and concluded there had been fifteen different versions of the event. This had to be number sixteen.

Just as he feared, the entire world was stuck in a time loop.

He had to put an end to this—but how? The obvious answer was that he could just not make the time machine ever again. But he immediately realized how this time was different. If the memory serum had worked for him, it likely meant that it had worked for Mr. Singh and Dr. Rostov as well. There was a very good chance that they now had everything they needed to build a time machine. He was longer the only person who knew the formula.

In all his memories of the events leading up to the time reversal, it was always Mr. Singh that sought him out. He had no idea where Mr. Singh was or how to find him. He needed the help of someone who could help him capture Mr. Singh.

Commander Stratford!

He searched his surroundings for his phone and found it on his bed. He placed a call, waiting as the phone rang twice before someone picked up.

"Stratford. Who am I speaking with?"

Knowing the commander wouldn't remember their history, he needed to find the quickest way to convince him of the imminent danger. "Commander Stratford, my name is Lance Everett. I'm a professor at Stanford University. You may not remember me, but please know I'm a friend. I need your help. I may be able to help you as well."

A brief pause followed. "Who is this and how did you get my number?"

There was no time to waste. Lance pressed on, eager to win him over. "Commander Stratford, am I correct in saying you just missed a critical mission that you have been working on for the last four years?"

"Who is this?" His voice was gruff and demanding. "How do you know this? That's classified information. I know everyone who was given information about that mission, but I don't know you. Stealing classified information can land you in jail."

"Commander, trust me. I didn't steal this information. If I had, I wouldn't have come to you. I'm here to help."

"Help? How?"

"About a year ago Abdul Azeez came to me and offered me a research opportunity."

There was a slight shift in his tone. "Go on, I'm listening."

"I wasn't aware of who he was at the time, but now I know he's been disguising himself as a successful businessman named Krishna Singh. I worked for him for over a year and only recently learned he's a high-ranking terrorist. He threatened to kill me, but as luck would have it, I survived. I believe I have some of his secrets that might help you with your mission. I hope we can partner together and capture him."

Commander Stratford sounded skeptical. "How do I know you're telling me the truth?"

"I can tell you things that only a few privileged government officials know. As I stated before, I know that just a few hours ago, you and your team carried out a critical mission, Operation Neptune Spear. You intended to capture the head of a terrorist organization, code name Geronimo. The location of the mission was in the southern part of Waziristan, a region of northwest Pakistan."

The commander's voice boomed in Lance's ear. "How do you know this information?"

"Trust me, I'm not the only one who knew; Abdul Azeez knew as well. He told me he tipped off the terrorist organization before your team arrived."

The commander swore under his breath. "Assuming what you're saying is true, what else can you tell me? Where's Azeez now?"

"I actually don't know where he is."

"If you don't know where he's hiding, how can you help me?"

"I think there is a reasonable chance that I can help you catch your number one terrorist again, and if we are able to do that, we will have a chance of catching Abdul Azeez as well."

"That sounds great and all, but how do you propose to do this? My team and I have spent the better part of the last four years tracking down Geronimo. Just hours ago, I lost him and we have no idea where to look for him now. You're telling me you worked for Abdul Azeez, but you now have no idea where he is."

"I believe Geronimo is still in Pakistan and I believe I've learned enough information from Abdul Azeez to know where he may be hiding."

Commander Stratford exhaled loudly. "Let's continue this conversation in person. Where can I meet you?"

"Stanford University, the physics division. Ask for Professor Everett. When can I expect you? Time is of the essence here."

"I'll hop on a military plane now."

"Will you be landing at Moffett Federal Airfield in Mountain View?"

"Yes," the commander answered, surprise in his voice. "How did you know?"

"Just a hunch," Lance replied casually. "I'll see you soon then."

"I'll land in three hours and be at Stanford in another thirty minutes."

"Great. By the way, speaking of Moffett Airfield, can you ask George to loan me his satellite? The Titan satellite, to be exact. I need it to start searching for Geronimo's new hideout."

"Wait—how do you know George? And how do you know about our satellite? What else do you know?"

Lance chuckled. "Not much more. But I do need that satellite for our mission to be successful."

Commander Stratford scoffed, clearly not amused by the situation. "This is your cell phone, correct?"

"Yes."

"Stay close by. I'll contact George to grant you remote access to the satellite. I'll see you soon," he added before hanging up.

Lance stared at his phone and shook his head in wonder. The day had sure turned around. The last memory he had of the commander was of him with a gun pointed to his stomach. The driver had shot him several times, but thanks to the time loop, Commander Stratford was still living and breathing. What a strange feeling it was to have heard his voice.

Pushing his emotions aside, Lance quickly gathered his belongings. He needed to get to his lab. He headed out the door then returned to grab his cell phone charger. The last thing he wanted was to miss a call from Commander Stratford or from George, the lead satellite operator.

His heart pounded at the urgency of the situation. He knew exactly what Abdul Azeez was planning, but the commander knew very little. He debated how much he should divulge, not because he didn't trust him, but for his own credibility's sake. Telling Commander Stratford everything he knew, specifically that he was from the future, would create more questions. He needed to think this through.

Lance reached the ground floor of the apartment building and located his car. He got behind the wheel and pulled out of the parking space. When he exited the garage, he spotted a familiar black car following him.

It couldn't be! Was it Azeez's driver?

Even as Lance accelerated, the gap between the two vehicles grew smaller and smaller until—bang! The car rammed into him from behind. One glance in the rearview mirror confirmed it was the assassin at the wheel. He wore his signature dark shades and a menacing smile.

Out of desperation, Lance floored the gas. He needed to speed up, and he needed to do it fast, before the driver hit him again.

He raced to the nearest freeway entrance a few streets away. After merging onto Highway 101, Lance attempted to lose the other car. Traffic was lighter now at a quarter after midnight, but being the Bay Area, there were still quite a few cars on the road. He wove in and out of the lanes, doing his best to drive safely, yet quickly.

Another glance in the mirror confirmed the car was still hot on his tail, following a few feet behind. Lance couldn't see the driver's face, but he imagined he was laughing at their little game of cat and mouse. Whenever he needed to slow down because of other cars on the road, the driver took the opportunity to remind him of his presence. The large, solid car crashed into him again and again, causing him to swerve. Several times Lance almost lost control.

Lance blew out a breath. This was not a fair fight. He needed a better strategy—and soon. His car wouldn't be able to take many more hits.

An idea came to him. The cemetery where Juliet was buried was nearby. Lance knew from his visits there that amateur street car racers often competed along the mountain road leading up to Skylawn Memorial Park. These illegal races attracted the police as well. If Lance was lucky, they might run into a cop along the way. At the very least, he would have a higher chance of losing the driver. Having taken that road every day for a year made him as skillful as those racers, if not more. He had no problem anticipating each twist and turn.

He swerved over to the junction to get onto Highway 92. Just as quickly, the driver changed lanes behind him.

Lance's heart pounded in his ears as he tried his best to maintain control over his car. Soon, he was only 500 yards away from the mountain road. Hope rose in his chest, only to dissipate with his next breath. The image in his rearview mirror made his blood run cold.

The driver had rolled down his window and was reaching his left arm out. He held a gun in his gloved hand. Despite the rushing wind, his hand remained steady and sure, pointed directly in Lance's direction.

Lance ducked, just as the first shot rang out. Shocked, his foot came off the gas pedal for a split second and he fought the desire to step on the brakes. He accelerated, but not before the car behind him caught up. The driver rammed into him again and fired a second shot, this time hitting Lance's back windshield. The glass shattered, producing a high-pitched, almost melodic crashing sound.

Lance didn't want to consider how closely the bullet had come to hitting him. Instead, he forced himself to focus on the road. He sped up and finally reached the base of the mountain. Traffic merged into two lanes here, forcing him to drive on the shoulder to avoid the cars in front of him. A couple of times, he drove in the oncoming traffic lane then quickly returned to the main lane. His strategy seemed to be working. The driver had yet to fire another shot. He had even pulled his hand back in and rolled up his window.

He knew he was still in grave danger, but Lance welcomed the brief reprieve. Driving like a madman on this winding road was a death sentence. Going uphill made steering still manageable, but things would get dicey once they started going down.

Lance had almost reached the mountaintop when, out of the corner of his eye, he spotted a lifesaver in the form of a black and white vehicle. Cops! He never thought he'd be so happy to see cops while driving above the speed limit. Lance zoomed past them, as did the driver. The wail of a siren resounded, and red and blue lights flashed in his rearview mirror.

Lance yelped for joy to see two cops, one on a motorcycle and another in a police car, trailing them. He expected the car behind him to slow down, but it did the exact opposite. The driver rolled down his window, extended his right arm out this time, and pointed his gun behind him.

Bang! The first shot fired, and the cop on the motorcycle immediately backed off. He slowed down and disappeared from view at the next curve in the road. The other cop, however, continued to chase them.

Lance grimaced. This was not how he imagined the situation turning out. The chances of him getting away in one piece now were slim. Not only that, he didn't want to see any police officers injured in the process either. The situation was not looking good.

He had no time to dwell on the negative though. The landscape was shifting now that he had reached the top of the mountain. Driving downhill required him to pay careful attention. Taking his eyes off the road could mean the end of him, and it would have nothing to do with driver at this point. Thankfully, Lance remembered these roads well. So well he kept his foot on the gas, only easing up on the pedal occasionally, but never needing to use the brakes.

His strategy worked. The driver was not familiar with these roads and their twists and turns. When the driver slowed down, widening the gap between their cars, Lance finally felt a twinge of hope in his heart.

To his surprise, the motorcycle cop caught up to the driver. Once again, there were two cops behind them. Lance began pulling farther ahead in hopes that he could get away. The driver, however, stayed hot on his tail. He reached out his window again, aimed behind him, and fired. He targeted the cop car, and this time he didn't miss.

The bullet hit the left side of the vehicle. The tire immediately deflated, and the car swerved to the right and slammed into the side of the mountain. The tail of the car flew up, and the whole vehicle flipped onto its side, violently and with great momentum. It nearly hit the cop on the motorcycle.

With one officer down, the driver aimed at the other one.

Lance watched the showdown in his rearview mirror and knew he had a split second to decide. He could either drive away…or do the unthinkable. Doing the latter could potentially result in ending his own life. But if he stood by and did nothing while the cop got shot, he'd never be able to live with himself.

He slammed on the brakes.

The tires screeched, creating the most ear-piercing sound as rubber burned against asphalt. Everything suddenly felt like it was happening in slow motion. Lance grabbed the steering wheel tighter than ever, his knuckles white. He set his jaw, bracing himself for the imminent impact.

To his surprise, the car behind him swerved. Instead of plowing straight into him, the vehicle lurched to the left, toward the mountain wall. Before it could hit the wall, however, the driver jerked the car to the right. The sudden movement, combined with the high speed, sent the car flying into the guardrail…then over it. The car turned onto its side and began to flip over several times, propelling itself down the cliff.

Lance blinked quickly, not believing his eyes. The cliff was easily 200 feet high. No person would be able to survive that fall.

He had no time to react because in the next moment, the police motorcycle came into view. The cop seemed to lose control, tumbling to the ground, while the motorcycle slid out from under him and across the pavement. It hit the guardrail and broke into pieces.

Lance got out of his car and ran over to check on the officer who'd been knocked unconscious. He spotted the area where the guardrail had been. Down below, he saw the driver's car resting on the bottom of the cliff. A crazy idea popped into Lance's head. Should he try to save the driver? But how? As he debated what to do, the car exploded in a large ball of flame.

Obviously, there was no hope for the driver now.

Sirens wailed in the distance. Lance checked the cop lying on the ground again. His breathing was even. Knowing an ambulance was on its way, he decided not to wait. He'd lost so much time already. He needed to get to his lab.

Lance returned to his car and drove away as red and blue flashing lights lit up his rearview mirror.

Back on the road, he held the steering wheel with one hand and his forehead with the other. His head still throbbed, reminding him of the alarming course of events he had experienced that day.

Logically, he knew it was April 30th, just past one o'clock in the morning, but he had multiple sets of memories stored in his brain. Specifically, memories from the future. Yet what he was experiencing now was not part of anything he remembered. If he truly remembered the future, shouldn't the current events be in his memory? But, of course, if the future was not yet written, then what he was experiencing was yet another version of the future.

Lance shook his head as he tried to make sense of these thoughts. These were not typical things that one thought about. It was one thing to read about time travel in a sci-fi novel, but it was another matter to believe you had just gone through a time-space disruption and come back from the future. Not only had he come back from the future, he had done so fifteen times. This was straight-up crazy talk! But Lance had to believe these memories were real. Otherwise, the only other explanation would be that he was in fact crazy. But how could he have made up all these things? How could he know so much detailed information about Commander Stratford or Abdul Azeez? No, he couldn't be crazy.

After what seemed like an eternity, Lance reached his lab. As soon as he walked in the door, he headed straight for the time machine. With his newfound memory, he recalled fifteen different ways he had built it. There were so many variations, he wasn't sure how the machine was built in this timeline. Seeing it now, he knew he had some adjustments to make. He frantically started working, in hopes of finishing before Commander Stratford arrived.

An hour or so later, his cell phone rang. He glanced at the time. 2:35 AM. Chances were high it was George calling from the Mountain View military site regarding the satellite.

Lance answered the call. "George."

There was a pause before George answered. "Right. Dr. Everett, I presume?"

"That's right," Lance replied with enthusiasm. He was glad to hear George's voice, or any familiar voice, for that matter. "Feel free to call me Lance."

"Sure, Lance. I'm calling to give you access to our satellite."

Lance was glad to hear that, too. "Great. Thanks. Sorry to wake you in the middle of the night."

"No problem, I'm sure this is important."

"It is. It's extremely important."

"Well, then, it's very easy to access the satellite. You just need the right credentials, which Commander Stratford has granted you. I've created an account and password for you."

"That's great."

"I'll email you your credentials in an encrypted email, but do you know how to operate our satellite?"

"I do. Don't worry, I've been fully trained by one of the best."

"Okay, but just so you know, our satellite uses a special computer language—"

Lance cut in, trying not to be rude. "Yes, I'm aware of that. Thank you, George, and don't worry, I'll take care of your baby."

George chuckled. "Okay, I trust you. You do have a Ph.D. after all."

"Thank you. If all goes well, let's have a beer together."

"Uh, sure. I hope it goes well for you." He paused. "This might sound strange, but you remind me of someone."

"That's not strange at all." Lance couldn't help but grin. "You remind me of someone I used to know, too."

"Well, before I go, may I ask what you propose to use the satellite for?"

Lance remembered in a past timeline that George had asked the same question of Commander Stratford. He thought it would be fun to use the same phrase the commander always used. He simply replied, "You know the drill."

George chuckled again. "Understood. Good luck, Lance."

After thanking George, Lance hung up. He immediately opened his laptop. On one half of the screen, he went through the steps to connect to the Titan satellite. On the other half, he connected to his time machine, then began making configuration changes to it. Scrolling through image after image, Lance made the needed adjustments, sometimes moving the satellite ever so slightly, other times moving it by large margins.

He was still analyzing Titan's data when his phone rang again. He picked it up on the second ring.

Commander Stratford's voice came over the line. "I'm here."

"I'll be right down."

Lance rushed downstairs and pushed open the double doors. He and the commander shook hands as if meeting for the first time, but for Lance, it was like seeing an old friend again.

The commander's expression was serious, almost suspicious. "Dr. Everett, I hope you have some useful information for me."

"I believe I do. Come up to my lab."

After a few turns and a flight of stairs, they arrived at Lance's laboratory. Commander Stratford's eyes immediately landed on the gigantic machine sitting in the middle of the room. "Is that what I think it is?"

"Yes, it is." Lance walked over to his computer and began organizing some data to show the commander his findings.

Commander Stratford's gaze was still fixed on the machine. "I'm assuming it doesn't work."

"We'll find out soon enough."

The older man's brow twitched. "I'll assume that's a joke that scientists like to tell each other."

Lance only smiled and finished typing. He then turned on a large projector that faced a blank screen. The image that appeared was from a satellite feed. The location appeared to be a large housing compound in a foreign land.

To untrained eyes, the image would not be easy to make out. But Commander Stratford took one look at it and remarked, "Where is this place in Pakistan?"

Pausing as he typed, Lance replied, "This is Abbottabad."

The commander crossed his arms as he studied the image. "There are a few things that don't look quite right here. The house in the middle doesn't fit in compared to the other structures in the neighborhood. What's the significance of this?"

"This," Lance answered him matter-of-factly, "is Geronimo's new home."

The commander grunted. He stayed silent but kept his eyes trained on the image. "This house obviously has had some serious security upgrades, especially compared to its surrounding neighbors. But what makes you think this is Geronimo's new home? Do you understand what you're claiming?"

Lance nodded. "I know he's there. I have the last few hours of satellite recordings which show a caravan of military-grade utility vehicles coming from South Waziristan to this location."

"There are many militant groups in Pakistan. What makes you think this belongs to Geronimo?" His voice was gruff, unbelieving. "You've only had access to Titan for a couple of hours. How is it possible that you have recordings of the feed from South Waziristan to Abbottabad for the past few hours?"

Lance was impressed with Commander Stratford's analytical mind, but not with his understanding of modern technologies. "Titan is a geostationary satellite, which means it stays in the same spot in the sky at all times. It will never see Pakistan from its current position, not without some major relocation efforts. I mainly needed Titan to get access to the U.S. satellite network."

Commander Stratford was listening intently now.

Lance continued his explanation. "The U.S. monitors just about the entire world. There are enough surveillance satellites up in the sky now to monitor and record everything at every second. Once I got into the satellite network, navigating over to the records for the location I was interested in was as easy as looking up someone's address on the internet."

Seeing that he had the commander's full attention, Lance quickly typed a couple of commands into the computer. The image on the screen zoomed out and focused on a larger map of Pakistan, then quickly narrowed in on the northwest region of the country. Lance slowly navigated the image to reveal more of the mountainous region of Waziristan.

Commander Stratford spoke up. "I know this area. This is where my team searched but failed to find Geronimo."

Lance looked at the screen's projection as he typed. "Your team literally just missed him. While you guys were hitting the area right here—" he zoomed in on two Black Hawk helicopters "—Geronimo and his men were escaping from a place about forty-five miles away. They had obviously been tipped off just prior to your team's arrival."

Commander Stratford's brows drew together. "These are classified recordings. You cannot go digging into this without proper security clearance. We have protocols in place, Dr. Everett."

"With all due respect, Commander Stratford, these files are on the server just like any other recording. There's no way for me to tell what is or is not classified." Not wanting to take away from the importance of his findings, Lance urged the commander to look at the screen. "See the three trucks and group of people there? That was Geronimo and his men."

The commander cursed under his breath. "We were so close. They ended up at his mansion in Abbottabad?"

"Yes, but..."

"But what?"

"I believe Geronimo will only be at this location for a short time. It's risky for him to stay in such a big city in Pakistan. It's not as ideal as being in the mountainous region where he can move about without being seen. He'll likely be moving to another location. According to Azeez, he plans on relocating Geronimo to his own island in the Philippines. There are approximately seven thousand islands there with a large

Muslim population in the Southern part. If Geronimo were to live there and put on a fisherman's hat, we would never be able to find him."

"How certain are you that this is Geronimo?"

"As certain as you were with your intel that it was Geronimo in the mountains of Waziristan."

Commander Stratford looked Lance square in the eyes. Emotions flickered across his face as he processed the information. "Dr. Everett, I believe you that Geronimo is indeed hiding here in this mansion in Abbottabad, but what do you propose I do? He won't be at this location for long. But for me to order another strike, it could take months. We're talking about a lot of government bureaucracy to navigate through. Our last strike in Waziristan took a year of intel with solid evidence and months of planning."

Lance blew out a long breath. "Well, no pressure here, but whatever you decide to do or not to do will determine how history will be written. If you choose to do nothing, no one will ever know, but if you want to be on the right side of history, you must act now. I'm committed to helping you however I can."

Commander Stratford raised a brow, a small smile forming on his face. "It looks like you've made my decision for me, Dr. Everett."

Lance grinned. "Please, call me Lance."

"Well, Lance, get ready to be busy for the next twenty-four hours."

Chapter Nineteen

Despite his earlier optimism, Commander Stratford struggled to formulate a plan. He sat in the middle of Lance's lab, surrounded by the most advanced scientific technologies, but he felt limited and powerless. Although he had planned and executed many military missions throughout his career, this was the most challenging one yet. Glancing at his black steel watch, he noted the time: 0700 hours, Eastern time. He simply didn't have enough time for this mission.

The President had long been informed of the status of the original failed mission that had taken place a few hours ago. Ethan was scheduled to give a full report at 1100 hours on why the mission had failed and what impact it would have on capturing Geronimo in the future. Once the report was given, it would be nearly impossible to have enough momentum to strike again in a reasonable time frame. The team assigned for the original strike would be reassigned to another mission. Who knew when or if they would ever have another chance of locating Geronimo. Now was his only chance, but how could he come up with a workable plan in four hours? He looked at his watch, wishing the hands would slow down.

"Commander?" Lance stood over his computer screen, a line between his brows. "What's the problem?"

Ethan sighed, frustration building in his chest. "I appreciate the second chance here, but I don't see how I can make it work. There just isn't enough time."

"Well, you happen to be talking to an expert on time." Lance smirked. "Is there anything I can help with?"

Commander Stratford chuckled as he rubbed the back of his neck. This guy had a surprisingly good sense of humor for a scientist. "I'm scheduled in four hours to give a full report on the failed mission. I'm willing to skip this critical meeting for a good cause, and I can't think of a better reason than catching Geronimo. The problem is, my team is still in eastern Afghanistan. It would take me fourteen hours to get there. Geronimo is now at his new hideout, and no one knows how long he'll be there. After 1100 this morning, my team in Afghanistan will be dismissed and we will need to start this mission over. This is our only opportunity to catch Geronimo."

Lance nodded. "I understand. Time is of the essence here. Let's get to work. Let's suppose if I can get you to Afghanistan, do you think your team would go on this unsanctioned mission with you? They would not only be risking their careers but their lives, and possibly even face jail time."

Narrowing his eyes, Ethan answered, "Of course they would. Those of us who make a career in the military don't do it for the money. We serve to protect our country and its people. We are ready to lay down our lives at a moment's notice. Every mission we go on may be our last. Capturing Geronimo is critical to our country's safety. I have no doubt that every person on my team would be willing to take the risk. Even so, I will not risk my team's safety. It is crucial that we accomplish this mission successfully. And right now, time is not on my side."

Lance straightened his posture and lifted his chin. "I'm willing to sacrifice my life for this mission as well, Commander. Trust me when I tell you that catching Geronimo is a big deal, but I'm on a mission to stop something even bigger. I don't have time to explain everything to you right now, but for me to accomplish my part, I need to first help you catch Geronimo."

The commander didn't understand what Lance was saying, but he sensed it wasn't the right time to question. He simply nodded.

"Are you ready to double down?"

"What? What exactly do you mean by double down?"

"When I said earlier I'm an expert on time, it wasn't entirely accurate. I'm actually an expert on time and space."

Ethan's ears perked up. He gestured for Lance to continue.

"I won't go into details as we're already short on time. The gist of it is that I know how to manipulate time, and knowing how to manipulate time is just about the same thing as manipulating space."

If the scientist was trying to be funny, he sure had bad timing. "You're right," Ethan scoffed, "we don't have time for this."

Lance was unmoved by his cynicism. "Commander, do you see this machine here? I'm able to use it to manipulate time and space. In other words, I can send both of us to Afghanistan, where your team is located, in an instant."

Ethan dropped his jaw. Now the scientist sounded plain mad. "That's not possible."

"It's entirely possible. As a matter of fact, compared to manipulating time, bending space is a whole lot easier and requires much less energy." His face lit up as he explained, "Space and time are intricately bound together. I have memories—they're slowly coming back to me now—of a time when I teleported myself from one place to another. It's possible, Commander!"

Possible or not, all this scientific talk was above his pay grade. He didn't know whether to believe it or not. Even if he wanted to, it was beyond his comprehension. "Look, I'm sure you're a brilliant scientist and your theory in time travel and teleportation might one day prove to be invaluable to mankind, but as of today, time and teleportation machines have not yet been invented."

Lance began mumbling under his breath, so lost in his thoughts that he didn't respond.

Seeing how he was preoccupied, the commander decided to politely excuse himself. "Dr. Everett, thank you for inviting me here. I'll pass along the information you gave me to the intelligence agency. Good day," he added before walking to the door.

"Hold on," Lance called out. "What do you have to lose?"

Ethan turned around. "Excuse me?"

"What do you have to lose? I can have the machine set up in thirty minutes."

"You're serious?"

"Yes! Of course, I'm serious." Lance threw up his hands in exasperation. He glanced around his lab, his gaze landing on a small refrigerator in the corner of the room. "I'll show you. I'll teleport that refrigerator outside." He pointed out the window to the grassy lawn below.

Ethan crossed his arms. "You are serious."

Lance nodded. "If you stick around a little longer, you'll be the first person ever to witness a teleportation. More importantly, I will teleport you to Pakistan, so you can complete your mission. What do you say?"

The commander raised his eyes to the ceiling. He couldn't believe he was considering staying. "Okay, let's see it."

"All right!" Lance rubbed his hands together and stepped up to the time machine.

Thirty minutes passed. Seeing Lance work on the machine was like watching a scene from a movie unfold. All the tubes going in and out, the four large pillars at the corners—everything appeared like they belonged in a comic book. The set up was impressive, but Ethan had waited long enough. After another fifteen minutes, the commander rose from the chair he'd been sitting on. He approached Lance, and with a last-ditch effort, asked him, "Do you need any help?"

"Sure, I'd appreciate it. Let's move the refrigerator over, on top of this rack here."

Ethan blinked in surprise. "You're done?"

"Yes. Let's test it."

They carried the refrigerator and set it on top of a wooden box.

"Uh, why the wooden box?"

Lance chuckled. "Well, when the machine teleports something, it's really exchanging the content between two spaces. When I teleport an object like this refrigerator over in a three-dimensional space, I'm pulling the same exact content from the destination. The wooden box is there because I don't want the bottom of the fridge to be cut off when it's teleported. As you can imagine, when we teleport ourselves, we'll probably want to stand on a box or something as well."

"That makes sense." Ethan shook his head in wonder.

"About as much as the other things that don't make sense to me right now."

Lance smiled. "Okay, we're good to go." He gestured for Ethan to follow him to the other side of the lab where they stood behind a glass window. He grabbed two pairs of protective headsets and handed one to the commander. "Put these on."

Ethan did as Lance instructed, his movements swift and steady, even as his mind wavered between doubt and belief. He had no idea what to expect. When he first came to the lab, he had minimal expectations, hoping only to gain a lead as to where Geronimo might be. Who would believe he was now witnessing a mad scientist teleport a refrigerator? The experience was surreal.

Lance started the countdown. "Five…four…three…two… one. Teleporting initiated."

The time machine came to life, generating a very high-pitched noise. Even with a headset on, the commander found it almost unbearable. Following the high-pitched noise came a strong and consistent vibration. Fortunately, both the noise and the vibration lasted briefly. A loud boom sounded, and like magic, the fridge vanished.

Lance ripped off his headset and rushed to the window. He whooped in excitement. "It worked!"

Ethan joined him at the window, not believing his eyes. Sure enough, the refrigerator that had been sitting in the middle of the lab was now sitting on the green lawn in front of the building. As the commander tried to make sense of what had just happened, he heard the door open.

"Come on," Lance called out, "we need to check the contents."

He followed Lance down the stairs and out the door. When they reached the fridge, Lance opened it up and pulled out a couple of bottles and jars to inspect. Everything looked to be intact, unharmed.

A big grin lit up Lance's face. "Our test was a success."

Even with the evidence before him, Ethan still had a hard time swallowing what had happened. "What does this mean? Are you going to teleport us to Pakistan?

"That's the whole reason why we did this test, wasn't it?"

"But isn't teleporting a refrigerator and teleporting people two different matters?"

"Yes, but this is the closest thing I can find right now as a test subject, besides teleporting one of us. You see, in this refrigerator I have liquids and other jello-like substances which resemble our brain and other organs. They all came out fine, under my very coarse examination, of course."

The commander eyed the scientist. How had he accomplished such a feat? But more importantly, why? "Why are you so eager to help me find Geronimo? Before tonight, I never even heard of you. But you're willing to use this machine and potentially risk your life for this mission? What's in it for you?"

Lance answered him with determination in his voice. "It's like I told you earlier on the phone. I worked for Azeez. I know he has plans to kill thousands of innocent people. If we miss this chance to catch him, we might not get another one. I wouldn't be able to live with myself if I didn't act on this opportunity."

Ethan nodded. He had the same conviction as well. "Just so you know, if we fail, you and I will both have to answer to the authorities."

"I understand."

The commander clapped Lance on the back. "Okay, let's do this."

They returned to the lab and began preparations for their teleportation. Lance recalibrated the machine, while Commander Stratford notified his team of his arrival.

"My men will be ready in twenty minutes."

Lance's fingers flew over his keyboard for a minute. When he finished typing, he stared at the monitor and declared, "Now for the moment of truth, do or die." He glanced at the commander. "Are you ready?"

Ethan took a deep breath. He had made many critical decisions during his Navy career, but this one was by far the perilous one. Here he was about to teleport from California to Pakistan, a distance of almost 8000 miles. He was placing his life in the hands of this mad scientist he had met only hours before. Strangely enough, however, he felt a bond with Lance. He also had faith in him. Seeing the refrigerator successfully teleported didn't hurt either. "I already gave my word to my team. There is no backing out, unless I die."

"All right." Lance typed one last command into his computer. He then grabbed two headsets and two pairs of goggles and walked toward the spot where they had teleported the refrigerator. He motioned for the commander to join him. "Let's go then. We have one minute on the clock."

"Hold on, Lance. While I appreciate your bravery, Pakistan is no place for a scientist."

Lance handed half of the gear to the commander. "Don't worry about me. I won't go into the building with you. I'll do what I do best—stay near a computer and monitor the satellites, make sure no one gets out. And by no one, you know who I mean. Also, as soon as we finish up with Geronimo, I need you to catch Azeez. Someone needs to keep you on task, you know. And besides, who else is going to teleport you back?"

Ethan did appreciate Lance's satellite spying skills. "Fine. Let's proceed."

Lance gave him an enthusiastic smile. "The process will take about thirty seconds. The goggles and soundproof headset should help minimize the effects of the teleportation, but nausea should be expected. Scream as loud as you possibly can to help decrease the pressure in your head."

They both put on their gear and stood on the wooden platform Lance had set up. Lance looked at his watch as he counted down with the fingers on one hand. Five fingers, then four…and three…two…one.

The commander's entire body tensed up. His joints locked in place as a strong force enveloped him from all sides. He opened his mouth to scream and suddenly felt his voice, along with the rest of his being, being pulled upward. A burst of white light flashed. In a split second, a loud popping sound consumed him and the environment changed.

They were now in the middle of a desert, standing in pitch darkness.

Ethan grabbed Lance by the shoulders, shaking him until he opened his eyes. "We're here."

Lance looked around, a grin growing on his face. "We did it."

Checking the GPS on his military-grade watch, the commander confirmed their location. "You did it. Your coordinates were impeccable." As he spoke, he turned and looked behind him. In the distance, he spotted the outline of the Combat Outpost. Seeing was believing. They had teleported to Afghanistan. His head spun at the ramifications of this new technology and how it could be used by the military. They could potentially teleport someone behind enemy lines with ease, bypassing all checkpoints and outposts. He was utterly amazed…then dismayed. He grimaced, imagining the potential dangers should this technology fall into the wrong hands.

Lance seemed to understand what he was thinking. He placed a hand on his shoulder and remarked with assurance, "The machine will be destroyed as soon as this mission is over. No one can ever possess this kind of power. I don't care who wants it."

The commander acknowledged Lance's comment with a grateful nod. "Thank you. Come on. The base is this way."

They walked toward a group of well-constructed tents about a hundred feet away. Two soldiers stationed outside the checkpoint spotted them and stood at attention. They saluted as he and Lance approached. "Good evening, sir!"

Ethan returned their salute. "At ease. Is the team inside?"

"Yes, sir," the first soldier responded as he pulled open the tent door. "The team is waiting for you."

As soon as he entered the room, someone shouted, "Attention! Senior officer in the room." Two dozen men, along with Cairo, their war dog, immediately stood. The soldiers acknowledged him with a firm salute.

The commander quickly replied, "At ease." He turned to the soldier nearest to him on the left. "Lieutenant, are we ready to go?"

"Yes, sir, yes. We're ready to go at your command."

"Lieutenant, please help our civilian, Dr. Everett, suit up. He'll be coming with us."

Commander Stratford looked around the room, making

brief eye contact with each of his men. These soldiers were the best of the best. If anyone could capture Geronimo, they could, especially now that they had Lance's intel. With full confidence, he gave his final command. "Let's move out."

Chapter Twenty

All around Lance, soldiers rushed out of the tent at a brisk pace, determination in their steps. He followed Commander Stratford outside and toward what looked like the outline of two military helicopters. Their black, non-reflective coating hid them in the darkness, making it hard for him to make out their exact shapes.

The team split up and boarded the copters, seeming to know who was assigned to which plane. Lance thought to ask which one he should take, but the commander tapped his shoulder and gestured for him to follow.

Once on board, a soldier handed Lance an all-black uniform, helmet, and goggles and simply said, "Put these on."

Commander Stratford glanced over and smirked. "There's no need to scream this time," he remarked, obviously referring to their teleportation experience. He managed to maintain a serious expression, although there was a twinge of humor in his tone.

Lance had just gotten his gear on and his seatbelt strapped when the helicopter began its ascent. Through the specially-designed communications helmet, Lance heard a conversation in progress. Someone in ground control was questioning the authorization of this mission. Commander Stratford forcefully responded, stating it was an emergency mission. When ground control pressed for more information, the commander stressed their need to go, and to go now. He ended the exchange with a command to cease all communication until he contacted them after the mission completed.

Commander Stratford reiterated his order. "Cut the feed; local com only." The radio clicked before he continued, "Team, we are on our own now. You have already been briefed by the Lieutenant Commander about this mission. Although the details have changed, we are here to do what we do best. No one else in the world can do what we do as well as we can. When we get on the ground, we will do what we've always done. Get in, get out. Remove any obstructions, keep civilians away from the compound, and ensure all civilians, especially women and children, are safe. Secure all computer hard drives, CDs, memory cards, video tapes, and any other intel you can locate back with us. And of course, our primary target is wanted dead or alive. Any questions?"

"No, sir, no."

"We are currently about ninety minutes from our target location. We will fly NOE as we approach the Pakistani border—that's nap-of-the-earth, a low altitude flight path, for our civilian helper here. We will monitor our satellites for any movement from the Pakistani government. Dr. Everett will watch the feeds for us."

The Lieutenant Commander acknowledged Lance with a firm nod and immediately handed him a military-grade laptop.

"We have forty minutes to get in and out, with a five-minute buffer. Should we stay on the ground longer than that, we risk encountering the Pakistani police or their military. Black Hawk One is targeted to hover over the courtyard as we drop into the compound. Black Hawk Two will land on the northeast side just outside the compound wall to offload our interpreter, attack dog, and handler and to deter any civilian onlookers and the local police. Is everyone clear on our mission?"

"Sir, yes, sir."

"May the Lord watch over your lives today."

In unison, the team shouted, "Hooyah!"

"Pilots," the commander added, "let us know when we near the border."

"Yes, sir."

Lance observed the scene in awe. While everyone appeared calm and confident, he couldn't help but feel overwhelmed. He remarked to Commander Stratford, "Impressive team."

"This is what we do." He glanced over at the laptop screen. "Are you ready?"

"As ready as I'll ever be." Having something to focus on settled the nerves in Lance's stomach. His fingers flew over the keyboard as he gained access to the necessary satellites to monitor not only their flight path, but all the surrounding Pakistani military installations.

"You seem to know the inner workings of these satellites well, like you've been doing this your whole life."

Lance picked up on the awe in the commander's voice. Now that he thought about it, he wondered how it was possible that everything seemed like second nature to him. Of course, he immediately realized why. He'd had multiple lifetimes of experience already. "Fifteen lives, actually," he mumbled under his breath.

"What did you say, Lance?"

"I just have a knack for all things computer-related." He offered a sheepish smile. "It comes naturally to me."

Commander Stratford gave him a curious look, but he didn't press the issue further.

After some time had passed, the pilots announced, "Commander, we are five minutes out from crossing the border."

Commander Stratford turned to Lance. "Any sign of movement at the border?"

"No, sir, no," he confidently replied, feeling like a useful part of the team. "I even tapped into Pakistan's military communication channels. All channels are quiet. Only a few regular check-ins are being communicated between checkpoints."

"Very good." Speaking into his communications helmet, the commander ordered, "Pilots, proceed with NOE flight course and activate stealth mode. Let us know once we pass the border."

"Roger that."

Lance stared at the monitor, keeping a watchful eye on the border and communication channels.

"Sir," the pilots spoke up, "we've cleared the border."

"Lance," Commander Stratford asked, "any activity on the Pakistani side?"

"No activities. I think we're good."

"A yes or no will do. We don't use terms such as 'I think' here."

"Sir, yes, sir," Lance quickly responded, understanding the seriousness of the situation.

Commander Stratford advised the team, "Double-check your gear. We'll be at the drop zone in forty minutes."

The team responded, "Hooyah!"

The soldiers busied themselves with their preparations. Lance recognized the different weapons in their possession from what his father had taught him as a child. In addition to long rifles, there were shorter machine guns, as well as handguns. They also carried chemlights, hand grenades, and breaching tools. To top it all off, they were equipped with ballistic helmets and night-vision goggles. The impressive amount of gear assured Lance the group was more than prepared to take down the target.

The pilots announced, "Sir, we are five minutes out to the drop zone."

Commander Stratford pointed to the corresponding teams. "Team one, follow me. Team two, station yourselves outside the northeast corner of the compound. Lance, you will remain on board for your own safety."

The pilots flew to the drop zone, with Black Hawk One hovering over the compound's yard. As Commander Stratford was about to give the order to jump, the pilot suddenly exclaimed, "Commander, we're losing lift."

The commander and pilot spoke over each other as they both informed the crew. "Hang on tight; doing a soft crash."

Lance quickly grabbed onto his seatbelt harness as the helicopter fell to the ground. The sudden drop caused his stomach to lurch. Before he could get his bearings, the Black Hawk's tail hit a wall, forcing the chopper to roll onto its side. After a moment, the commotion finally came to a stop and Lance released the breath he'd been holding.

"Everyone okay?" Commander Stratford called out.

The crew, along with Lance, answered in the affirmative.

The commander spoke to Team Two. "We've crash-landed

inside the compound; everyone is okay. I'll need you to fly Black Hawk Two in here for our return trip. Team One, let's go."

At his order, he and the soldiers exited the helicopter.

Before the commander exited, he turned around and told Lance, "This bird's going to be destroyed. Stay with the pilot."

Lance nodded his understanding.

The pilot rushed over to the back of the plane with several explosive devices in his hands. He began setting them up around the cabin, flipping over the red cover on each one and pressing a button to arm the bombs. He motioned to Lance. "Grab your things. We need to go."

Lance released his harness and stood up, holding onto the frame of the helicopter for support. He grabbed his computer and maneuvered his way to the door. The pilot jumped out of the plane, and he followed suit.

Suddenly, a loud explosion sounded from outside the Black Hawk. Commander Stratford and his team had breached the compound. It would be a matter of minutes before they needed to leave this place.

Lance found himself in a world of noise and darkness. Muffled, sporadic gunfire filled the air, interspersed with screams from both men and women. Dogs barked fervently in the distance. A crowd had gathered outside the compound walls, creating a loud commotion. The people shouted in a foreign tongue, their voices raised in protest.

The radio communication coming through his helmet was strangely calm and quiet. Lance only heard bits and pieces of the team's conversation as they moved about. *First floor cleared. Moving to second floor. Room cleared. Second floor cleared. Moving to third floor.*

More gunshots rang out.

Target acquired…

Above him, through a third-story window, Lance saw flashes of white. Shortly after, a voice cried out, "We got the son of a gun. Target down! Confirmed, target down."

Indistinguishable cheers soon followed. Lance and the pilot exchanged a quick glance and pumped their fists in the air.

Commander Stratford's voice came over the radio. "Roger that. Good job, team, good job. We have fifteen minutes to grab all intel. Team Two, get ready to enter the compound."

The second Black Hawk was inside the compound in a matter of minutes. A large cloud of dust swirled in the air as the chopper hovered over the area.

The pilot next to Lance spoke into his headset. "Stay clear of the wall. I think I hit a vortex ring that brought down the bird."

"Roger that."

Lance and the pilot ran over to where the helicopter had safely landed, its rotors and engine still running. Soldiers began running out of the building with everything from laptop computers, hard drives, tapes, and notebooks in their hands. The team boarded the Black Hawk as the commotion from outside the walls grew louder and more frenzied. Commander Stratford was the last to come out. He and another solder carried a large black body bag, which they loaded onto the plane. Everyone had climbed on board, except for Lance and Commander Stratford.

The commander called out to the team, "Well done. You have all made history today. You should be proud of yourselves."

The team responded with a resounding, "Hooyah!"

Commander Stratford turned to the Lieutenant Commander. "You know what to do from this point on out. Dr. Everett and I have some unfinished business to attend to."

The Lieutenant Commander saluted. "Yes, sir, I do."

Commander Stratford saluted him and the team before the helicopter door closed.

The lieutenant commander commanded, "Pilot, detonate the charges on Black Hawk One. Let's go home."

"Roger that."

Black Hawk One exploded as Black Hawk Two took off.

Commander Stratford looked over at Lance. "Thank you. We couldn't have done this without you. From now on you will be an honorary member of my team, my family."

Lance reached for Commander Stratford's outstretched hand and gave him a firm shake.

"So, where do we stand?" the commander asked. "We don't have much time."

Lance opened his laptop and located the control to remotely activate the teleportation device. "We're already in the right place."

He pressed the key, and a bright flash of white enveloped them.

Chapter Twenty-One

A moment later, Lance and Commander Stratford found themselves back in Lance's lab on the Stanford campus. Still dressed in military garb, they appeared out of place, but they were dressed appropriately for the event about to take place.

After making a call to his team on the ground, the commander gestured to Lance that he was ready. The two of them made their way downstairs and out of the Engineering building.

Lance winced as his eyes adjusted to the early morning light. He breathed in the crisp spring air, cleansing his lungs of the desert winds they'd just experienced.

Several students walked by along the grassy lawns to their first classes of the day. Among them, a well-dressed man in a high-end, tailored suit strode toward them.

Lance recognized Azeez right away. It seemed Azeez did so as well because he paused for a moment before he continued his approach.

A man in a dark suit and shades followed closely behind Azeez. Could it be? Lance gasped in disbelief. Somehow, the driver had survived the car crash. His face bore some scratches but also a familiar smug smile.

Looking up, Lance spotted several snipers stationed on the roofs of the adjacent buildings. A sense of satisfaction swelled in his chest. There was nowhere for Azeez to run. They would stop him once and for all.

Commander Stratford called out, "Abdul Azeez, this is the end for you."

A smile played on the older man's lips as he stood within arm's reach of them. Acknowledging the snipers with a quick nod, Azeez replied, "It does appear that way, doesn't it?" He turned to Lance and remarked, "Dr. Everett, I presume our special cocktail worked for you and your memory is intact."

"It certainly did," Lance affirmed.

"Well, good." Azeez sneered. "That makes you and I the two most powerful people in the world. You should know that one day your friend here—" he gestured toward the commander "—will turn on you because of how much you know."

Lance stood firm, his voice steady. "Your friends may turn on you, but I have nothing to worry about."

Crossing his arms, Command Stratford barked impatiently, "Azeez, you can come with us peacefully or you can come in a body bag. Your choice."

Azeez looked around him, seeming to assess the situation. He finally declared, "I will come peacefully."

Commander Stratford ordered the two men to turn around with their hands behind their backs. Azeez did as he was told and allowed the commander to handcuff him.

The driver turned as well, but as he reached back, he drew out his weapons with one swift motion. He aimed one gun at Commander Stratford and one at Lance. Neither man had time to register what was happening or to move out of the way.

Gunshots suddenly rang out, echoing throughout the quiet campus. The driver hit the ground like a fallen statue. Two bullet holes pierced his chest.

Commander Stratford looked over at the rooftop and waved at the sniper who had taken down the driver. He held onto Azeez's arm and turned to Lance with an appreciative nod.

Lance released a long, labored breath. He finally let go of the weight he'd been carrying on his shoulders. The world was safe again.

Suddenly, he heard a woman screaming in the distance. Lance turned in her direction and felt his throat constrict, making it hard to swallow. He couldn't believe his eyes. He ran toward the vision, willing it to be real.

When he reached her, he recognized the woman he'd only seen lately in his dreams. The sunlight shone on her hair, highlighting its vibrant shade of red. Her blue eyes shone with unshed tears. He reached out to touch her, threading his fingers in her hair as he stroked her cheek with his thumb. Her skin was so soft and warm, full of life. She looked more radiant than ever.

Juliet, his Juliet, was alive.

He stared at her, so overcome with emotion he couldn't speak.

"Lance, are you okay? Were those gunshots? What happened?"

Hearing Juliet's voice confirmed her presence even more. He finally found his voice. "I've missed you so much."

"What's going on? We just talked last night."

Lance didn't know where to begin. So much had happened;

he didn't even know how to process half of it. He wanted to tell Juliet everything, but the stories could wait. What he longed to do right now was pull her close and hold her. So, he did. He drew her into his arms and murmured against her hair, "I'm fine. Everything's fine."

Chapter Twenty-Two

A week later, Lance walked up to the table where Juliet sat at their favorite hangout on a Friday afternoon. He greeted her with a soft kiss on the lips then lifted a hand to brush back the hair from her forehead. Pausing to gaze into her eyes, he murmured, "You look absolutely amazing."

"You look pretty good yourself. I ordered our usual." She motioned to the sandwiches and blueberry cake donuts on the table.

"Thanks, I'm starving." Lance took his seat, not taking his gaze off the beautiful woman sitting across from him.

As they did every week, they ate dessert first before eating their sandwiches. It was just a small reminder of their first time together. When they had finished their meal, they stacked their empty plates to the side of the table.

Lance pulled out their engagement pictures from his laptop bag.

"You remembered!" Juliet clapped her hands in delight.

"Of course, my darling." Lance handed the photos to her. "Did you doubt me?"

"Well, there is a reason why someone coined the term

absentminded professor." She grinned and moved aside her glass to make room for the photos. "I've been checking them out on the photographer's website. Let me show you the ones I like, and we can compare them with the ones you like."

Lance continued to look at Juliet with a dopey grin on his face. It didn't matter what she was saying, he was just so happy and at peace in her presence.

"Hey, pay attention." She cupped his chin and turned his head toward the pictures.

Lance chuckled at how easily she could distract him. "Yes, yes, absolutely, honey." He reached over to take Juliet's hand and placed a soft kiss on her palm. Nothing could beat spending time with the woman he loved.

A beeping sound interrupted their intimate moment.

Juliet frowned as she glanced at his cell phone on the table. "Is it already time for you to go?"

He turned the alarm off and shook his head. "Nope, I'm good."

"But I thought you had a speaking engagement in So Cal. Don't you need to catch your flight?"

He tilted Juliet's chin up to look in her blue eyes. He still couldn't believe he'd found her—time and time again. There was no doubt he was the luckiest guy in the world. "I canceled it. I'm not going anywhere."

A smile lit up her face. "You did?"

"Yep. I'd rather be here with you."

"Me, too, Lance." Juliet leaned in to kiss him. "I wish I'd known earlier though. I could've taken the afternoon off. You should've told me."

That was an understatement. There was a lifetime of stories

he had yet to share with her. "I should've. I just didn't get a chance to."

"It's okay. We'll have to make the most of our time then."

"Sure thing. That's my area of expertise," he quipped as he kissed her palm again.

Juliet laughed. "It sure is."

Lance sighed a happy sigh. Everything was as it should be. He had Juliet back, and he couldn't wait to start the rest of their lives together.

But, first things first. "I'm going to get another donut. You want one, too?"

Epilogue

Somewhere in the world, in a state-of-the-art scientific facility, a man stood in the middle of a lab. Complicated machines and computer equipment surrounded him. He clutched his head with both hands as he screamed, "Something's wrong. Make it stop! Make it stop!"

He fell to his knees, doubled over. He was being tortured from the inside out. The spasms in his head were so extreme, he ached to stop them. He would do anything to end the pain. He looked around the room frantically, his screams echoing in every direction.

He saw the solution in the form of a surgical saw on the table. With one swift motion, he grabbed it and jammed it into the back of his skull. The pressure from within his head was so strong, the bottom half burst open upon impact.

The relief was immediate. Blood trickled down his neck and clothes, but he could care less. The pain had lessened enough for him to stand. He braced himself against the table and looked up. A mirror hanging on the wall across from him caught his eye. He slowly walked over and stood before it. From the front, he looked almost normal, yet when he turned around, he was shocked to see his brain exposed. The brain stem and part of his cerebellum hung outside of his skull. He placed a hand at the back of his head, feeling the soft matter that had doubled in size.

The serum was to blame. He had fallen into the time machine as he was still injecting it into his bloodstream. Perhaps the energy from the machine had caused a reaction in his brain, resulting in this physiological change.

Still in shock, he carefully bandaged his head. He also searched the lab for materials to create a helmet for himself. Using clear fiberglass, he covered the exposed part of his brain. When he was finished, he stared at himself in the mirror, long and hard.

Despite his new deformity, he was oddly satisfied. As the hours passed and the pain gradually subsided, he felt a heightened sense of processing. He recalled facts stored in his memory from long ago. Numerous scientific formulas and theories suddenly became clear to him. His ability to think and reason expanded in a way he had never experienced before. His intellectual capacities had grown along with his brain. There were no limits to what he could do.

Looking in the mirror again, he gazed deeply into his own crazed eyes. He chuckled as a realization came to him. The sound of maniacal laughter—loud and wild—filled the entire room.

He, Dr. Rostov, was now the most brilliant scientist in the world.

ACKNOWLEDGMENTS

David and Liwen would like to thank the following people for taking time out of their busy schedules to help bring this book to life:

Deborah Bradseth of Tugboat Designs, for her work and dedication in creating a cover that goes so well with this story.

Our amazing beta readers, Lia London-Gubelin, Jewel Punzalan Allen, and Alex McGilvery, for their insightful and thorough feedback.

Our two awesome ARC readers, Jim and Margaret Nelson, for their help in catching a dozen typos.

Heather Hayden, our wonderful editor, for taking on this project under a tight timeline.

The Clean Indie Reads author group for their endless support and encouragement.

About the Authors

David H. Ho and Liwen Y. Ho are the brains and beauty behind this book; more specifically, David created this story and Liwen made it sound pretty. An IT guy by trade, David enjoys watching sci-fi films and dreaming up stories of his own. Fortunately, he married someone good with words who not only edits his emails but understands the ins and outs of indie publishing. A chauffeur and referee by day (AKA a stay-at-home mom), Liwen is an author by night. She writes sweet and inspirational romance, but bravely ventured into the sci-fi world for David's sake. They have been happily married since 2001 and reside in California with their two children. They are proud and relieved to be finished with their first book baby together.

Contact

Find out more about Liwen's books at the following links:

Amazon: www.amazon.com/author/liwenho
Facebook: https://www.facebook.com/2square2behip/
Blog: http://www.2square2behip.com
Newsletter: http://eepurl.com/bt2nEL

Made in the USA
Columbia, SC
08 April 2018